LOVE
OF A
QUEEN

LOVE
OF A
QUEEN

SHAIN ROSE

A
NEW REIGN
MAFIA ROMANCE

To my readers…
buckle up.
It's about to get wild and hot in here.

She may be an ignorant creature,
degraded by the system that
has brutalized her from childhood;
but she has a mother's instincts,
and is capable of feeling
a mother's agonies.

HARRIET ANN JACOBS,
Incidents in the Life of a Slave Girl
Written by Herself

CHAPTER 1

KATIE

THE DOOR SLAMMED shut. The sound ricocheted through me, a loud reminder that I was leaving behind my family and the love of my life.

Rome had knelt before me, begging me not to leave. How could I not, though?

Freedom comes at a price. Breaking away from the shelter of your chains means you risk your life to see your true potential.

I'd been comfortable, stagnant, bound to the life the family had built for me. I'd allowed it. I'd actually respected and even defended it.

But it only took one trigger for the emotions to surface, and I'd been suppressing them for too long. I walked out into the darkness of the night and felt the wind whisper

1

through my hair, the night sky blanket my skin, and the sound of the city swirl around me. I felt the world, and for once it felt like it had opened itself up to me, that every possibility was available to me, that I, alone, was good enough to carve out whatever piece of it I wanted because I, alone, deserved it.

Freedom, though, comes at a price.

I stood on the edge of the sidewalk as the dark SUV rolled down the street. The rubber of the tires crunched over the pavement. No man stood by my side, and no one would protect me if Dimitri, the man who was said to be my uncle, rolled down the window to take my life right at that instant.

As the vehicle came to a stop and idled there, my heart raced. Adrenaline pumped through my veins enough to make my hands shake against the duffel bag I clung to my shoulder.

A large man got out of the driver's side and rounded the back. He opened the door, waving me in. "Hurry up."

Without hesitation, I left behind the comfort of the Armanelli family for the unknown. I'd find a way to prove to everyone that I was worthy of standing on my own, that I deserved a place in power just as much as any of them.

I folded into the SUV and came face-to-face with Dimitri, the heir to the Russian bratva. The seats wrapped around the back of the limo, allowing him to face me with his glacial blue stare. He waited for me to take him in: his white collared shirt, his black slacks and shined shoes, with little else to accessorize. It reminded me that he was cutthroat, straight to the point with no flair.

Two men sat on either side of him. One of their suit jackets folded over awkwardly, showing me just where he was carrying a gun. Neither of them smirked or offered any expression.

I knew the bratva for their low profile. No jewelry was worn, they barely had tattoos, and they didn't flaunt what they had. The Russian bratva had only just started to spread since Dimitri stepped into power. Sure, the family was disorganized, but they were ruthless and smart enough to work their way to the top with the resources they had.

The family was worth billions just like the Armanellis, and only the bloodline had access to it.

I'd heard the stories of Dimitri's father, how he'd killed children, how he'd tortured them in front of their parents just to get his way. He'd embedded his bratva within the government by breeding fear in its officials, by doing away with morals. Lines were made to be crossed, and he'd done it without hesitation.

Then, supposedly, his memory failed him. Now, he lived in a nice little suburb outside of the city.

"Introductions are in order, Katalina." Dimitri leaned back and straightened a cuff of his sleeve, giving me a moment to respond.

"You seem to already know my name." I sat back too, studying him.

His jawline cut like mine, and the slope of his nose was the same, but his eyes were too blue, his stare too vicious and cold as he sat there without responding.

Dimitri and I weren't related, not in the way I wanted to be, anyway. "We can skip the bullshit. You wanted me; you got me. What are you going to do with me?"

"Maybe I should keep it a surprise, yeah?" He smiled like a snake would at a mouse, his thick Russian accent heavy on his tongue. The frigidity of his eyes, how they pierced deep down into my being, showed me just how well this man could play games.

"Our lineage stems from the Romanovs, I've heard."

"What of our lineage? You won't have that blood in you for long."

"Ah, but can't a Romanov defeat the odds?"

"Or they're destined to be executed. You tell me." One of his fingers tapped his pants, slowly, to an imaginary rhythm.

"What do you want me here for? I'm not going to beg to know. If you planned to kidnap and kill me, you'll have an embarrassingly easy job, but I'm guessing a drive-by would have sufficed for that. So from the looks of it, we're going to see your father."

"And your grandfather," Dimitri said, lifting an eyebrow and gauging my reaction. When I didn't flinch at his words, he slid from his seat to come sit right up against me. His breath was hot on my shoulder, and he breathed in my scent against my ear. "Pity we're related."

His muscle shifted in their seats; one frowned while the other smirked like he might get a show. Neither of them knew their leader well enough to guess his next move, which meant either Dimitri was that unstable or they were green.

"Both your boys here coming to visit Granddad too?" I asked, not looking Dimitri's way. If he caught fear, he'd feed off it, and I didn't need him mistaking my disgust for that.

"Why? You want them to? You like something you see in one of them more than me?" His hand went to my jaw and yanked my face toward him.

We glared at one another, his eyes bouncing back and forth over mine.

"When I speak to you, your attention is on me. Don't make me teach you manners, little niece." His hand clamped down on my thigh and inched upward over my jeans. His thumb dipped into a hole in them, and my skin crawled.

"Dimitri, your father wouldn't be happy." The frowning muscle was trying to defuse the situation. He probably got queasy about incest.

My mind raced away, though, finding my safe space in case they decided to torture me. I scrambled to find the jar that had held all of my emotions for so long, but maybe I'd truly smashed it when I stabbed Georgie.

The frustration in me crackled like a fire just waiting to catch onto the dry forest ahead of it. I couldn't bottle it if I tried. All of a sudden, I was free, and I wasn't going back to whatever they wanted me to become. I wouldn't become anything for anybody ever again.

Taunting a woman who had nothing to lose except the freedom she'd just gained wasn't wise. "Do you know Georgie's dead?"

His hand stopped moving in the hole of my jeans. He yanked it away to grab his phone and, at the same time, flung Russian at the two across from us. They jumped to get their phones, everybody moving fast for information.

"What is it you're hiding from everyone? We know you traffic, we know the government is involved, we know that—"

Dimitri slapped me across the face hard enough to make my ears ring. "Don't speak unless you're spoken to. Father wouldn't argue with me on that one. You're out of line."

"Whose line?" I whispered, not sure if my question would earn me another smack. When it did, I found the weakness in the car. The muscular man that was frowning flinched like beating a woman wasn't in the cards for him. He wouldn't make it long in this family, and so I wouldn't feel bad about swaying him to become an ally of mine. Identifying connections came at a price tonight. Enduring pain meant I'd get to the end of this charade though.

It was the most justified pain I'd felt in a long time.

Dimitri fisted his hand. "Father thinks blood is blood. You are going to prove to him right or wrong when we get there. Set him straight so his mind can rest."

"He has dementia. A mind like that never rests," I corrected him. It came automatically because Parkinson's had taken my father and I wouldn't have anyone, not even the devil, walking around with false hopes about a terminal disease like that.

"His mind is worse because he knows you're running around with the Armanellis. He focuses on it all day and night. His lucidity is dominated by it. So we solve the problem by dragging you in."

"So, you're just the son who cares?"

"I'm the son who runs this bratva, niece. Once father sees you're nothing more than a mutt, I'll kill you."

"No bargain?" I wondered if he would negotiate my life with me.

"After you giving up Georgie's phone? You betrayed us—"

"I didn't know I was a part of the bratva when I shared that information." It wasn't well hidden evidence anyway.

"It doesn't matter." He waved off my reasoning. "I'll end the nonsense, and it'll be the start of the end for the Armanelli Family. Have they known all along? Were you the only one in the dark?"

I didn't answer him, just sat there breathing in the stench of Russian blood. The air within that SUV was so unbalanced, I could barely take a breath. My uncle was a man without a moral code, and I was about to test him in every way.

One of us would be spilling our family blood by the end of this.

. I knew damn well it wasn't going to be mine. I'd just gained my freedom, and I wasn't about to hand it to a man who didn't deserve it.

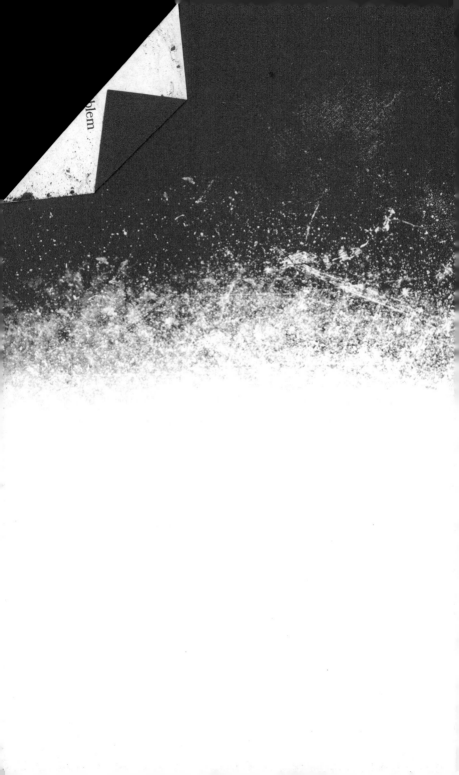

CHAPTER 2

KATIE

DIMITRI'S MUSCLE THREW a black cover over my head to drag me from the SUV. I wiggled as they hauled me out and onto some sidewalk. "Is this necessary? I came willingly."

Dimitri exchanged Russian with them both, and then I heard his footsteps get farther and farther away.

One of them grabbed my elbow and yanked me forward. Walking beside another individual should have been easy, but I tripped two or three times before the man swore in his native tongue.

The other grabbed my opposite elbow. "Just get her to the room, yeah? We don't have to do anything but keep her there until Ivan is comfortable bringing her in."

"Ivan said day or night," whispered back the one I was sure would crack under the pressure tonight. "We should be delivering her straight there. He wants—"

"Dimitri's in charge. We watch her for the night, huh? What's the worst that could happen? Just a little bit of fun for us, if nothing else."

I'd be killing him first. I knew his tone, the one that slithered the wrong way up your spine and sent shivers everywhere. My insides revolted at the mere thought of having to withstand his advances. A whole night meant I'd have to outsmart them or use everything Dante taught me. I'd been lucky enough to have training sessions with him, to know that I had a chance at defending myself in this situation. I knew I would have to and knew that if I got through all this alive on my own, I'd make it a mission to continue training with Dante.

My chances were slim, though; two armed against one unarmed wasn't great odds. The little girl in me, the one who'd cried in that small room when Marvin didn't come to her bed at night, was shaking. The woman in me knew I'd be able to live with it. That woman was like a sword: burned and beaten until she was so sharp she could cut through anything.

I stumbled over some cement steps and counted each one they dragged me up. We only climbed half a flight. The metal click of a lock and the carpet under my shoes told me they'd brought me to an apartment of some sort, not a warehouse or somewhere to kill me off.

It seemed my grandfather still made most of the rules. "Do I get to meet my grandfather tonight?"

"She's going to tell him if we don't bring her tonight. Ivan will—"

"Dimitri is the boss."

"Are you so stupid, huh? Ivan owns us. He's making us escort this woman to him. Not Dimitri. Dimitri doesn't want that. I'm not being a part of this shit." He shoved my elbow away from him.

I yanked my other arm to see if I'd be able to maneuver out of their reach.

The second guy let me go without much fight because he was arguing. "Maksim, just settle down. Want a drink, huh?"

Maksim scoffed, but I heard genuine concern from the other guy. They were close enough for him to want Maksim to stay. I wanted Maksim to stay too.

"Can we remove the head cover at least?" I asked. "I'll drink you both under the table all night if we're just waiting on Dimitri." Confidence went far with men, especially Russians who liked to drink. I remembered how Georgie's friends would eye me up when I downed a shot.

"You heard Dimitri—a few hours aren't going to hurt if he's gone for the night." Maksim sounded like he was getting rid of his shoes, and then his hands were at my neck, loosening the binding.

"I'm not taking ownership of that if he finds out," his partner replied gruffly.

The light blinded me for a second, but I scrubbed my hands over my face and combed my fingers through my waves. "You might be stuck with me for a very long time. Blood's Russian, you know?"

11

"Half Russian," he shot back as his blue eyes scanned my face. They hovered on my lips like any creep's, and I licked them just to taunt him.

The game we were about to play would begin with taunting. Maksim pulled out a bottle of vodka, and I took in the small room. The carpet was old like the rest of the small apartment. It looked like a stopping point for the bratva. They might check in and out of here, but no one lived in the space. The wooden table was worn with scratches and stains, and the chairs wobbled badly from years of abuse, but there were no photos on the walls and no food in the refrigerator, just alcohol.

And glasses in the cupboards.

Maksim poured generous helpings, and we drank.

Three shots in, I was looser than I wanted to be but keen enough to know that Boris, Maksim's friend, was enjoying my company a little too much.

He drank double what I did and made a show of it as if to impress me.

His hand had been rubbing my thigh for the past five minutes, and he'd just gotten up the courage to tell Maksim to leave us. "Katie wants a couple hours with me to herself, right?" His eyebrow rose, and his hand squeezed hard over my jeans.

Had I mastered everything Dante had taught me? To the point I could execute every move perfectly? It was all about the right timing, no mistakes, making sure I was committed to the outcome.

I had to be ready to kill. You didn't pull a gun without knowing you were going to pull the trigger.

"Why not, huh? The Italians never gave me much to write home about. Let's see if Boris packs a punch." I winked at Maksim, and he squinted at me like the whole thing made him queasy. In another life, we would have been friends. He would have read my wink for what it was.

I'm going to get rid of this man. He'll be the first of many who will never hurt women again.

"Get the fuck out of here, man," said Boris. "I'll call you if I need you. Be back in an hour?"

"You sure?" Maksim was already getting off the worn chair, like a dog finally let off his leash.

"Sure, go." I shrugged and flipped my hair over my shoulder. I locked eyes with Boris and smirked at him. The looks I had mastered... I could trick any man into thinking I wanted him.

But I had to have mastered Dante's escape and survival tactics too.

I didn't know which was better, a surprise attack or one where I looked him dead in the eye. My little girl was shrinking back into the corner of the room, cowering in fear, but the woman wanted to show her how to be brave, to stand up and fight.

As the door swung closed, I poured myself another shot without giving Boris any attention. I downed the whole thing and then backed myself against the door.

"How do you want to die, Boris?" I asked, staring into his eyes, the smile I had for him a second ago completely gone.

"I could choke you out or break the bottle over your head before I stab you to death."

"Twisted." He groaned and rubbed his pants before he got up to come toward me. "I like it. I think I'd like to make you scream once or twice before you try to scare me, though."

Adrenaline whipped through me, shooting off in every direction before Boris descended upon me. My palms sweat, my heart beat at the speed of light, and every thought sprang from my mind like hair full of static.

Instead of letting him touch me, of letting any part of this happen, I grabbed his hand and brought it to my throat like I was playing a damsel under a strong man.

The position was one Dante had taught me. With the perfect pivot and a palm strike to his wrist, I would be able to throw him off balance and, with the right amount of leverage, get him in a chokehold.

Before his other hand could come up to touch me, before his hot breath could mingle with my own, I executed the move.

I believed in myself.

I stood up for me and the little girl in the corner.

I put my strength, my hate, my repulsion into it. I gave it all I had.

Pivoting hard into my palm strike, I forced all my momentum into his wrist. He yelped and fell toward the wall, a little unsteady after all the vodka, right where I needed him to be. I swung my arm up and around his neck to garrote him. He started swinging immediately, but my body could take the punches and the pain. I clamped down harder because, if I were to let go now, I'd die.

Him or me.

My death or his.

The amount of energy he was exerting by flailing, wiggling, and flopping around like an idiot had hope growing in me. Dante said the more they moved, the less I had to.

I guess the bratva was still disorganized, because Boris hadn't been trained to deal with me.

Punching me over and over again in the side was his main defense. He tried throwing us into the wall, but my garrote was tight.

Never let go if you want to live.

He bent at the knee, then to the ground; then his breathing stopped.

I held on for minutes. Maybe twenty. Maybe a hundred. Maybe I would have stayed in that position forever.

I'd killed again, and I wanted to be sure the life was mine before I released the hold.

That's how Maksim found me when he returned. "Fuck, Katalina." He bent down to loosen my grip, eyes full of something that looked like remorse. "Did he attack you? I shouldn't have left. I wasn't sure...You seemed—"

"It's not your fault, Maksim." I slid up to sit against the wall and pulled my legs toward me. We stared at the lifeless body. "He had it coming, right?"

"Most of us have it coming.?"

Thinking of all the things the mob had done, of lines crossed, laws broken, lives taken, the only answer was yes. We were trying to outmaneuver one another, but in the end we all had it coming one way or the other.

"From what you can see, I'm not long for this world," I said. "Take me to see my grandfather now, please. I'll owe you. Maybe he'll owe you, too."

"You can't hand out favors from the grandfather of the bratva, Katalina."

"How do you know?" I shot back. "You ever met his grand-kids before?"

"Well, no." He sighed over Boris's corpse. "And I'm thinking you're the only one I can handle meeting. Dimitri is going to kill me anyway. Let's get you there quick before I have to provide an update."

I nodded and we left, man down, drinks gone, and plans completely ruined. Maksim drove fast, city lights whipping past us. We crossed over the river, through fields outside the city lights, and into a small suburb.

A white cedar house appeared in the distance. As we neared, I saw the lawn was taken care of, and the cedar shake gables with a wraparound white-stained porch looked welcoming. Understated but expensive. I wondered if Ivan had picked the place out himself.

We drove up onto the cement driveway, and a floodlight came on. Not a second later, the front door light flicked on too.

Ivan had been waiting.

Now that we were idling just twenty feet from the man

who had given life to my mother, whose blood ran through my veins, my body wouldn't move to open the door.

Maksim cut the engine and waited. "I'm not sure if you want me to shove you out or drag you in, but I'm pretty sure you should walk."

A laugh burst out of me. "You've had about as bad a night as me."

"You could say that. I'm a little fucked in the head right now, probably why I gave you as much leeway as you got."

"Fucked in the head from what?" I inquired, maybe because at that moment, he was the only person I felt safe with. I wanted to be in that car with him where I knew he wouldn't kill me. At least, not yet.

"That's a story for another day, Katalina."

"If I see the light of another day," I grumbled.

"Be happy you got this far. It could have been worse."

"How so?" But I knew there were worse things than a Boris rushing me.

"I should have called Dimitri. If I was smart, it's what I would have done. I would have had to let him torture you, fed you back to the bratva where we aren't sure you belong. Normally, if we aren't sure, we just kill you. There's no real soul to this brotherhood, not like with the Armanellis. You know that right?"

"But Ivan wanted to see me. He didn't want me dead. There's some hope there, don't you think?"

"Ivan's going insane, probably. Still, no one's sure. No one's sure about anything anymore, and you're the wild card. I couldn't take the risk of not listening to Ivan this time."

"Guess that's good for me. Or for Ivan. Should I call him that when I meet him?" I stared straight ahead at the white garage door we'd parked in front of.

"Ask him yourself." Maksim pointed at the front door, and there stood a tall, older man with a full head of silver hair and a smile that was deceptively comforting.

"If I'm still alive after all this, I'll owe you." I whipped open the door and went to meet Ivan with strides that ate up the sidewalk. I'd face whatever the man had in store for me.

He swung the door wide open and waved me in. "You made it tonight. I'm pleased. Dimitri said tomorrow morning instead."

"Dimitri had other plans for me tonight."

Ivan peered over my shoulder and nodded at Maksim. "Ah, that one shows the true loyalty, then."

Ivan closed the door behind me, and I took in the sleek wood floors, the arched doorways, and the delicate blue china in the dining room across the foyer. "You have a nice home."

"It does what it's supposed to." He waved away the decoration. "I had a wife once, your grandmother, and she loved this type of china. Silly woman went and bought hundreds of thousands of dollars' worth during one of our fights."

I hummed as I walked toward the mahogany dining table chairs. He motioned for me to take one and sat at the head of the table. We stared at each other, his ice-blue eyes studying me like I was a science experiment.

"You look a little like your mother," he said.

"I doubt it." I shrugged, knowing I had a lot of my father's features.

"You'd be surprised." He pulled at his ear and then got up to grab a picture from inside one of the built-in cabinets behind him. He set it on the table, and the picture clattered against the wood. He slid it across the table.

The woman in the picture wasn't smiling. She stood against a tree, her mouth downturned and her blonde hair blowing in the wind. Staring off into the distance, she looked like she didn't want anything to do with the person behind the camera or the world in general.

I'd had that look before.

I shrugged. "If you say so." I set the photo down and let it sit between us. The silence stretched, a good indicator that blood didn't mean instant closeness.

Ivan's phone buzzed, and from his raised eyebrows, I could only imagine that Dimitri had texted him about Boris. "Dimitri is on his way," he said.

My blood should have run cold, or my heart should have sped up. Was this really where I was supposed to be? Instead of with Rome, Bastian, Cade, and Dante?

No.

That family wasn't really mine. They'd made that very clear.

"I guess more Russian blood will be spilled tonight," I said. Dimitri wanted me dead, and now he had good reason to kill me.

"Your loyalty lies with another family. I didn't ever want that for you."

19

"But my mother left me to my father. What did you expect?"

"She'd run around with Douglass forever." He waved off the notion of my mother loving my father. "Those two thought love could conquer everything."

"It didn't," I finished for him. "It never does."

"Your mom came to terms with that before your father. She didn't tell anyone about you when she was pregnant. I thought she was just hiding away with your father for a time. Then she came to me in the middle of the night, determination in her eyes. She wanted to learn from me, be in Russia with me, and leave for there immediately. I was so happy, thought she and your father had broken up, so I took the opportunity. I trained her and Dimitri for years. Until they turned on each other. The night she died, Dimitri admitted it all to me. He wanted to prove his power and desire to take over the mob, so he made a deal with the Armanelli family."

My hands shook, and my heart turned cold and black. "Mario was—"

"—always making deals, Katalina. But your father worked closely with Mario so that Mario wouldn't do much else to you. I found that out much later. It's only been a few years that I've known I have a granddaughter. Had I got to you before your father died, you'd never have been embedded in the Italian family."

"I don't understand," I whispered.

"Mario didn't pay your father to take care of lightbulbs. He threatened him into staying nearby so he could keep an eye on you, make sure we didn't come for you instead. I

20

would have too if I'd known you'd been born. Mario swore he wouldn't take your life, because you'd be a part of his family instead. Your father said no. And then he died, or so I'm told."

"He didn't want me to be a part of any of it." I shook my head, everything starting to click into place.

"Mario always had a soft spot for children. And what better child to hold over my head than my own grandchild."

When the body is given too much to handle, too much to bear, it looks for outlets. I found mine by snapping up from the table, by pacing the floor in denial. "My father, he would have told me at the end, he would have..."

His letter, crinkled now in a little box I kept, with words so straightforward but cryptic at the same time, made all the more sense.

"You're beautiful. I choose death so you can live. I won't tell you to stop working with them. I know you're in too deep. Make me proud, Katalina. Show them you were meant to stand out or get out from under them."

My grandfather didn't look at all anxious like me. He sat there, hands folded on the table, blue eyes bright and full of too much life for someone who was supposed to have dementia as he retold the story. "Dimitri's not good at much, but he's good at being a snake, at bringing everyone to his level. He devolved and got angry when he found he couldn't have children, that he couldn't carry on the Russian Family.

He was furious when I told him he wasn't worthy of much if he couldn't do that. So he slithered around this city, trying to ruin your mother just as he'd been ruined. He found you. You were his golden ticket, a baby she'd hidden from the family. He ordered you both killed. By then, Mario had other plans for you, but not your mother. He's steered you his way from the beginning."

I shook my head, closed my eyes, and breathed in deep, trying to calm the quaking. They'd delivered blow after blow as if I were empty inside, as if I couldn't feel the pain. "He's not steering now."

"Maybe. Maybe not." Ivan narrowed his eyes. "I think that's up to you."

The front door clicked and then swung open. Two seconds passed. I listened closely to the footfalls of the man who'd ordered my mother to be killed.

They called Rome a monster, but now I knew the feeling, the stirring deep in my bones and the wild shaking of the cage where I kept my emotions locked up. The war in me had begun. I wanted vengeance, and I wasn't sure I would ever be able to tame the beast of that desire.

"Dimitri, you made it," said Ivan.

"I texted you that I would, that this niece of mine already brought down a man in our family. We end her now."

"I don't think so, son." Ivan closed his eyes like he was frustrated with him already. "Sit down."

Dimitri spat furious Russian words at his father.

Ivan's cold stare turned frigid, and the room dropped ten

degrees. I longed for the power to control the room with just a look. "Sit down, son. Or I'll make you sit down."

Dimitri's eyes jumped behind him and around the room. No one was there, but then two men came from the shadows. One was Maksim, and he stood behind my chair while another man stood behind Ivan.

"You'll die for the way you left Boris." Dimitri pointed behind me, and a vein popped on his neck as his face turned red. "That bitch—"

Ivan's hand slammed down on the table. Then he stood, and as old as he was, when he curled his lip at his son, the predator in him showed. "You don't speak to family that way."

"She's not family. She's a bastard child, a mutt."

The cage that had been holding my emotion broke. The door came unhinged and the beast flew out. "Careful, uncle. A mutt's bite is always worse than a purebred's."

"Is that so?" He laughed maniacally, turning in a circle so he could look at each side of the room. One eye twitched, and he scratched at his arm aggressively. He was sweating, eyes bolting every which way, and then he ripped his gun from his belt. "Why don't you show me, then? What's that bite like, niece?"

"We won't be doing this," Ivan mumbled and waved a hand behind him. "Dimitri, if you're going to fight, at least do it when you're sober."

The man behind Ivan walked slowly toward Dimitri, who swung to aim his gun at him, eyes wild. "I am sober! I've been sober this whole damn time."

"You got addicted to the drugs you were selling a long time ago." Ivan tsked. "Put down the gun."

"No!" Dimitri screamed and waved it. While the gun wasn't aimed, Ivan's man quickly advanced and disarmed him like he'd done it a million times before.

Ivan pointed to the table, and the man set the gun there. We all stared at it once Dimitri stopped struggling.

"A long time ago, I would have killed you myself," Ivan whispered, his tone sending shivers down my spine. "I'd have killed both of you. I would have thought I was invincible, that I would lead the family forever."

Dimitri struggled in the guard's grip. "I can lead. I'm good enough. It's been in my blood from the start."

"You've been nothing but a cancer to me from the start!" Ivan snatched the gun and aimed it at his son. "You've been a disappointment, Dimitri."

"No! Your daughter was the disappointment, Dad. Look at what she left us! A woman mixed with God knows what. She won't even provide a decent bloodline!"

Maybe it was that freedom to finally do whatever I wanted, maybe it was the girl who'd never fit in coming out to scream she was worth something, but I wouldn't sit there silently. "What's a decent bloodline, Dimitri? Just so we're all clear. Earlier tonight you were ready to have your way with me, no?"

"I wouldn't have you bear my children. I'd have shown you how to submit to a man. It's what you're good for."

"Is that what every woman is to you?"

24

He panted out short breaths and shook his head, a frown across his face. "I don't have to explain anything to you."

Taking his time, Ivan placed the gun on the table, and we watched as he glanced at his only child, then shoved the gun my way. The sound of steel sliding across wood was heard for miles, across the city, across the mob. "I either give this bratva with all the businesses and money tied to it to you or to her. You're both my blood. This is what we do. When my mind fails me, my bloodline will not. So I think you do have to explain yourself to her, as she's a new generation, my son."

"Those businesses are mine. She's not a damn thing!" he shrieked and struggled against the man holding him in place. He was out of control, drops of sweat forming on his brow, his arms whipping about until he finally caught hold of his captor's face and gouged an eye.

He took his freedom quickly and flew at me in a jealous rage, screaming, "You're a bastard child. A mutt. Your mother was nothing, and so are you."

"She was your sister." I flinched at the spittle flying from his mouth, but the cold weapon in my hands held most of my attention.

"She was exactly what you say all women are to me." He cackled in his mania. "I fucked her and I'll fuck you. I'll show you your place whether—"

The shot rang out, and the bullet ripped a hole in his flesh, just like the devil in me wanted to.

His blue eyes widened as he grabbed at his heart. He whispered, "You shot me."

25

The red spread like a virus across his shirt and his hands. I watched him realize his fate.

I never looked away, not when I was taking a life. Deserved or not, the man got my attention at that moment.

"How could you...I need a hospital." He looked at the men in the room.

No one moved.

Then he screamed it again, "I need a hospital."

Not even his father loved him enough to tell him he would live, that he would be okay. The men at his side stepped back and away.

As Dimitri crumpled to the floor, tears and wails of agony escaped him. He didn't hold on to his pride in death; he begged and pleaded instead. I searched everyone's eyes, and not one held an ounce of emotion. This was the bratva I would inherit.

I stood from my chair, laid the gun back on the table, and crossed the room to my uncle. I knelt before him and grabbed his hand. He repeated over and over again that I was nothing as he took his last breaths.

But he held my hand, his fingers clutching mine like he was scared and needed the comfort. He pulled it close to his bleeding chest as he disappeared from the world.

Did he take my soul down to hell with him when he left? I wasn't sure.

CHAPTER 3

KATIE

T HE CRIMSON COLOR of blood washes away easily. Cold water rinses it from clothing, erasing the stain enough that you'd never know it had been there. And yet, it never really disappears from your memory, not when a whole life bleeds out.

Not when you sit watching to make sure every ounce needed to cause death leaves the body.

Pint after pint of Dimitri's blood ran into the wood flooring. Ivan and I sat there in silence after he waved off the men.

"He was a good boy only some days, Katalina. Most days, he was evil. I will not mourn his death." He clapped his hands as if we'd wasted enough time on him. Then he grabbed his cellphone and started texting away.

"Did you mourn my mother's death?" My heart dropped, thinking of how she may have died: in her own blood, alone, without a soul to tell her she mattered. Had I felt like her all this time? Did I matter to anyone really anymore, or was I climbing through all this hell for nothing, for control of something I didn't even know I could handle?

"Oh, very much." He squinted off into the distance as if thinking about it, and for a few moments I had hope. "She would have led the bratva to rule the city if she'd taken the last step needed."

My blood ran colder at his words, my heart hardened, and my skin crawled. She'd been another tool to him, like I'd been a tool of Mario's for so long.

He shrugged at me like he knew why I was furious but didn't feel any remorse. "Way of the world, Katalina. I was born into all this. I mourned what I knew. I knew she would be powerful; I knew her potential, and that's all I can give. She knew that about me, huh? I wasn't a father to her like your father was to you."

"Nobody could be a father like him."

"Maybe." He nodded and scratched his head. "But I was proud of her. She believed in herself, unlike Dimitri. He wasn't brave, not intelligent either. He made all the wrong connections at all the wrong times. The Armanelli family had nothing to worry about once my son was in power. They knew they would rule this city forever with the way he did deals." The man cringed at a memory and then shifted in his oak rocking chair.

28

He spoke with clarity in his eyes, and his voice was strong, without hesitation.

Without a sign of dementia.

The slow spread of his smile had me walking toward him to study him more closely. I bent forward, hands on my hips, and squinted. "Is it early onset or did you stage it all?"

"Ah, sharp like your mother." He rubbed a hand over the white whiskers on his face. "Once you pass your prime, you have to see how your kingdom will rule without you. I staged a few bouts of memory loss to sway them, sure. The onset is there, though. I just needed to speed it up. I wanted your mother to show me she could fight for her bratva. Yet her heart beat for her family first, for a brother that was no more than a—" He spat at the ground next to Dimitri.

I looked over my shoulder at Dimitri's cold body, at the blood pooling on Ivan's wood floors. "Do you have a clean-up crew?"

"They're on their way, and their blood is your blood now, not the Italians' like you thought." He chuckled at the twist he'd put on the Armanelli's oath. "You'll learn quickly how well they will listen to you. They've all been waiting for you, for someone who could take on Dimitri. Your mother couldn't. She couldn't kill him. She hoped he wouldn't be able to kill her either. Coward."

"I don't want to know any more, Ivan. What's done is done." All the emotions rattled around in my bones, and something angry ran wild in me. The ground seemed to wobble beneath me as I aimed for my chair.

"You will know. She was your mother. She was found beaten, assaulted, naked, and alone."

I fisted my hand, pursed my lips to stop the ball of fury that built in my throat.

"He had some no-name do it, said he'd worked closely with Mario after, and Mario leapt at the chance."

I shook my head. "Mario wouldn't—"

"Mario did whatever he had to do." Ivan slashed his hand through the air. "You'll do what you have to do too. The bratva will rise with you, and you'll implement what you want. This is your chance."

I pictured my mother, how she must have been found, how so many women had been a victim to the pain on the city's streets. I pictured Marvin standing over me unbuttoning his pants, myself being bait over and over again. I thought of Jimmy, of Georgie, and others too. Then my uncle, how he'd grabbed my thigh, how he'd told me I was nothing. I stared at his lifeless body on the floor and how the vibrant red turned a darker and darker brown with each passing minute.

"I'll change everything." I narrowed my eyes and swung my gaze up to him. "I'll rebuild the whole bratva the way I want it. Women in power, men underneath us, and every single one of them will have to answer to me if they step out of line."

He bowed his head and held his hair in his hands. This was the moment he'd find a way to kill me. I thought he realized what I was saying, that I wouldn't be told what to do by anyone if I was in power, not even him. Instead of pulling a weapon to end my life, he got up and hobbled over to me with open arms. I stood and he pulled me in for a hug. I didn't embrace him back but stood stiffly there, listening to his words. "Your mother's heart was too big, Katalina, but yours is cold. Powerful. And strong. The blood on your hands is proof. You have your inheritance at your disposal now, huh? Let's see your reign. I bet it will be like mine."

I rubbed my palms against my jeans, instinctually trying to get rid of the evidence. I took a deep breath, though, reminding myself that I wanted this. It just had to be my way. "I'm not like anyone. I'm me."

"You're a queen, willing to do what it takes for family, for blood, for your bratva. You spill to protect. The bratva will bend to you, and you'll rule better than you ever would have on the arm of another."

"Is this bratva strong enough to stand without you, Ivan?" I wondered.

"Why not? You're my granddaughter. You've made ties with our enemy. That's beneficial, isn't it?" He smiled and it was one with sick satisfaction.

Didn't he know that Mario had built his family like an organized military structure that led the world? He was the general, he had his officers, his sergeants, and a thought out military that wanted power. They didn't need us. "The Armanellis won't bend for anyone."

"But they already have, haven't they? They gave in to you. They'll take down Mario too." He sat, thinking over his next idea. "You and Bastian could create a new city, a new empire.

Yes, I'll help with it. I'll teach you what I know, and I'll watch you build until I can't anymore. This bloodline is made for the greatness we'll construct."

I shook my head and backed away from him. "You just said he helped kill my mother?"

Ivan rolled his eyes like I was naive. "Way of the world, Katalina. He was quicker to get his power because of it. If you want to be ruthless, you need to let go of revenge. We focus on what we want."

"What's that?"

"Power to change things, access to money, to deals. When you have that, you can do anything." His voice sounded far away, like he was dreaming of what could be.

He'd never reached that status. The bratva was too scattered and he'd never controlled it like he should have. I bit my lip. "I don't trust you. And your dementia—"

"Will take hold soon enough. And even still, you came here today. You took your uncle's life today."

"That was self-defense." I pointed out.

"That was you seizing power, and you know it. You stepped out onto that street and waited for his SUV to pull up because you wanted something more. This is the more you wanted. Take it. Be greedy. Be bold. Be brave. You're capable of greatness."

I tripped on the Persian carpet and then righted myself immediately. "I don't know how to run a bratva. I don't know...I only know how to be bait." I sighed and closed my eyes. The burning in them and in my throat was a clear indicator that tears would spill over soon. I tried to pull back the emotions, closed my mouth to hold them in. "I'm not ready."

"I'm going to teach you, Katalina. What's another member going to do, huh? You want to leave your legacy to someone else? Make your claim on the throne now. Tell me you want this so that we can bring the bratva back to life. You and the Armanellis can rule together."

I shook my head slowly, but my mind raced as fast as it could to put the pieces together. I'd been used for too long, and I'd wanted power for even longer.

My hand was on the gold knob of the front door, but it fell to my side. I stared at my grandfather, his silver-gray hair an indication of the stress over the years. I took in his blue china in the dining room and the grandfather clock in the corner. He was living a beautiful life retired from the bratva. But when I glanced down, Dimitri's dead body was a reminder of what it would really be.

"I'm not like any of you," I said.

"Ah, so my son's words got to you. You think you're a mutt and a mutt can't rule?"

"No. I think a mutt will rule better." I paused. "I know it. Because I've been a part of it all and yet not included in any of it."

Ivan tilted his head at me, trying to understand. It'd take the world a while to catch up, but I wouldn't be waiting.

"The throne is mine."

CHAPTER 4
ROME

DAYS. SHE'D BEEN gone days.

I'd called her the first night only to notice her phone was still on the counter. She'd left everything, and the only thing we could do was listen. Cade kept eyes on her and gave me phone access to the men who had taken her hostage. Yet I had to trust her. I had to let her go like she asked.

We kept our ears to the ground for news and focused on our own cleansing.

I told Bastian that very night, "We're cleaning this damn family up. That means you're about to become the real leader of this country." We'd been his men of honor, his soldiers, his musketeers. The day had come where he chose to stand with us now. Was it our blood or was it the family's that mattered?

He'd nodded at me slowly, taking in the words I was saying. "I was thinking the same thing."

"It's time our family got to work. If red splashes the streets, we turn that red into a river so they can be cleaner the next day."

Dante, Cade, and Bastian had nodded. We'd agreed that we were fighting for a change. It would be brutal, but it would be worth it.

Now, I stood in the room with another man I didn't trust.

"Sergio, begging isn't something I do well. I won't plead with you to tell me what you know," I told the man in front of me.

"You don't have to, Rome. I wouldn't lie to you." Even the moles on Sergio's bald head looked like they might be sweating. His buggy eyes and pursed lips were perfect indicators that he was keeping something from me.

"I've known you my whole life." Words that should have been said in anguish rolled off my tongue without an ounce of emotion.

"Right! I knew you when you were just a little boy," Sergio yelped, willing to jump on anything that might save him. He was tied to a chair in his own house, his buggy eyes darting back and forth, searching for an escape from the secret I knew he was hiding from us.

Maybe I should have felt a pull to spare him. We were close enough. He was part of the family.

Did no one understand though? Katalina had left. She was gone. With her, she'd taken all that was good, all the hope, all the dreams of the future.

All of my heart.

She'd left only the monster.

I couldn't have kept him caged if I'd tried. He erupted out of hiding, and we went on a rampage.

Katalina didn't just stir my demon though. She'd had everyone in our unit vibrating with devastation over losing her.

This time, I couldn't intervene any more than I already had. I had to let it play out, or she'd never ever come back to me.

I didn't wait well.

I killed exceptionally, though. All I needed was a list, and Cade did a fine job of providing me with that.

One by one, Dante and I went down the line. It didn't matter if we'd known them a day or a year or our whole lives. We needed a new family, and my immediate unit and I were going to clear ours out until we had the one the city and Katalina deserved.

"Cade pulled your bank statements from the year of Katalina's mom's disappearance. A lot of big numbers." I disclosed to Sergio. "Did you and Mario have something to do with it? Did you know about her?"

"I don't know what you're talking about. The money we moved back then, Rome, it's all so confusing. We had a lot more—"

"Sergio, remember how my dad would hand you a dollar and you'd say, 'No, no'?" I knelt down in front of him, trying to get on his level one last time. I motioned behind me to Dante, and he placed Sergio's sawed-off shotgun into my outstretched hand. "You'd tell him he only owed you ninety-five cents. You counted each and every penny. Your memory hasn't failed you."

"My memory isn't what it used to be. I don't recall…"

So much time we could have had growing a better family, a better unit. I didn't have any more to waste.

I aimed the gun at his jaw. "Stop playing games. You know I don't like them."

His eyes bulged. "Dante!" he called out.

Dante just straightened one of his black gloves. "Answer the question, Sergio. I don't want to call the cleanup again today."

"Look, I only set up her foster care. Mario wanted her somewhere she wouldn't last, okay?"

My stomach turned at his words.

Marvin.

Mario had known that man was a pedophile. He'd known just where to get Katalina placed so that she'd go running straight into his arms.

"I thought he'd spare Jimmy, you know?" he wheezed. "Jimmy was supposed to be good to her, but he got too close to her. It all worked out, though, huh?"

I pulled the trigger. The sawn-off shotgun blew most of his jaw clean off.

"God damn it, Rome." Dante sighed and wiped a splatter of blood from his cheek. Teeth were scattered across the floor. "Couldn't you have at least warned me? I would have stepped back."

"I'm sick of playing games. He didn't want to talk. Now he doesn't have a mouth to do so."

"Or a life, for that matter," Dante grumbled and started to type out a text that was surely about cleanup.

"We got what we needed from him." I undid the latch of my chain and removed it from around his hands, then rolled it up my arm to tuck back under my jacket sleeve. "We should just let the cops handle this one. He didn't struggle enough to have marks on his wrists, and it's his own gun."

Dante waved me off. "You're right, not that it matters. The chief of police called this morning. He knows we're on a killing spree, and the squad is capable of keeping it under wraps."

Dante and the chief went way back. Their friendship—along with the security of having the family on your side—was enough for most of the cops in the city to cover up what we wanted. "Then, I'm not messing with cleaning today."

"I don't want to be near the fucker, anyway. Damn, man. They all twisted her life. She was a pawn." He pulled at his hair and then swiped a hand down his face. "I don't know if she'll ever come back. Not after we tell her this."

"We clean out everyone involved. We make her see we're family." I pointed at the dead man, his head hanging sideways as blood dripped from the top of his mouth. "He wasn't."

Dante nodded and grabbed the gun, shoving it into the corpse's hand.

I pulled open the front door. "On to the next."

One foot in front of the other. One kill after another.

Each body was a testament to my love for her. This family had been hiding things for too long. Now, I would bury myself in their darkness and clean up. I was the one who was supposed to live in the shadows and listen to the whispers. I was the one Mario was supposed to trust with his secrets. He'd kept this from me—his biggest secret of all. He'd prepped me all these years to rip apart those who disobeyed, who omitted the truth, who threw their bones in a closet where we couldn't find them.

Didn't he know that I lived in that grim closet now? That I collected those bones and hunted down the ones who'd hidden them?

The monster in me had eyes that saw better in the dark, saw the secrets more clearly than anyone.

I was ready to pull down the whole family. This was about trust, now. Our family had a new ruler. Bastian had given us the go-ahead, and it started with transparency. The ones who couldn't clean up and be open about their past would be wiped out.

"I'm picking up Mario alone," I told Dante as we got back into my vehicle. I steered us toward the highway that led to Dante's place.

"I don't like the sound of that, man." He pulled his gloves off and shoved them into his leather jacket. "Do Bastian and Cade know?"

"What's there to know?" My hands gripped the steering wheel, and the leather creaked underneath my grip. I squeezed it harder, like I was squeezing a neck. Turmoil waged a war in all of us. We'd been putting Katalina in the line of fire for far too long. This family had taken advantage of her, of others, even of me.

Dante shook his head. "We should all be there. He's the man we need to stop if it's true."

"If he killed her mother and only took her in for her blood-line, for the union of the bratva and the family, he's as good as dead today."

"Then, let him sit in the chair. Let us make that decision together."

"I'm still going to pick him up alone. Get the unit to the facility. We do it as soon as he lands." I drove in silence as we passed over a bridge where the river drew a line between upper and lower class for most of Chicago society. I dropped off Dante and headed straight to the airport.

I dialed Mario's number and listened to him greet me like we were still family.

Yet my blood for him had run cold.

"Mario, I'm positive now that love runs deeper than blood." I shifted the phone so I could cradle it between my shoulder and neck. "I'm on my way to get you from the airport."

"Rome, I'll get one of the units to send me someone. I want you to keep working on tracking down those who need to be cleaned up."

"Nah. I'm already on my way, Mario. Keep me company. I'm tired of being on the job today, you know what I mean?"

The line crackled, and I pictured him switching ears, something he did when he was a bit nervous. Mario knew I never really cared for company. Or maybe he just knew by my tone. He hadn't stayed alive so long as the head of the family by being unaware.

"How far out are you?" he asked.

"I'll be there in five." I paused and turned onto the airport exit. "It's good you came home, Mario."

"You know I love Katie as a daughter. I heard some things."

"Oh, I know, Mario, I know."

I pressed the red phone icon on the screen to end the call. Maybe he'd run, get back on the plane, and set up in New York. He had to know that it was the smart thing to do.

Mario held himself to a standard, though. Every plan he'd ever implemented, he stood behind.

As I drove up to him on the tarmac, he stood tall, the inner silk of his navy suit flashing in the wind. The gold buttons on his cuffs glinted in the light of the setting sun. For all he'd been through, for all the years he'd endured as the head of the family, Mario looked well.

I rolled down my window as I pulled up to him, and he started lugging his suitcase toward the back. "Should I throw them in for you?"

"You're our monster, not our valet, Rome." He chuckled, but I wondered if he knew about the last two men I'd killed.

Was the rage building in me the monster we all thought we could control?

He got in and turned his mud brown eyes on me. "Bastian wants us to meet at the facility."

"That he does." Itching to crack my neck, I tightened my grip on the steering wheel instead. Then I adjusted the air, trying to cool the temperature within the vehicle.

The weather was gloomy, raining on and off, so there wasn't a need for air conditioning. Still, it cooled down the heated temper flowing through me. Cade had continued to text me, call me, send me more information on Mario.

Mario had dug his own grave. Even his sons had turned on him. I knew from the texts. They'd started with:

> **CADE:** I found a few things about Dad.

Then it'd progressed to:

> **CADE:** I don't know what the fuck Mario was thinking.

Then even his name was dropped:

> **CADE:** This fucker needs to explain.

From there, Cade hadn't even added his own commentary. He'd just send encrypted files for me to look over. Billing statements, phone calls he'd found within the phone service system. Nothing was off limits for Cade. He could break into anything, which had me confident that he'd continually been able to block our own lines.

Technology was dangerous in our field, but we had one of the best hackers to cover our asses. The only thing that could save you was him or the trust of the family. Unfortunately, Mario had lost him and our trust. We scoured everything we could for intel on him.

"What's this all about?" He chuckled, but I saw him squirm in his seat. Mario hadn't been called home by his son for nothing. Bastian didn't exert his power over his father ever, nor did he want to sit down for a meal with the old man. Their problems ran deep, and this had made them near impossible to overcome.

"I'm the monster and the valet today, Mario. Not the explainer. I won't be the one doing that today."

"Come on, Rome." He clapped a hand on my shoulder.

I dipped it so he quickly lost his grip. Connecting through a familial touch wouldn't work, not when it felt like a snake's.

His bushy eyebrows pulled toward the center of his face. Lines from years of stress deepened across his forehead. "You're my son, Rome. Just like Cade and Bastian, huh? Tell me what's got you this way with me."

He probably could have pulled at Cade's heartstrings with that one. Bastian and I had always been more distant from Mario. Bastian had to live up to being the heir to the family, and so Mario hardened him with constant pressure and gruesome work. I'd been his right-hand man, the one he turned to for most things. I knew too much to have heartstrings.

When I didn't answer him right away, his right hand started twitching. He'd risk jumping out of a moving vehicle because Mario had stared death in the face enough times to know he was in trouble.

"Don't spend your last moments being a coward, Mario. Stay put." I punched the door lock for good measure.

Mario gulped loudly but didn't respond. He leaned over and turned on his favorite oldies station, cranked up the music, and shrugged when I looked over at him. "One for the road, huh?"

CHAPTER 5

ROME

H E WASN'T BEGGING; he wasn't really even shaking. From the middle of the room, Mario stared at his sons, at me, at his bloodline and the world he'd built, like a god looking down on his creation.

"I won't apologize," he said.

"It wouldn't help now, anyway," Bastian said from one of the chairs encircling him.

Dante cracked his knuckles, next to him. "You should have been stopped long ago."

"The only people willing to stop me were the people I made strong enough to do so." Mario stared at the arm that always had my chain coiled under the sleeve. "Are you going to do it, Rome?"

I shook my head. He'd been more of a father figure to me than my own, and he was the father figure of the mob, of the family. "I don't understand how you could do all this."

"You do what you have to for the family. Katie was a piece we needed."

"Tell me that placing her at Marvin's was coincidence." I shook with a wrath I couldn't contain and circled him like a shark ready to rip apart a wounded animal.

"Do you want me to lie?" Mario asked and then picked at his teeth. "Deals were made. That wasn't the only one. We got a lot of protection out of me agreeing to a lot of things over the years."

I raised my head to make eye contact with Bastian, and he nodded along with Cade, who sat by his side. I swung my fist fast hard into Mario's jaw. The old man crumbled in the chair. He breathed in and out quickly, sucking on air as if he were trying to get his bearings.

Then the man laughed, hard and loud. "Wow. That's real. That's some real shit I've given my enemies over the years. The monster in you doesn't come to play."

"I never did play when it came to the family, when it came to her."

"She always was able to hook every man she came in contact with, huh?" Mario rubbed his jaw in thought. "I've always been proud of that girl. Tell her I was proud, will you?"

"Marvin raped her. He tortured her. Katie was just a girl. You want me to tell her you placed her there knowing that he would?" As I said the words, acid rose so high in my throat, I contemplated spitting on him.

"I'd do it again, Rome. Let me be clear to you all here and now. I don't have a single regret, not one. Katie is ours. I did what I had to do to get her. Being the boss"—he looked at his son—"means making the hard choices. I made them over and over again. You all know by now we have money from drugs and trafficking. I halted other families from doing it."

When I turned to stare at Mario's boys, Cade's face was ashen. Bastian was vibrating with another emotion. We'd all been duped into thinking we'd been cleaning up when really Mario had fooled us all.

"You made our family a lie," Bastian responded quietly, but his words held malice.

"I made us untouchable," said Mario. "Look what we have now. I got Katalina here with us. So she had to sleep with Marvin and Jimmy. She's fine now. She's the heir to billions in the bratva. Just marry her, son."

Bastian's eyes flared at his father's admission, but I'd already known. Mario had moved Katalina like a chess piece, willing to have her fall victim time and time again. He'd used her like she felt she'd been used, and he'd made her feelings about the mob true.

Bastian walked up to his dad, bent down to look him in the eye, and said without an ounce of emotion, "Blow this man's goddamn head off."

"No!" Katalina stood in the doorway, hair tied up on her head, exposing the sharp features of her face. She was free of makeup, in combat boots and a plain tank top hanging over her jeans. In her simplest attire, she exuded with the most power I'd ever seen from her. "Don't any of you listen? I said let me go and stop what you're doing for once."

"Oh, Katalina," Mario groaned. "Now's not the time. We've already decided what becomes of me."

"Without me? Because my choice doesn't matter even when the choice is about me?" She stalked forward. "I don't want death, Mario. I want life. I want all of you to see this can be different."

"Different how?" Bastian whispered like he wanted an out, like he wanted to rally behind her, but the choice had already been made. Mario had wronged us, and Katalina most of all.

"I can forgive him if all of you can."

"I can't." The words flew out of me and held the gun to Mario's head. "I'll never forgive him. It was the one secret he should have told me and the one he kept from me instead."

Mario nodded, no remorse playing over his features. "He's right. I chose this path for the family. I'd choose it again."

Bastian cringed, and Cade stumbled back as if hoping their father would redeem himself.

"I don't care." Katalina shrugged. That shrug, that deceptive hitch in her voice like it was no big deal... The beast in me roared.

"I do." My finger pulled the trigger.

The shot rang out loud and clear, explosive within the expansive space.

She jumped forward into his blood while Cade and Bastian took a step back. Dante sighed and hung his head before he dialed a number on his phone.

Mario's death was instant. He slumped in the chair, and the temple where the bullet entered poured blood.

Katalina lunged toward the wound immediately, the savior in her bigger than all of us. Her hands tried to hold in the blood and her gaze cut to mine. "How could you?" she whispered, and her gray eyes held not an ounce of love for me. Gone was the longing, gone was the lust, and gone was the connection.

I threw the gun to the cement. "I choose the family every time, Katalina. You're a part of it, and I'll protect you whether you like it or not. That man was never going to protect you."

"You killed our father," she screamed in agony and held her hands up with the blood of the mob king on them.

"We didn't need him anymore." I crossed my arms because if I didn't, I'd go to her. I'd try to calm her, soothe her, wrap her up while she fought me enough to remember that she loved me.

Yet the fury in me was still tearing around my body and the monster wasn't silenced. I wanted more blood. I wanted more revenge. I heard her screams and saw her pain and knew that all of this life had caused it, including me.

I couldn't subject her to more of that.

I couldn't go to her.

I had to let her go.

"You need to walk away from this life," I said.

Her cries wracked her body as she held up Mario's face and then pulled it to her bosom to hug him one last time. No one approached them. We let her feel the pain for us all. Mario had been one of us and she mourned him like that.

When enough time had passed, when her cries turned to silence, she leaned him back on the chair and turned to Dante. "Get the best to clean him up and give him the funeral he deserved." Then she spun to look at the facility, wiping the blood onto her clean white shirt, staining it with dirty, lost life. "I always think I'll learn to love this place. And yet I step foot in it and want to burn it to the ground every single time."

"It's not a place of happiness." I tried to ease her.

"It's a place of death and it reeks of it. It's a place of misplaced anger and judgement." She shook her head and laughed. "I wanted for so long to sit beside you all and make these calls. For *what*? For blood on my hands and no reward? No true ownership or power?"

"Katie, we need to—"

"We don't need to do anything!" She cut her hand through the air when she whirled to look at me with hate in her eyes. "I took the bratva. Dimitri's gone. It's *mine* now."

Something hard, solid, and cold dropped into the pit of my stomach. "No," I said so low, maybe she didn't hear. "Where are they then, huh?"

"Your guards won't let them pass. I'm allowing it for now."

"Katalina," I whispered. "You shouldn't be allowing for anything here. You can't do this. The bratva, they aren't like us."

"I can and I will." Her voice boomed around larger than life, echoing back at us. "I intend to rule, not walk away," she continued.

"What the fuck are you thinking?" I bellowed, and my voice matched hers now. By then, men had started to filter in.

Bastian grabbed her arm. "We need to talk, Katalina."

She shook her head and held her bloodstained hands out in front of her. She glared at me and nodded, looking straight in my eyes. "Yes, we do. I need to make alliances with you for my bratva. I hope to protect them from monsters like him."

I lunged for her faster than Bastian could pull her away and threw her over my shoulder. Dante stepped forward as she wailed into my back, but the sound that erupted from deep in my chest stopped him. I turned to face them with Katalina struggling as I pulled a gun from behind and swung it toward all of them. Every man's hands went up. Whenever I fired, I didn't miss. Everyone knew that. "Do *not* come for her. This is our fight with each other. I bleed, she bleeds. Back the fuck off."

She threw out obscenities at every single one of us as I carried her across the room to the back doors we'd entered so long ago together. The same trash can was to the right of them as I swung open the door.

This time, I wanted to be the one puking in it.

When I got to the bathroom, I set her down, and she tried to stomp my foot. "I don't want to be back here with you! I don't want anything to do with you at all." She screamed at me so loud, she must have wanted everyone to hear.

53

"Same. You think I've wanted anything to do with you since the first time I met you?"

"You left your damn PO Box, not me."

"You needed someone," I explained.

"Not you. You can't love. You killed your father and Mario. If you can't love them, then who the fuck can you love?" She was throwing blows lower than ever before, but the pain in her eyes was there, was almost palpable. I saw our connection renewed, burning brighter in her anger than ever before.

"You!" I screamed. Or the monster screamed. Or my soul screamed. I wasn't sure who anymore. She'd ripped me all apart. "You left and I crumbled. Don't you get that?"

I wanted to crumble at his words. My heart did, I felt the pain of it. Knowing the one you loved loved you back should have been a happy moment. Instead, we knew we couldn't be together. There was too much behind us and too much in front of us. Sometimes the complications around that burning flame of love snuff it out. "You deserved for me to leave. Look at our past, Rome. We can't come back from that. You all deserved my desertion."

"This family needs you. We need you to stand with us and be a part of what—"

"Stand *with* you?" Her face turned ashen. Her little nose wrinkled up as if she was disgusted that I'd even suggested it, even though she'd done it all these years until now.

Before we could continue, she whirled and vomited in the waste basket near the bathroom door.

The motion was violent, wrenching from her soul like she wanted to exorcise everything from it.

She gripped the edge of the waste basket, knuckles turning white. "I should be used to this by now."

"Used to what?" I walked over to rub her back and she tensed but let my hand glide up and down her spine.

"Used to those around me dying. Losing every single person I care about."

"You haven't lost anyone tonight."

"I lost Mario." She glared up at me. "Because of you."

"He didn't care about anyone but himself." I tried to leash my anger by balling my fist and pressing it into the palm of my other hand.

"And yet I still cared for him. I still wanted him alive. You take a life and they're gone forever, Rome. Wiped clean from the earth." She shook her head at me like I should be ashamed.

"So they can't do any more damage."

"Was he all that bad? He loved me in the only way he knew how."

"Harden your heart, Katalina. If you think ruling that bratva out there is going to be easier than this, it won't be. You're going to need a stronger stomach."

She stepped back from the garbage and took a moment to wash her mouth in the sink. "Like déjà vu being back in this bathroom."

"It's more like a nightmare," I grumbled.

Her silver eyes watched me over her shoulder in the mirror. "I think I'm in love with you. And that's not possible. Especially not now." The words fell as whispers from her lips, floating like light feathers over to me. And still they shattered and destroyed every part of me. I wanted her love but not like this. "It shouldn't be possible after what you've done."

In the movies, the novels, the fairytales, we could work it out. We'd find a way and kiss and make up here. Suddenly, I wanted that with her.

"You don't have to walk into the bratva's open arms," I said. "We're possible if you want us to be."

"Do we ever really get what we want, Rome?"

I wish I could have told her that the mafia gave us exactly what we wanted. We got the money, the cars, the luxurious lives. Yet we were too far in, too deeply rooted in the family to think the money and infamy on the surface was all it was. Down in the dirt, the grit and power and responsibility of a city weighed on your shoulders.

"This doesn't have to be our fight," I said.

"It's the only one worth fighting now. My family and my blood will be for something."

"For what?" I whispered. "You can't change a whole city by yourself."

"I won't be by myself. Bastian and the family are going to align with us. We're going to clean up, Rome."

"He won't agree."

"Why?"

"Because it's not safe for you! Or anyone. The bratva can't be trusted." I snarled and slammed my fist into the wall. She didn't listen, she didn't even attempt to. "Look at this logically."

"Logic keeps you stagnant and I'm not aiming for that." She turned on a heel and made her way to the door.

As she was about to swing it open, I slammed my hand on it and shoved it closed. "Did you ever consider I might not let you walk away so easily? You're the damn enemy now, Katalina."

"Or an ally. Bastian makes that call."

"We all do. Bastian's never ruled as a dictator."

She leaned her back on the door and crossed her arms to look up at me. "And what? You're going to sway him to kill me? To lock me up and treat me as the enemy? You don't want the bratva as an ally to the family, and yet, you know as well as I do it's the best thing for the family. We could crush all the gangs and other families in the city. The power would be ours."

"And the responsibility."

She bit her lip as if thinking for a second. "Who better to have that responsibility, Rome? You grew up on these streets. We all know them. I know how the men operate, you know how the gangs slither through the shadows of the city alleys. I want to grab them by their heads and hold them out in the light, make them stare at the damn sun and confess their sins."

"We aren't gods, woman. We don't make the rules."

"I do now," she shot back. "I have to now, Rome. Or else, everything I've ever done is all for nothing."

"For nothing? It was to help the family and to survive." I fisted a hand and tried my best not to let her words grate on every nerve I had. I wanted to find every man who'd made her feel this way and rip them apart so they felt her pain and then felt nothing at all. I emphasized it again, "You did what you had to in order to survive. You can be proud of that, you can be—"

"I can be more than just a survivor. I can be a savior. I can be a damn enforcer. And I'm going to be one. You either get on board or stay the fuck out of my way."

"I'm in your way, woman, because you set me there. You fucked me and I fucked you so far into our own oblivion, I'm stuck in love with you."

"Stuck?" Her eyes narrowed. "I'm not asking you to be stuck."

"And yet here I am in this bathroom with you again after all these years. Let's stop this."

"Are you going to stop being Bastian's right-hand man?"

"What?" I stepped back at her question.

"You want me to give up my place for what? To stand next to you? After all this? Right now, all I've gotten from you is a fucked-up version of 'I love you' in a little bathroom I just puked in. Is that what I'm supposed to want? You've shown me that you will swoop in to save the day and ignore me the next. You let your damn monster out to play to save my ass but then tell me it's the reason we can't be together."

"Katalina, I have to keep things in line for the family."

"I don't give a flying fuck!" She stomped her foot and the words thundered out with fury. "I'm not here to be by your side, to be a pawn on the chess board; I'm here to rise above it. I should have done it long ago. I never should have given my heart to you when you couldn't quiet this viciousness. You were never ready. None of you are."

She'd already taken my heart, and now she squeezed the life from it with those words.

"You're making a mistake," I whispered.

"No, the only mistake I made was trusting anyone to do for me what I could have done myself. Had I been sitting in the room making decisions with all of you, I like to think we wouldn't be where we are. If Cleopatra ruled an empire, so can I."

"That bratva isn't the empire you want."

"It's the only one I have. I was only this family's tool. Did you love me for that or in spite of it?" I took a step toward her, but she held up her hand. "No! You don't get to come to me now. Not after this." She waved toward the hall. "You couldn't hold back killing Mario. You couldn't let me make that decision. And you want me to keep standing by your side as if it's okay, Rome. It's not."

"I won't apologize."

"You can't even see why he would have been an asset alive. That in and of itself is a problem."

"I don't need to think rationally about him, Katalina." I walked into the hand she hand between us, I held it to my chest. We both stared at it as I said, "He hurt you. He should have been six feet under the first day he even thought to."

"You can't unleash your monster any time you like based on how you feel about some girl, Rome." She wanted to hurt me, but her hand had curled around my shirt, like she was holding on, like I was a lifeline.

"You're not some girl, Katalina," I whispered. "You're my fucking world. You're the queen of this family and now the bratva too. You're the one thing I hate to care for but still do. I can't cage the animal in me that's willing to fight for you, wouldn't be able to even if I tried."

"Then we can't work."

Rage at her words flowed through me. I wanted to strangle some sense into her, but our emotions were vibrating off the walls and I was sure the tiles would shake and fall off soon. "We can if you stop this. Don't put yourself in a position where I'll have to fight to keep you alive day in and day out. A bratva queen is always in danger."

"Good thing I'm not an Armanelli queen then, right? You're only their monster, not mine." She dropped her hand, turned and swung open the bathroom door. This time I let her.

"You stay with the bratva, you leave this family behind, Cleo." I let the words fall from my lips as a warning, but they were filled with anguish too.

She froze mid stride before she turned and looked at me. Her eyes glistened like stars shining on metal in the night. "I leave you behind too, Rome. You aren't just the family. One day you'll see that. One day, you'll get why I'm doing all this. We're more than what everyone has made us out to be, huh?"

I could chase her, but I knew if I did it would only be to rip her apart for what she was putting me through.

We were destroying each other, and one of us had to stop. We couldn't keep fighting, especially when neither of us was willing to give an inch. If we continued this, we'd both end up dead. She was too important to more than just me now. She was an heiress. A Russian Princess.

The monster in me lay down and surrendered to its queen.

CHAPTER 6

KATIE

THE SICKNESS ROLLING around in my stomach
didn't subside as I left Rome without looking back. I
was destroying the bridge that connected us, burning
it up and watching it disintegrate into ashes. The dizziness
that overcame me had me leaning against a wall.

My adrenaline was subsiding. I'd watched a man close to
me murdered by the one man I thought loved me. We were
causing more destruction instead of building a foundation.

I pushed off the wall and righted myself before I walked
back out. "Bastian!" His dark head of hair snapped toward
me, and he nodded as I walked over. "We need to talk."

"That we do." He didn't raise his voice, but his words
were measured. He didn't relax when he looked at me now.
I wasn't just his friend anymore, he didn't have power over

me like he did the family, and suddenly I realized the fear my shift had brought.

I glanced around at all the faces who'd once joked around me, who'd come in for hugs and kisses on the cheek. They all looked at me with caution now. The men cleaning up Mario didn't try to say hello, Dante didn't pick me up off the ground in a bear hug, and Cade didn't throw out a smart remark. They were all coiled to react instead, like we'd never been family at all.

"It's probably best to do this with everyone," I said. "I can bring Ivan in too. I'm voting for transparency rather than secrets and deals behind doors."

"Should I call the Stonewoods too, then?" Bastian chuckled as if what I was saying was a joke.

I stood taller. "Bastian, we've had men like your father leading since the beginning of time. And"—I motioned toward him—"do you think his secrets did him any good?"

"Katie." He pinched the bridge of his nose. "More hands in the cookie jar make for a mess, no?"

"Allies are better prepared to go to war with you when they know what they're going to war for, right? We build this based on trust. Dante and Cade want to hear what we have to say, huh?"

Dante didn't say a word, but the smirk on his face told me all I needed to know.

The low voice from behind me was the only one that answered, though. "I'm not sure I want to hear it, but I intend to either which way."

"Let's just invite the damn government too," Bastian grumbled.

Three men stood and carried Mario's body out in plastic. I winced at the scene.

"Better get used to that and more, Cleo," Rome warned.

"I'm used to it already from being around you," I snapped back.

"Now, now, lovebirds." Cade looked up from his phone at the most ridiculous time to say, "I think it's best we schedule a time for the meeting. Your bratva is getting antsy outside."

"How would you know—"

Cade held up his phone. "Tapped their text messages. Some of the guys are asking Ivan what's taking you so long. We'll need to work on their tech privacy if we go into business with them…Or should I say you now?" He winked and dropped his head back into his device.

Dante chuckled, but Rome and Bastian's silence rattled the room with tension.

"I have a new phone," I whispered, not sure how to navigate not really being a part of them anymore. It was my choice, it was my calling, but it still felt foreign. I was suddenly a fish very much out of the sea I'd always swam in. "You'll text me your availability if I text you my number, Bastian?"

"Sure." He breathed in once, then twice. Before the conversation went any further, he strode toward me with purpose. I didn't pull a weapon, didn't even think to.

Maybe it was my love for him or my pride that kept me from cowering. Either way, he wrapped me in his arms tight

65

and hugged me like a man hugging a puppy he'd lost. "I'm happy you're alright, Katie. You scared the shit out of us."

I squeezed my eyes shut and gripped his shirt. Cade and Dante were suddenly behind me too, arms wrapped around me, squeezing me tight.

"Don't ask us not to follow you again. Watching from afar was fucking painful," Dante grumbled.

"You can't follow the bratva. I'm a different breed now." I poked at him and laughed through a sniffle.

"All we do is follow the bratva," Cade joked, but there was truth in his words. "I'll have more eyes on you than I ever did before, woman. Just you wait."

We all laughed at that, and then Rome killed our moment. "I'm happy you're all having this Kumbaya time but we have enemies to make alliances with. Hugging it out won't do that. Ivan's been a thorn in our side for a very long time."

"Give us a break." Dante rolled his eyes as he stepped away from the group hug. We followed his lead and rolled our eyes at Rome too.

"I'll text you, Bast," I said.

"See that you do. We'll make it work, huh?"

"That's all I can hope for now." I shrugged and began my walk back to the SUV that would be deemed as mine.

Suddenly, a world I never knew existed was my own.

I didn't know how to be happy and sad and scared at the same time. More emotions flew through me than ever before. I just had to find a way not to drown in all of them.

CHAPTER 7

KATIE

I DIDN'T TALK TO any of them for another week. I worked closely with Ivan. We found a penthouse that I could set up in. He'd already introduced me to the men within the bratva that needed to know who I was.

None of them welcomed me.

They eyed me up and down like a piece of meat. All except Maksim who'd helped me that first night while being held hostage by Dimitri.

The only thing I had going for me was that I'd killed my uncle. The bratva respected that, like it was survival of the fittest, like I was suddenly stronger than I looked.

It only took a week and we were all standing at Mario's funeral dressed in black, driving in black, make-up in black. Even the cops that showed up wore black instead of a uniform.

The chief of police shook hands with Bastian, then Rome, Cade, and Dante. The Stonewoods shook hands too. They were the leaders of this city, the men who pulled all the strings.

The women among them stood tall, though. Each of the Stonewoods had married or were tied to women they cared about. Jett held Vick's hand like she was his lifeline and Jax never took his eyes off Brey.

I wondered if Rome would ever look at me that way or if he had in the past and I'd just missed it.

The ceremony was large, green grass sprawling across the cemetery where Mario wanted to be buried. He'd bought a plot next to his mother and father.

The priest said all the right words, praising Mario's drive to always do right by the city. He mentioned he was a businessman but never touched on what type. Every person there knew but didn't say. We didn't bother sweeping our secrets under a rug because we didn't have to. Standing in plain sight was how our family worked now, loud and proud and full of power.

The priest mentioned Mario's love for his family, his boys, and those he'd taken under his wing. Rome was just that, his brother's son but someone he'd looked at as his own. Rome had been the one to kill him too.

Was that death for me or the family?

The lines were so blurred and mixed up at this point, I didn't know.

We all made the sign of the cross and then the priest asked for last words. No one spoke.

Not Bastian. Not Cade. No one.

I stepped forward. I didn't need to give Mario words of kindness, but everyone deserved love at their death.

"Mario knew, like we all do, that his blood was our blood. In his death, a part of all of us died." I took a breath. "Let us pray."

The priest cocked an eyebrow at me before he bowed his head along with most everyone.

Except Rome. His heavy, dark stare caught mine. My heart seized at the sadness I caught in his eyes. Heavy was the burden of a monster and a friend who had to take the life of the one he cared about.

His strong jawline flexed as I rolled my lips between my teeth, trying to keep in the emotions that were bubbling up. We'd complicated things beyond repair but my body still wanted to run to him, to feel his skin against mine, to find a way to be with him even if the bratva was where I belonged.

I cleared my throat and tore my gaze from him to stare at the casket. "Let us pray for ends that are cruel like Mario's death and new beginnings that bring life and love between us all in this city. Let the demons he took to his grave find peace there and let the lessons he taught us take flight to bring light to his family. Let us all bind together to make sure his death wasn't in vain. Amen."

The men and women all dressed in black followed my prayer with the sign of the cross and more amens.

Rome stepped forward. No one said a word as we watched him hold his arm over the casket. He rolled his wrist, and the chain he always had under his sleeve dangled out and dropped onto his casket. Rome draped it over the smooth surface.

I gasped as I watched and covered my mouth when a sob almost escaped. Rome was letting go of some past he had with those rusted links. I knew his father had trained him with it, probably beat him with it, and he'd definitely hurt others with it. It was a symbol of his pain and the pain he inflicted on others, something that made him the monster he was. Maybe he felt the emotion, maybe he'd mourned the loss of the life he took too. He had to. He'd taken his father's and now his uncle's life, and most everyone had to see him as a ruthless animal.

I wanted to go to him.

Knew I couldn't.

I wanted to mourn with him, for him, and by him, but knew I had to be stronger than my desires now. They normally led me astray anyway.

I let him stand on his own and give his gift to the dead.

As they lowered the casket, the chief of police walked over to me. He held his shoulders too high and his back too straight to be anyone but law enforcement. His stride held purpose and his bushy eyebrows frowned when he stopped right in front of me. "We haven't formally met. Shall I introduce myself?"

In the past, the question would have been for the man whose arm I'd been placed on. I was used to men discussing their place around me but had never been approached as though my place mattered.

"No, I know your name." I stuck out my hand. "I'm Katalina."

His eyes didn't widen, not that I expected them to. Everyone knew by now. "Ivan never disclosed he had a granddaughter."

"And yet you know all about me."

"It's my job to know those things. We should probably have a private conversation. It's normally best to have an understanding." He eyed me up and down and I immediately knew the type of man he was. He didn't think I could hold my own and he was ready to make that known.

"Katalina doesn't have private conversations unless she requests them. Even when she does, you can believe I or someone similar to me will be present." The deep timbre of Rome's voice still sent shivers up my spine even though he'd been the one to take the life that warranted this funeral. We were burying the man he'd murdered and still my heart beat faster knowing he was right beside me.

"Rome." The chief nodded and slid his hands into his suit pockets. "It's my understanding she's not a part of your family anymore."

"She's a part of me."

I shook my head, knowing I needed to interject. "We aren't—"

"He doesn't get to know what we are or aren't, woman. Chief Brown gives us the right to remain silent, right, Chief?"

"Rome, why make things difficult?" the chief asked. "Do you want to talk about how difficult Mario dying here was?"

The smile that spread across Rome's face was menacing and slow, like he could take his time with whatever he had to say, like he knew this man in front of him would wait. "Why was it so difficult for you, Brown? You want to share something with me?"

A silent stare down took place. I was sure the police had to cover up Mario's murder, sure that they'd covered up a lot for Rome in the past. I didn't understand, though, why Rome was taunting him. It was just clear that the upper hand remained with Rome, that it always had and it always would.

"I can have a private conversation with the girl here. What's the harm, huh?" He rested his fingers on his belt buckle and pulled at it a little, like it was something he usually did with the gun holster he wasn't wearing today. I made sure to scan him and most everyone else at the funeral for weapons. I needed to be aware of the target on my back at all times now.

This wasn't a normal funeral. I'd worn a garter that my knife tucked into nicely. Weapons were mandatory along with black attire.

"There's harm because she may be Ivan's granddaughter but, first and foremost, she's mine."

"I'm not yours!" I felt myself heating up at his words. He shouldn't be claiming me, not after I told him we were done, that we were going our separate ways.

"You're mine, Katalina. Whether you're my savior or my demise, my prey or my predator. You're *mine*. You'll learn that one day, even if it's after everyone including Chief Brown here."

The chief shook his head at us. "I'm thinking she'll be the

demise of all of us. If this points to a partnership between Ivan and Bastian, we'd like to know."

"We'd *all* like to know." Rome had shifted his stance so that he was blocking me from the chief.

I peeked my head around his body. "One day soon, we will. Until then, nice to meet you, Chief Brown."

I spun away and made a conscious effort not to beeline toward Bastian, Cade and Dante. They'd been my crew for so long that my feet almost carried me there automatically.

Instead, my heels sunk into the grass as I measured each step I took toward Ivan.

"I need a minute with you." The rumble and strain in Rome's voice had me closing my eyes and sighing. My heart wouldn't let me take another step away from him without giving him something. "Rome, what's there to talk about?"

"Your phone number, for starters. I can't even get ahold of you, woman."

"You don't need to get ahold of me. We have nothing to discuss."

"The chief of police isn't someone you talk to alone. Anyone over there tell you that?" He motioned toward Ivan who was sitting in a cherry oak chair, smiling at both of us. My grandfather tracked every movement I made and corrected it when it was out of line. I was learning the bratva way quickly enough, but the men had to learn to respect me too.

It wouldn't happen overnight. It might never happen at all. Tradition was rooted deep in their bones and the tradition was to have men in power.

"We're going to figure it all out, Rome. It takes time to learn everything." I looked at the grass rather than him, trying my best to disconnect from the pull he had on me.

"I'm trying here, Katalina. I know this world and I can't have you getting locked up or ending up dead because Ivan wants to Mr. Miyagi you in his free time. Is he even sane?"

The rumors had spread about his dementia or Cade had hacked a phone or two. "It doesn't matter." I looked toward the sky. "My wellbeing isn't your concern."

"How can you say that? If I was bleeding out in the grass here, would you walk away from me?"

That barb had me snapping my gaze his way and glaring at him. "I'd never walk away from you."

"You did just a week ago!" he yelled and then winced when two of Ivan's guys walked over. "I'm not going to make a scene. You and I both know these two wouldn't hold me if I didn't want them to. Give me your number."

I shook my head. The hair I'd straightened fanned out around my cheekbones. "We don't need to have contact."

"Who are you planning to have contact with then? My cousin? You going to set up with Bastian all over again?"

A frigid voice sounded from behind me. It cut through the air like a blistering cold wind and I now knew it as my grandfather's. "I think she'll do what it takes. This is a bratva and Armanelli Family matter at this point."

Rome never took orders well. He never took advice or direction of any sort from any leader in the family ever. I didn't expect that this would be any different. He basically growled at Ivan when my grandfather extended his wrinkled hand. "I think Katalina does what she wants, not what it takes. I've witnessed that more often than anyone here."

I crossed my arms over the sweetheart line of my black dress as Bastian, Dante, and Cade ambled over. They moved with precision, each of them appearing so put together in their suits that both men and women watched in awe as they moved. Even if they didn't want to, they would always cause a scene when they moved in sync like this. Their dark, thick hair, their athletic builds, and their confidence magnetized people's attention. They didn't care nor even acknowledge another's gaze. They were focused on me, on Ivan, on the heartbeat of the city shifting as we all stared one another down here at the cemetery.

"Is it time for a meeting?" Bastian asked, glancing at Ivan's extended hand and then Rome's disgusted scowl.

My grandfather dropped his hand as I stepped in front of him. I'd grown attached to him quickly in the last week. He'd showered me with pain, not gifts. He'd been brutally honest to the point of cruel most days too. Yet I found that success wasn't built on love or kindness. It was built on respect and equality. That was the basis of a relationship really. For one to truly believe in another, they had to respect that person, have confidence in them, and treat them as equal.

Ivan wasn't a kind man. He wasn't even an okay one. I saw how he watched his son die. I saw that under any love he tried to show, there was emptiness. The bratva had created a callous, hard-hearted leader just like the Italian families had. I stood amongst men without souls and hoped to make it out of this life with one.

"If we need a meeting, now's the time." I shrugged and peered up at Bastian. "We know what makes the most sense."

"Our families from LA and New York are here."

"Let's meet somewhere more private." I eyed the chief of police who watched us with his body tensed.

"New Reign's will suffice," Rome offered as he glanced around, waving over a few men. "The work on it is almost done."

"New Reign's?" I tilted my head, not knowing what place he was talking about.

"The Stonewoods and I are putting the finishing touches on a new club."

"Not one you ever mentioned to me." I cocked a brow, caught off guard by how little he'd told me about his side businesses. I knew most of the businesses managed by and for the Armanellis and I was used to the few bars Rome had on the side but this was new. With the Stonewoods involved, it would be epic too.

"When would I have mentioned it, Katalina?" He sounded exasperated.

"Oh, I don't know. When we were in the car together, when you kidnapped me? I could name a lot of times."

"It just happened. I needed to preoccupy my mind with something other than losing your smartass." He shot back.

I opened my mouth to argue, but stuttered on my words. His voice was laced with a pain I knew very well, because I was feeling it too. My heart was yearning for him, begging for him, beating for him with him in front of me. I'd missed his dark stare, the rumble of his honest words, and the way he touched me like he wanted to cause me pain and pleasure at the same time.

"I'll tell you whatever you want to know. It's a business venture for all of us," he replied. "The Stonewoods asked me to invest and I took the opportunity with most of the legwork already done."

"Not exactly neutral territory, Rome," said Ivan. "You've taken out men of mine in your bars and clubs before. You've let them bleed out on your floor."

"Don't send your bratva in as spies, Ivan. Or I'll do worse next time." Rome cracked his knuckles and I tried my best not to clench my thighs at how good he looked, talking back to the head of the bratva. The man had a death wish or maybe death was what he wished upon everyone else.

Ivan mumbled Russian under his breath and then announced, "We'll meet there in two hours. We'll bring the bratva leaders who are in town for Mario's funeral too. If this goes as planned today, I'll disappear from all of your lives. Katalina understands my wishes."

I understood more than ever now. His mind would fail him. He saw it in tiny little pieces throughout his day but had most of his marbles at this point. He knew Dimitri had left the bratva a mess and was handing it off to me. I could sink or swim for all he cared. The other bratvas throughout the country would absorb us one way or the other. This was the only way I made it out alive and the only way he felt his family would get some recognition.

"She rides with me." Rome gripped my arm right above my elbow. I glared at him, but the electricity in his touch made me hold back my initial retort.

Ivan beat me to the response because of it. "It might serve you both well considering it may be the last time either of you get to sift through whatever disgrace of a relationship you have here. It will most likely be done after the meeting. So Katalina, cut ties now."

I glared at them all. "Rome and I already cut ties."

"Not according to him," Cade grumbled.

"Just go." Dante sighed and gave me a look. "Put us all out of our misery."

I threw my hands up at the ridiculousness of the situation. Bastian even waved us away as Rome started dragging me to one of the black limos. "This is fucking fantastic."

"It is, isn't it?" Rome said with a high-pitched tone that let me know he was being condescending.

"I don't want to ride with you!" I pouted like a petulant child as we continued across the freshly cut blades of grass.

"Tough shit."

I tore my hand from his right as we got to the limo door. The driver rounded the hood of the vehicle and opened it. He didn't hang around to close the door behind us and with good reason. He knew I was about to put up a damn fight.

"Say what you need to and I'll go with Ivan, the way I came."

"Say? You think I need to say something to you?" He leaned onto the limo and dragged his black, ominous eyes over my body, all the way up and then all the way down. He took his time, like the most powerful men of the nation could wait. "I don't need to say anything."

"Well then..." I turned on my heel to give him my back, but he spun me around and then pulled me close so that my breasts were in his chest.

He leaned down so that the scruff of his jaw was tickling my earlobe. "Words won't fix what's been done now, Katalina. I've suffered for days without you. I haven't tasted your mouth, owned your pussy, or dragged my hand across your skin. And I'm saying this the nicest way I know how because it's all mine. You took away *my* mouth, *my* pussy, and *my* damn skin. You're fucking mine and I want you back. Even if it's for a second in that limo."

"You can't have me back. You threw me away when you—"

"Enough." He slammed his hand on the roof of the vehicle and then breathed out slowly. "Get in. Now. Do not make me carry you."

"You wouldn't be able to even if you tried," I threw out, but I stepped past him to get in. I didn't want to make a scene, not when every single person at the funeral was still watching.

He slammed the door after me, then ducked his mess of beautiful dark hair to my window as he mouthed a thank you.

Why did my heart ache at that one small gesture when it should have been beating in rage at him bossing me around?

I knew right then that I wasn't going to handle this ride well. I missed him. I missed his commands, his eyes on me, the little glimpses of the gentleman under the beast that he gave me.

I just missed *him*.

I took a deep breath and focused on what I knew couldn't be anymore. We were enemies now. He was the reason we were all burying Mario today.

He deserved my hell, not my longing for him.

"Drive until I tell you to stop," Rome announced to the man in the front seat and then he pressed the partition button. I watched it rise in silence and then turned to the man I craved more than anything else in the world.

Nothing about the day was going as planned. I'd lost complete control when all I'd wanted was to maintain it. Now, I sat with the one man I lost myself with and felt my blood pressure rising. "Why keep driving, Rome? None of this is of any importance at this point."

"We could change that if you'd let go of your anger toward me. Why not show me the same grace you showed Mario in his death?"

I rolled my eyes. "You're not dying."

He pulled at his hair and then stared out the window before mumbling, "I could be from the way I feel without you around."

His voice fell to such a small, soft tone that I almost didn't hear the agony in his words. It was enough to remind me that my heart hadn't hardened toward him at all. Instead, it gravitated toward him, wanted him, longed for him. I wanted to jump across my seat and touch him again. And I almost talked myself into it.

But I'd be back to what I was then. Or worse. Because now I had the bratva on my back. "You say those things like you're willing to die for me, like you love me."

"Because I do." His voice echoed through the vehicle loud and vicious. He announced it from the pain deep within him. It wasn't a statement of beauty, but one of agony.

"So you're telling me like this in the back of a limo?" I whispered, trying to hold on to the fact that I should be angry, but my eyes welled with emotion I didn't want him to see.

"Yes, because you won't give me any other line of communication." He saw through my façade and a string of curse words erupted from him before he slid across the middle seat to me. "Don't cry, Katalina. I'm not here to make you cry. I'm here for you to see we can't separate. You know we can't. This arrangement isn't going to work."

"Why not?" I bit out as I leaned my head back on the arm he'd wrapped around my shoulders. I closed my eyes and wiped away the wetness on them so that I could try to relax, try to take in his presence all around me and have a moment where it was just us again.

Ivan may have been right. Maybe it was our last moment.

I didn't want to spend it bickering.

"Do you love Bastian enough to take his arm instead of mine forever because that's what they'll ask you to do?"

"It's not the worst thing."

81

"It's not a thing at all."

"Dare I ask why not again?"

He pulled me so close his lips were on my ear, and then he did what he knew how to do best. "You tremble when you see me, Katalina. I know you're not scared. It's just your body's reaction. When I touch you, you jump away because if you don't, you'll lean in for more. When my hand goes between your legs, your pussy is wet. It's not for anyone or anything else. I own that part of you while you own every other part of me."

"Rome—"

"I'm done talking." He pulled his arm out from under my head and unbuttoned his suit jacket, then slid it from his shoulders and draped it on the seat next to him.

"But…"

"Take off your panties and spread your legs." He said it while rolling up his sleeves, one measured fold at a time. Those strong fingers moved quickly with purpose and precision.

"I'm not in here to fuck." Yet I wanted to obey so badly that I wiggled in my seat trying to cull some of my need.

"That's fine. I'll do the fucking." He sighed. Before I could stop him, he was undoing his tie and unbuttoning the top button on his collar. He pulled his Glock from where he had it tucked into the back of his belt. I thought he was going to set it on the seat beside him, but he unloaded it before placing the cool steel on my thigh.

"What are you doing?" I whispered.

"I wonder what you're carrying today, how good our weapons would look next to each other?"

When he eyed the space between my legs, I knew that he could tell where I'd placed my knife. It was his job to know those sorts of things. His hand went right to it, on my left outer thigh and he wiggled the handle of it. The leather was buckled tight, but he slid it slowly so my knife rested right below my pussy. He tapped his gun against it. Then he pointed the barrel higher and higher. The knowledge that he was holding a weapon that took lives right next to my knife and near enough my clit that it might graze it had my breaths coming faster and faster.

"I wonder, what's the most powerful thing under your skirt right now? Your knife, my gun, or that pussy of yours?" He lifted my skirt and we both stared down at the view. My knife was tucked in a leather garter belt made specifically for my weapon. His gun was just a centimeter from touching my core.

I whimpered as he moved his hand the last tiny bit. The barrel hovered over and then covered my clit. I gasped at the cool sensation. He let the feeling sink in before he rolled it back and forth.

Back and forth.

My hips rocked immediately. "This is dangerous."

"It's only dangerous because I'm watching you ride my gun. Because I'm sure more than ever now that you belong to me. You ride what's mine. That's it."

My hands were at his shoulders and I arched when his other hand moved up my thigh to test my entrance.

"You going to get the leather of this seat cleaned, Kate-Bait? Seems like even though you think you want to be on the arm of another man, you can't stop getting wet for this one."

"Want and necessity are two very different things. It's a necessity for the bratva."

"We'll see," he murmured, but his eyes were laser focused on the barrel of the gun rolling over my clit, his fingers starting to slide in and out of me, and me riding them uncontrollably.

I'd lost my sense of power here. I always would because the enigma that was Rome always consumed me, maybe the same way I consumed him.

He holstered the gun behind him again and knelt before me, never stopping pumping his fingers in and out. "I'm going to feast now while you contemplate how to end this. And remember that while you scream my name in ecstasy, no man will ever bring you to this high."

"Rome, I can get myself there. It doesn't take you or—"

"You think of me when you orgasm every single time, woman. I know it because I do the same. You going to deny it?"

My mouth slammed shut, not willing to argue. I knew he was right, but I didn't agree immediately. Instead I shrugged, knowing it'd piss him off.

The smile that crossed his face was sinister, then he smacked my pussy like he owned it. I should have been offended or in pain, but instead it throbbed for him and I gasped at the tingling sensation that shot through me.

"Don't make me punish you, Kate Bait. We'll both like it too much," he said, eyes still locked on my center.

"Not true, Rome. I don't enjoy pain for pleasure." I'd always made that known in my sex life but here in this limo, I questioned myself. I was panting harder, riding his fingers faster, and grinding into him more roughly after that slap. I couldn't make myself stop. I'd build a wall later, create a barrier of some type then. Right now, I was chasing a high of love and pleasure that couldn't be ignored.

His forearm flexed and the veins popped from him moving his fingers in me. I watched the way every muscle tensed like he meant to work every part of himself just as he worked me. "You'll enjoy the pain if I lick it better, baby. I know this pussy better than you know it yourself."

I opened my mouth to protest, but he moved like a panther starved for his next meal. His tongue flew over my clit, and then he sucked on me until my nails dug into his shoulders, until I screamed that I couldn't take anymore. Then he dove into my core and lapped every charged inch of me.

Over and over again.

I clawed at him, ripped my fingers through his hair and rode his face like I would never have him again.

It was honestly what I thought.

My whole body convulsed around him as I saw everything we were made of exploding beneath my eyes.

I clutched him to me and he stayed between my legs for long moments after, massaging my ass with his fingers and letting me relax before he slid up my body. He gripped right under my jaw and turned my face up to his. "Is my girl satisfied?"

I bit my lip and glanced down to his length between my legs. With his suit pants still zipped, I saw the strain there, wanted to undo it, and realized that if I didn't get my sex drive under control, we would never be over.

I nodded and closed my eyes as I clenched my fists. "Satisfied."

He quirked a brow. "Really?"

It only took that word, just one extra push and my hands flew to unbutton his fly. "We stop after this, got it?"

He was laughing, no remorse or confirmation coming from his lips. Rome was a different type of monster to me: one of my own indulgence. He brought out my greediness and my emotion. I wanted all of him and I didn't ignore my wants and feelings with him. He didn't let me.

We were playing a dangerous game because of it.

I wrapped my legs tight around his ass, my knife still on my garter digging into both of us, and slammed my core right on top of his cock. He entered me fast, meeting my momentum with his.

He gripped my straight hair and yanked it back so my neck was exposed to him. Then he bit down hard, taking another piece of me for himself. I let him ravage my neck as I sucked on his earlobe and rode him for all I was worth.

We hurled our aggression at one another in those moments. There was clawing, yanking, shoving, grinding. All of it. He was my enemy, my lover, and my best friend. I needed him to feel it all.

I'd never screamed out as loud or felt such a tsunami of emotion as I did then when I climaxed. Rome wasn't far behind. His neck tightened and he growled into my neck, a string of curses coming from him before I felt his cock pump his release into me.

"Why does this get better every time?" he asked as his breath returned.

I laughed at his bafflement. "You'd think as we neared complete chaos, it'd be worse."

"I think we thrive in the dark and forbidden, Katalina. It seems we were both born into it."

I dragged my nails down his back before I gently pushed him away and he pulled out of me.

Empty. Lost.

The feelings flew into me the moment he left my body.

What makes a happily ever after and a fulfilled life? Was it finding your soulmate? Was there such a thing?

He grabbed a Kleenex from a console between the limo seats. I watched him clean up, took in his relaxed posture, how his neck finally fell smoothly down to his shoulders without bunched muscles. His jaw wasn't flexed but still as square as ever and there wasn't a line between his eyes creating a frown. The tattoos peeking out from under his collared shirt didn't seem alive with tension anymore either. They just snaked around his tanned skin, adding to the beautiful masterpiece the man already was.

He tucked himself back into his pants and sat back into the seat to the side of mine, putting distance between us.

When he glanced down at me, I realized I was still open to him. I jerked upright and closed my legs, then put my hand out. "Kleenex, please?"

"You wiping me from you so soon?" He smirked as he grabbed a Kleenex and held it just out of reach. "Maybe we should let me linger on you to warn away anyone else."

"You just did the same thing, Rome! What about warning away women from you?" God, he was a freaking caveman sometimes.

"If you want, I can tattoo your name across my neck, so they know I'm yours." He handed me the Kleenex.

I chuckled at the joke and then shook my head at my crazy desire to immediately tell him to go get it done. "We have to get it together. This isn't smart or something I want to indulge. You shouldn't either."

He waved me off. "I have what's mine whether it's smart or not. By the way, you on birth control still?"

"What about how clean I am? You're not nervous I'm sleeping with someone else?"

He side-eyed me. "You better not be on someone else's dick that fast, woman."

I rolled my eyes at the deep warning in his voice because we both knew I wasn't. "Yes, my birth control is still going strong. A word of advice, though. It's a good idea to ask a woman if she's on birth control *before* she has sex with you. It defeats the purpose to ask after."

"You're the one who dove onto my dick." He shrugged like he didn't care either way and smirked at his joke.

"Oh, please. Get fucked. No one's jumping on you that quick," I shot back even though I knew it was a lie.

He laughed at my quick retort and I joined him. He raised a brow as if to question me. "Sure about that?"

My gut clenched. Rome was a freaking god amongst men and I could imagine the women who would throw themselves at him. I looked down at a nail, acting unfazed. "Yep. You got me off first. Got on your knees for me. In all actuality, maybe you had to coax me onto there, hmm?"

His smile stretched full across his face at me goading him. "I think you want real punishment. I'm happy to deliver too. You got a nice enough ass that I could lay a few good slaps over it without causing any real harm."

I found myself breathing faster and clenching my thighs together at his words. I glanced out the window quickly so as not to give myself away.

He caught me, though, and moved to sit right next to me, putting his arm around my shoulders. "I'm inclined to not make this damn meeting at all at this point."

"It's the biggest meeting of our lives."

His tongue dragged from my bare shoulder all the way up to my ear where he bit me softly. "I'll table your punishment for later then."

My nipples tightened and I had to clench my fists to stop from responding physically to him. I closed my eyes at the reminder of the meeting, of the fact that we were going to another new club that was under Rome's name and housed the family's events.

We were dancing on thin ice, playing with fire, walking on melting rock and hoping it didn't turn to lava as the volcano erupted in the background.

"We have to be stronger than our connection to one another, Rome." I said it with my eyes closed, my body rigid in denial.

He sighed and I felt him pull away. There was a long silence. I heard the roll of his deep breaths through the limo and wondered if he was even going to respond.

"Maybe you're right." He wiped a hand over his face, and I heard the scruff on him I loved so much scratching at his palm.

My core clenched again and I ran my fingers through my hair before I turned to look out at the city rushing by as we drove. Hearing him agree with me sent an unexpected shock through my heart, one I couldn't even begin to interpret. "We know what they're going to ask of us in the next hour."

"I know what they'll ask of you." He emphasized 'you'. "You get to decide."

"Does that mean if I choose to be on Bastian's arm so all of us can survive, you'll table the monster in you and let it happen?"

"You expect that I'll be the only problem here, woman? You can't control the pull I have on you either."

"Well, we have to try. We can figure it out as we go."

We'd hidden in the shadows before, taken our passion in the night. We could do it again if we needed a fix. I'd have to get stronger, but as I looked at him, I knew I'd give in to weakness time and time again.

Rome shook his head like he could read my mind. "I won't have you like that again. I won't hide, Katalina. You're either mine or you're not."

"Bastian and I could have a partnership, Rome. That's what the bratva and the families will respect. You know that their tradition is buried so deep in their bones, they'll barely look at me as a leader because I'm a woman. If I don't tie my blood to his, there won't be much of a partnership at all. If I'm yours, the bratva ceases to exist. You get everything you ever wanted and I, nothing. I can't make an impact without ruling and I can't rule without taking the partnership. I'm left at your side while you put the family first. Can you say otherwise?"

He growled into the palms of his hands. "You're the family. I put you first too."

I shook my head. "You don't." My throat tightened at the thought of Mario bleeding out in front of me. "Mario's a testament to that. You took his life after I asked you not to."

"That was as much for you as it was for them."

The ball in my throat grew large at the image of Mario lifeless in my arms. "He was a good uncle to you."

"He was what he had to be to get power."

"How can you say that? You shared meals with him, you stood beside him for years, you—"

"I was his weapon and I was his downfall. The last was for you."

"Not for me!" I pounded a fist into my thigh. "Stop saying it was for me when I said no."

He stared at me for long seconds, reading every part of me. He peeled back every layer he could, took me in for maybe the last time alone, and then he cleared his throat before he said, "I had to wonder for days if you were dead. Dead, Katalina. The muse to my monster was gone and she asked for time like I could quiet the beast. I went fucking insane. Mario did that to us. He pushed us all too far. I can't cage anything that pushes the family to that point."

"Maybe." I shrugged, trying to rid myself of the emotion I felt at his words. I wanted to scream at him that I needed to go, that it wasn't his fight. I had to learn about my family alone, make my decisions without the Armanellis making them for me. I'd been their pawn long enough. "Maybe we're all a victim to the tradition of these families. We have to be more than that though. We're all broken and we need—"

"We need you!" His voice cracked through the air like a whip.

"You need the old me and that's not me anymore!" The words flew fast and furiously from my mouth. "I won't be bait anymore. I won't walk through this life without a cause or let the cause pass me by. I'm not the victim; I'm the fucking savior now."

My body shook and I felt my skin dampening from the memory that was flying through my thoughts.

The odor hit me first. His stale breath panting into my lungs like an oversized walrus, trying to perform an act he hadn't in a long time. My eyes shot open, because the smell was different. Marvin would brush his teeth like he thought I cared. The past few nights, he'd told me to kiss him and asked if I enjoyed it.

When someone takes everything from you, you don't feel anything anymore. When every single hope is gone, you don't contemplate what feels good or what feels bad. I only knew I wouldn't lie. So I told him the truth. I didn't know what joy was anymore.

He laughed in my face, his minty breath mixed with cigarette smoke filling the air as he said he would reintroduce me. I lay there and let him have me.

No tears fell.

Tonight, though, was different. This was a man I didn't know, one whose sweat slid over my naked body. The rolls of him slapped against me as he floundered to get ready for whatever he'd paid to do with me.

He whispered how much he liked my mouth, that it was all he paid for but that he might sneak a few fingers in me to get me off too.

Did I fake it to make the time go faster? Try to find pleasure where I knew I would live out the rest of my life?

My mind recoiled at the idea. It was the first one it had actually responded to in a long time. I wasn't a willing participant. This wasn't something I could ever enjoy.

Revulsion hurled through my body as I lost more of myself that night to that man. I cried as he took what he wanted. Tears streamed down my face when I realized not that I was being raped, but that I'd had more to lose in the first place. I'd thought every part of me was gone already. Would it happen with every man that came here? Would I be stripped of more and could I handle it?

I remembered the words Rome in the dark of the night had said to me. "You'll survive. Because if you don't, you'll die."

I repeated them over and over in my head.

The stench of him lingered when he got off me and left the room. It grew sour with shame, weakness, and self-loathing.

People cope with rape and abuse in different ways. My only way was to accept it. I didn't have a shower to wash the stench away. If I got up and did that, Marvin would most likely come to ask if I needed help. I didn't get up to write to Rome again either. I'd written to him once about Marvin but I wouldn't again. Not like this.

I'd already lost everything.

I'd lost myself.

And I vowed that if I ever got the chance to get that control back again, I would take it viciously, without remorse.

CHAPTER 8

ROME

MY HAND SHOT out to wipe one lone tear that escaped her glassy eyes. They looked far off and I needed her to come back to me. "Hey, you've never been a victim, Katalina."

"I have." She cleared her throat, blinked away her fog, and wiped at both her eyes before shutting them tight. She was probably trying to push away all the complications I was thinking about. "I have, Rome. And I won't be again. I want to change what's been done. I want to make waves in the bratva, do good instead of bad."

We all wanted to make changes. But change took time and lives. I wasn't about to lose her because of it. "None of us do good," I pushed back at her. She knew that. She knew what this life was.

"I'm going to change that."

I swear the woman made me want to punch and break things every minute of every day. I took a deep breath and tried to relax. "Have it your way, Katalina. And remember you chose this."

Her glistening eyes held mine. She fisted her tiny hands and then crossed her thin arms over her chest. "I'll remember. And remember you're agreeing."

The woman was tiny all around and yet she was about to take on the bratva. She wanted to be something that was impossible. She couldn't change tradition and she couldn't change greed. The bratva had them both and they enjoyed them too. I knew her end goal, knew that sex trafficking was on her radar and that she wanted to put an end to it while leading a disorganized group of idiots. That's all the bratva was.

She didn't understand that a woman wouldn't be able to accomplish what she planned, that those men wouldn't give her the respect she deserved.

Which meant our family was about to go to war for her.

I was about to rip apart the people that would come for her.

We would all be fighting the war on sex trafficking and it was about to be the biggest one we'd ever fought before.

I grunted as I pressed the button to speak through the soundproof partition a little harder than necessary. "Take us to the club now."

I lifted my finger from it and she tried for a lighter topic. "How is this new club venture going? You never mentioned it."

"I just bought in and took the offer to own majority stock in it after Mario." It'd been a week ago that the Stonewoods offered it to me.

"Why take that on? You don't need it."

"It's good for the family."

"Is it? They don't need it either."

My bars were just small businesses that we could run dirty money through if need be. Yet this club was exclusive. It would be one of many and it was going to bank millions from membership costs. "It's an elite access club. People will pay millions over time just to be a part of it. Both men and women will indulge there and they'll share secrets, business deals, and more there. It's an investment that will solidify a lot."

She narrowed her eyes and I saw the questions flying through her head. They were legitimate ones. "Is it a venture I should be involved in?"

"The bratva or you?"

"I don't operate without the bratva anymore." Her response was quick enough to show me that Ivan had already ingrained some sense of belonging in her.

I wanted to snatch her back, wanted to cage her in with just us but knew I had to let her fly. Either way, she was bound to do so. I'd either lose her or get to witness her in her glory. I wanted the latter, even if it meant accepting the pain along with it.

"We'll see." I didn't say more or less. She'd be given the option soon enough but she had to see the club for herself.

The bratva would decide with her if they wanted to turn over a new leaf. This meeting would be the sure sign of it.

We pulled up to the Stonewood Skyscraper. They'd built the club underneath the highest building in the city. It was dark, wound underground like a coiled snake, and took navigating to enter. Our black SUVs and limos filed into the Stonewood Enterprises parking structure one by one, but we drove past the expensive cars already parked there. At the end was a steel, matte black garage door with two armed guards manning the security system. They scanned our licenses and the parking tags that were hanging from our drivers' vehicles.

The system had multiple security checks. I lowered my window when one of the guards tapped it and gave him my finger to run.

"She with you, boss?" he asked.

"Yes. Scan her in. She'll have access whenever needed."

Katalina hesitated only for a second before offering her fingerprint. The guard's pad read and logged her print quickly.

"All set." He tapped the hood of the limo and we drove through.

"A little much?" She scratched the side of her face in question.

"Not when you've got international politicians and leaders sharing secrets here."

She didn't say anything more. We knew where we were going. We knew the men we were about to meet with ruled a lot more than a mafia in Chicago or a big business. They made calls to presidents; they pulled the triggers on lives metaphorically and literally.

I got out just as we parked and my shoes clipped across the marble flooring. The parking structure inside the garage doors was extravagant like the rest of the club. Right now, it was empty, but it would soon be filled with luxury cars and money. The Stonewoods spared no expense with the design and even now when they asked how any design should be handled, I chose top tier.

I went to open Katalina's car door for her, but two men speaking Russian were already there ushering her out. She glanced my way and mouthed goodbye.

I wouldn't say it back, wouldn't even acknowledge it. That woman wasn't going anywhere away from me ever again.

We moved separately for now. Ivan studied me before he made his way to her side. Two hosts were at the front plated doors near a fountain. They rushed to open the doors for us and we walked through. Inside, diamonds and stones glittered from the ceiling but the lighting was dim, even dark in some places to allow for privacy. The marbled flooring met with dark carpeting near VIP areas, and the velvet seating had gold silk threading throughout.

I watched Katie take it all in. She scanned it like a hawk noticing every detail. When her gaze landed on the first tantra sex chair, they flew to mine.

I hadn't divulged to her the type of club it was. Sex sold but I wanted a different take, a place where it was consensual, exclusive, and open to whatever the customer wanted. Every member would sign legally binding documents to participate, to bring guests, to be recorded, and more. And exclusivity sold. With our names, we already had a waiting list.

The chains, the whips, the poles, the hoops hanging from the sparkling ceiling didn't deter anyone except those who may not have wanted to enter in the first place.

Katie curled her lip and walked over to me, stopping her men from following with a hand in the air. "Sex club and I wasn't invited?"

"You're invited if you want access." I turned around the room to see most everyone who was of importance being served and mingling.

She hummed low and cut off what she was about to say when one of our servers approached me with a drink on a tray.

"Your usual, Rome?" The server purred it out like a feline ready to rub her body through my legs. Instead of watching the tall brunette in a leotard that shined like the ceiling, I watched Katie's reaction.

Her whole body tensed like she wanted a fight. "You enjoy the help while working here, Rome? Maybe I was too quick to assume you were as clean as me back in that limo."

"If you want to test out the furniture for that smart mouth of yours tonight, we definitely can. I seem to recall you being the one telling me to check my jealousy over you and other men."

"I'm never going to flaunt them in front of you."

"Your partnership will be enough."

She growled in frustration before turning away from me and staring at the entrance where the Stonewoods had just arrived. Jax and Jett walked hand in hand with the women they had decided to take leaps of faith with. Together, they appeared to own the bar, the room, the world. Every family and bratva member silenced as they strolled in.

None of them hurried; each took their time and each of their women walked with just as much ease and composure, like they owned every bit as much of the empire as their husbands.

They were right to think so.

The women had their men's hearts from the beginning and most likely called most of the shots.

Jett moved his wife, Vick, forward first to sit at the side of the long table we had set up. She waved him off to run over to Katie and hug her though. Some of the distant families whispered, especially when the other Stonewoods made their way to her. Katie had belonged before she knew she did, and somehow she was a thread that was weaving us all together.

She'd befriended Brey and Vick long before we all had. Her bond with the Stonewoods and her friends was more solid than any she had with bratva members, maybe even some of the Armanelli Family too.

Ivan ambled up to me as everyone took in the scene. "She's something else, no?"

"She's everything else."

"I never imagined the depth to the girl or the sheer intelligence. Her mother was smart but that one...she has the potential."

"She's not a tool, Ivan."

"She's a ruler and that makes her a tool for the bratva, just like you're a tool for the Armanellis. We've all got a place."

"Or maybe we decide to leave the place behind and make our own somewhere else."

"At this point, someone would find and kill her. You and I both know that. You can't live your life in hiding with her. You weren't built for that. Neither of you were. Look at her."

She radiated power. Her earrings, strands of gold hanging from her lobes, swung back and forth as she shook her head, laughing at something Jax said. Her black dress fit her like a glove, wrapping up her curves in one delicious package. More than a few of the men stared and surely wondered what it would be like to bend her ass over one of the chairs. I had. It made me want to usher her out of the club immediately.

"I hope you've both figured out your issues," said Ivan. "We're about to create more."

"I'll advise you not to create any that you want me to fix. I'm not a good fixer. I erase and seek vengeance, but that never really fixes a damn thing."

I left him to greet the Stonewoods. I shook each of their hands with Jax's being last. He grunted and nodded at me while Brey held her hand out for me to shake too.

I lifted a brow. "Really?"

"Oh whatever." She waved off the whole charade and moved in for a hug. "I was trying to be formal for the whole situation."

"Formalities became a waste of time after we slept together, no?" I said.

"Don't make me angry before the meeting, Rome," Jax warned.

"Or me." Katie folded her arms over her chest and stood beside him. She was making a statement to them and to me, that she wanted me, that she felt the jealousy, that she was bold enough to admit it.

I respected her fire and how she wielded it.

"Shall we?" Bastian clapped his hands and motioned to everyone to take a seat around the massive mahogany table. A few of the other men murmured about Katie, Vick, and Brey attending. We heard the whispers but let them go. The Armanellis weren't the ones bringing women to the table. The Stonewoods and bratva were.

"It's been brought to our attention that we're all in the same place due to the unfortunate circumstances of my father passing," Bastian started as he took a stand at the head of the table.

I stood next to him while Cade and Dante sat on either side of us. We had the head of the LA Italian Family beside Dante. He was only a few years older than us. The head of the New York Family sat next to Cade, older than old, with his brother beside him. Much of the bratva were a similar age, seated on the other side of the table with Ivan at the foot, Katie right beside him.

The Stonewoods filled out the middle of the table but it didn't dim their power at all. They lounged in their chairs, bigger than most of the men here and definitely in better shape. I'd almost come to blows with Jax in the past and had wondered whether I'd have won that fight. He'd have put up a good one, that's for sure.

The bratva only had three other heads at the meeting. Each of them were old enough to be our father; each of them looked completely out of place and unhappy to be in our presence.

"Since we're all here," continued Bastian, "it's best we meet and discuss what's come to pass in light of my father's passing and how we should handle it."

A mid-tier member of the LA Italian family mumbled, "Not sure we can call it passing."

Bastian let the comment roll off his shoulders but I was already on edge, too charged to let things go. "You got something to say, Giovanni?"

"You may be an Armanelli, Rome, but I'm a Valentino. We own the West Coast, and I just think we should all be a part of life and death decisions."

"It wasn't a decision as he'd broken a code of conduct." I cracked my knuckles. "He knew that, even admitted it when we brought him to the chair."

"You're just in love with the bitch he wronged," he sneered at Bastian.

At this point, the leaders knew who that bitch was.

Every eye looked her way. She waited and let their stares sink in. Katalina was made for a throne even if she hadn't known it before. She rested an elbow on the table and put her chin into her palm as if completely bored by the man's statement. "Am I that bitch, Gio?"

He grunted and mumbled in Italian.

"Don't tempt me to put you in the chair too. I got no problem killing you when you talk to her that way." I warned.

Bastian cracked his neck and let out a breath.

"Chill," I whispered to him, because I knew he felt pressure, could read my cousin like I could have a twin brother. Bastian had never wanted to be the head of the Armanelli family but he was and he was good at it. He didn't want to argue with anyone though. It irritated him. His time was more valuable than that, and so was the rest of the family's.

"I'm not here to throw barbs and none of you are either," said Bastian. "We have a group of men—"

"And women," Katalina said to no one in particular.

"And women now," Bastian included her as whispers sounded again throughout the bratva and Italian families. Jax and Jett both sat back in their seats smirking as if they were above us all.

In a way, they were. Their hands were cleaner than clean and yet they profited greatly from our families. We profited from them having our backs too but our fathers and the fathers before them had climbed a dirtier ladder, one we couldn't scrub quite as clean as the Stonewoods' ladder would always be.

Bastian continued, "None of us here need to rehash the past, Giovanni. We've all discussed it at great lengths. Katalina is here to discuss the future with us."

"What about them?" Egor, the older man next to Ivan and head of the bratva on the West Coast asked pointing to Brey and Vick.

Vick, always the optimist, smiled widely at him. "We just came along for the fun of this meeting."

Jett chastised her with a look.

"What?" she asked. "It'd do everyone some good to lighten up. The classical music for one is pretty ominous." She turned toward me. "Probably should have had them put on some hip hop."

The music that hummed low in the background would ramp up at night once we opened. Now, though, it played the popular favorites of Mozart, Bach, and Beethoven.

I lifted my drink to my lips to keep from chuckling at her boldness.

"This is not time for women, huh?" The old man glared at her. "Talk of music and frivolous things we don't bother with."

Vick sat back completely undeterred and lifted a brow while raising her hand to her husband's shoulder, signaling for him to let her handle it. The mood in the room had shifted.

Stonewoods weren't talked down to, and Vick was just as much a Stonewood as Jett and Jax. "Maybe you're unaware, because we haven't met, or maybe my husband didn't make it clear to everyone here, but I'll do the work right now so there aren't any misconceptions. I walked in here with the knowledge that this was family business. Family is created equal at Stonewood Enterprises. You want to be a part of our success, it would be smart to take that into consideration."

Katalina smiled at her friend and then glanced at the other bratva heads. "Let's be clear, we're not here to be on display for all you men. If we sit at this table, we're going to eat at it. We make the decisions too. Am I right, Bastian?"

He nodded.

"You agree, Jett and Jax?" Her grey eyes cut to them.

They nodded.

"How about all of you?" Katalina looked at Gio. The Valentino family fell in line because no one wanted to contend with Bastian and the Stonewoods.

"It's for the best that we're all sitting here now. Us together means we have control that can't be penetrated." Bastian explained.

"Our crews need to fall in line first." Ivan spoke up next to Katalina, tapping his calloused hand on the table. "I want to believe our leadership will sway them, but we know that's not the case. My blood only gets her so far. We're telling them to listen to a woman…"

Katalina didn't rear back. She knew it wasn't tradition. She knew she'd have to protect herself. Still, his words slammed into me hard. I spoke from behind Bastian. "We need eyes on her twenty four seven."

Ivan waved me off. "We have that, of course."

"Better than just a man or two. You need real security. It won't just be your own who want her dead."

"But will they risk it when they know it will bring the wrath of the Stonewoods and the Armanellis?" Ivan countered.

"If they can get away with it, why not?" I shrugged. "Put a bullet in her head and drive away with no trace. Make sure she always has enough eyes on her to protect her."

"I don't need you to tell me how to do my job," Ivan grumbled like his pride was at stake.

"Your son was doing your job for a long time and he learned from you. It took Katalina one night to get out from under his men, no?" I'd destroy his pride if I had to. Cade had updated us on security footage and word spread of her taking a guard's life.

Katalina cleared her throat. "The bigger question is how we solidify my role."

"You take your place next to Bastian," Ivan said, like they'd already agreed on that, like he'd already decided and her question was outrageous.

"What does that mean exactly?" She squinted at him, her silver eyes suddenly hard and fierce. "Our bratva shouldn't be overshadowed by the power of the Armanellis. We have specific requests, necessary ones that I think need to be acknowledged before we all agree to a consolidated power."

Ivan hmphed like she'd blindsided him. "I suppose you want lawyers and signed in ink contracts too," he said like she was crazy.

She nodded without glancing away from him. The struggle for power was happening between them already. Her life would always be in jeopardy now and she would have to obtain power over and over again to keep herself alive.

Still, the woman didn't think about it that way. Instead, she wanted her cake and to eat it too. I respected her for coming this far and pushing her agenda immediately. She wanted sex trafficking off the table. I knew that was going to be her first ask.

Yet I wasn't sure everyone would agree to it. The Armanellis had never pushed all of the families to wipe their profits clean of it, and the bratva probably hadn't even considered it.

"Katalina, I can only agree to so much without the other families." Bastian was already leaning back on his heels as if ready to walk away from the deal.

"Do what you want," she replied. "Without us, you make an enemy of us."

"Don't threaten the family that fed you for years." His tone was harsh but I would have said the same thing. She belonged on this side of the table and we all knew it.

"The bratva gave me a seat at the table, Bastian. I didn't have one before."

Cade cracked his knuckles but kept his mouth shut. Dante winced at her accusation. I stepped forward before Bastian put a hand on my shoulder to stop me. We all hurt when she hurt. She was one of us even though she acted like she wasn't.

We'd put her in the box that tradition had made over time. Learning was the first step and change was the second.

"We need more time, woman," I said. "You never gave us a chance."

"How many chances are women supposed to give?" Brey, quiet as ever throughout the whole meeting spoke up then. "How long have you truly known her, seen her, included her within your family, Rome? Bastian?"

Bastian rubbed his forehead and answered before I could. "We've all made mistakes. You do that when you're growing up."

"Seems some had to grow up quite a lot faster based on the actions of your family." Brey's emerald stare weighed us all down, along with her words.

Bastian's hand slammed onto the table, his palm smacking the wood hard, the sound cutting the tension in the room. His glare turned hard on Katie. "What's your angle? We all bend your way so that we can have an alliance rather than a war? We'll kill you, Katalina."

The bratva tsked and muttered obscenities. Ivan balked at the threat. "I won't deny that. We'd die in the end, sure. Yet, your families..." He waved at both us and the Stonewoods in disgust. "You would fracture. We'd pick off a few. Maybe one good one. One that would wound you enough for the others to turn to vultures and jump in."

Bastian's eyes narrowed at Ivan.

Mine were on the woman I knew better than anyone else in this room. "You're sitting on that side, Katalina. You willing to go to war for them? Take lives for them?"

"It's bigger than that, Rome. My allegiance to my bloodline affords me the power to change what needs to be changed."

I hummed at her response. "Tell me then. You willing to take my life?"

"What?" she whispered as I left Bastian's side and stalked toward her.

"If we can't have you, prove it. Prove your loyalty."

The other Bratva Pakhans nodded in agreement. "Good idea," one said, completely on board with my taunting.

She stood up to face me right as I reached her chair, like suddenly she didn't trust that she could have her back to me. I searched her eyes and found a new kind of fear there.

"I'm not taking your life," she said. "I'm not spilling blood."

I pulled my Glock from the back of my pants' waistband. She gripped the table and leaned back on it as I held the weapon out.

When she didn't initially reach for it, I pressed it up against her chest. Her breaths were coming quickly and her heart was going a million beats a minute.

Good.

I took her wrist and set my gun in her hand; I said the words I knew she would finally understand. "Just like Jimmy, huh? Show me what you're made of."

She squinted. Her hand still shook, but slowly and surely Katalina's thin fingers curled around the gun one by one. "You forget that I've killed for much less than this."

Her finger hovered over the trigger but she glanced around the table first. She wanted someone to object, to call my bluff.

"Me and you, Cleo," I whispered. "Pull the trigger and show them what you're made of."

I didn't know if her trust in me was that great, didn't know if our connection was that strong after everything that had just happened.

She lifted the gun another centimeter and pointed it right at my head. She rolled her lips between her teeth and said,

"I loved you more than I would have ever loved Jimmy. He got in my way though. He didn't do as he was told. It's best this way, right?"

I lifted a shoulder just as she pulled the trigger.

The sound of the click punctured the room like a needle does a water balloon. The explosion of gasps throughout meant they had believed our show.

Dante, Cade, Bastian, and I were the only ones who knew different. Katie had caught on. Ivan whooped with laughter in the same way Mario had with Jimmy all those years ago. The other men, leaders of the biggest mafia families, joined the shocked laughter.

"She's one of us now, no?" Ivan nudged Egor next to him and he lifted his glass to her.

She shoved the gun into my chest. "Playing games will end up getting your head blown off one day, Rome."

Bastian looked between the two of us, then he and Ivan locked eyes.

"Draw up whatever papers you want," Bastian said. "Let's let the lawyers iron out the details of this partnership between us all. We'll see what we can agree upon."

"Katie should be seen with you in public," Ivan announced as others started to stand, ready for the meeting to be over. They were all sitting ducks, leaders that were vulnerable without their security. It made them antsy; it made them pussies.

"We'll sit at the table together, Ivan," Bastian replied. He glanced between Katie and me before he continued. "She won't be fucking me though."

"Why not?" Egor said. "Good for show to those under us."

"They can learn what a leader is," Katalina shot back at him. "It's not a dick or a pussy. It's a person."

Jett was the first of the Stonewoods to stand. "It seems Katie knows her way around all of you. I'm not questioning leadership, especially when I know them. I'm happy to do business where needed with her crew, but only her crew and only under her circumstances."

"Interesting." Ivan quirked his head. It was an angle he hadn't considered. "You trust her more than you trust what I've done in the bratva."

"Katie's been my wife's friend for a very long time, Ivan. I trust their judgement on what will make my business prosper. Above all else." He turned to his wife. "Anything else you'd like to add?"

"Yup. Katie, call me. Girl's night soon." She winked and threaded her hand through Brey's before they all turned to leave.

The meeting was over. The negotiations and the turmoil that would come with it had just begun.

CHAPTER 9

KATIE

ROME IDLED IN the background as Bastian walked over to me while I took in the large space. Beyond the doors of this room, a club beyond my wildest dreams had been built with a dance floor, two floors of beautiful luxury, winding staircases, and an extravagant bar.

A bar at the sex club I hadn't even known about.

That I'd just pulled a trigger in.

It'd been for show. Still, my heart had pounded and sweat trickled between my breasts before I did. No one holds a gun to someone's head and pulls the trigger without the idea that they may kill them. But Rome had dropped enough hints.

I doubted anyone had bought the display. How could they when we'd entered together after driving around the block together for an hour?

Still, we'd got the job done. Most of the attendees had agreed or witnessed agreement to our alliance. Hopefully, that agreement would trickle down through the hierarchies. Some would accept me out of sheer loyalty to their families. In the case of the others, I hoped I'd earn their respect, but if not, I would have to fight for it or die.

Bastian straightened his black suit and combed a big hand through his full head of hair. Then, he leaned in to ask, "Want a drink at the bar?"

"You want me to drink with you at a new bar no one thought to mention to me? New Reign has a nice ring to it."

"It's Rome's baby, not mine."

I hummed at that assessment and glanced around the space. The large mahogany table with a crystal chandelier hanging above added a rich, luxurious feel. With the leather seating and the gold-framed portraits lining the walls of this room, you felt important just being in it. I understood the appeal.

I watched Ivan stand up and saw him already shaking his head in response to Bastian's invitation. Yet I found myself agreeing. Not because of power, not because I wanted to build our connection, but because I missed Cade sitting near us on his phone and Dante throwing in some inspirational comment half way through the meeting and Rome's heated stare.

That, I missed most. "I'll stay for a soda."

Ivan's face scrunched like he didn't have time or patience for any of it. "I'm tired."

"You're old," I retorted and smiled thinly at him. "Go home. Or retire, huh? I'm stepping into your shoes whether you want me to or not."

"Your mother was just like you," he grumbled as he started to walk away. "Maksim will be at the entrance to take you home."

Maksim had become a friend, a faithful bodyguard I'd hoped I could trust ever since he drove me to Ivan's that very first night. He didn't say much, but I didn't need him to. I just needed him to keep me alive.

"Where precisely is home?" Rome's murmur was deep behind me and had the hairs on the back of my neck rising immediately.

"You'd like to know that, wouldn't you?" I kept facing forward, not giving in to the need to look at him, to touch him, to feel him again.

My gaze stayed on Bastian, who shrugged his shoulders and winked at me like I should throw Rome a bone.

I'd thrown him enough in the limo. I'd indulged way too much.

Bastian abandoned me and made his way to the bar. I sighed and closed my eyes, readying myself.

"Just give me your address, Katie."

I knew that if I turned around I would be overwhelmed by the beauty of his dark features, lured in by the sheer size of him, and feel the gravity of his aura pulling me toward him. I tried to steel my nerves and my desires, but his stare still hit me like a jet going full speed when I faced him.

There was expectation in his eyes, and the way he stared at me like he knew me, like we could conquer everything together, made me weak at the knees, in my heart, and in my soul. "Probably not a good idea to be sharing addresses, Rome. Especially when you don't even share with me things like the fact you own a sex club."

"Oh, please. We don't talk business."

"Maybe we should," I threw back at him. I was pushing his buttons because the sex club omission pushed mine and I was letting off steam, adrenaline. Fear, even. I hadn't ever had to sit at the table where the decisions were made before. Now, I did. Now, I was one of them, and I wasn't sure I knew what to do with it.

"I told you what there is to know already," said Rome. "I bought in and agreed to manage the place. We'll open in a few more weeks, but we've obviously got staff on site for meetings and for initial set up. It'll be a lucrative venture, good for all parties involved. I'll involve you however you want."

I peered up at him. "As in, you'll let me buy in?"

"Do you want to?" he asked, like he didn't care one way or the other. The thing about Rome was, he always put me on that pedestal, and he believed I should have been there all along. He'd offer me this like I deserved it.

"I guess I should consider it." The fact that I could do that with the wealth I was inheriting turned my stomach with anxiety.

"It's worth it. We can have the lawyers draw it up."

I hummed and let the idea rest as I glanced around. "It's big," I said almost to myself as I took in the high ceilings, the shimmering poles that reached from them all the way down to the floor, the deep red ropes dangling throughout. Staircases flanked the open area and curved up to more seating and more private spaces. They met at a beautiful waterfall that cascaded down to the first floor behind the bar. A chandelier encircled that water. "The base of the waterfall a VIP area?"

"Of sorts."

"Interesting," I murmured, thinking of what this place would turn into when the doors opened to the exclusive clients on the list. It'd be a labyrinth of luxurious debauchery.

It'd be heaven and hell.

"Tell me what you're thinking," Rome commanded.

I didn't exactly know. But a part of me wanted to find out. "I want to come to the opening."

He looked me up and down. "I guess you can. What for? I'm not sure."

I didn't answer him but headed toward the bar and everyone else.

"If you're coming, I can come get you once you give me your address."

I sighed. "No, Rome."

"Why?"

"Because we aren't exactly great at practicing self-restraint."

"I don't see a reason why we have to." He followed so close, I felt the heat of his body behind me.

"The bratva need to trust me. They can't do that with you between my legs."

"They need to respect you. And bow to you. Nothing else. Those men will never trust you because they don't trust each other, probably don't even trust themselves."

"Well, we have to restructure, rebuild, and start anew."

"And what's the first step in that?"

I turned to him just before we reached Bastian, Cade, and Dante, who were drinking at the bar. "Probably the little stunt you just pulled. An empty chamber in your gun? Why?"

"I didn't reload after the car ride." The man took that moment to wink at me.

I bit my lip at his mentioning it, my core heating at his words, at his playful way of messing with me.

"Don't think about it in a sex club, huh? I'll have to take you over my knee."

I ground my teeth at him catching me. "I'm guessing no one bought that. Not after us arriving together, anyway."

I tried to play it off, tried not to think about him in all the ways I wanted to. Holding a gun to him had jarred the thought of losing him right to the top of my mind. Really losing him. It made me want to grab him and announce we were official and exclusive. And I wanted to cower at the same time.

Loving somebody, breathing in their air and realizing they are breathing with you: that's a gift, it makes you want to hold on to them so tight that even God can't take them away.

When death creeps into your life, it scares you into the arms of everyone who loves you and makes you wrap up those you love back. And you like to think your love is sacred, that you'd get a pass from turmoil.

But death is fickle. Death is mean and predatory. I swear it seeks those people out that you love and pulls them down into the darkness, rips them from your arms, and makes you choke on their loss.

Losing him, even the thought of it, I couldn't handle.

Was it right to back away, to cut the tie in the hopes that it wouldn't hurt as much when that end came? Or was that selfish?

For me, it didn't matter. For me, the answer was much simpler.

"Either way, it bought you their attention," he said. "If you won't give me your location, give me your number."

"No." I gripped Cleopatra around my neck, trying to remain strong. I needed to stand on my own, show the bratva that I could, and maybe show myself too because Rome could be gone in an instant. We all could. Our lives were fragile objects surrounded by wrecking balls of destruction. "We need to break the link, Rome. We need to move on, at least for now."

"You don't break the link, woman. What for? Because you don't trust me? Or because you've got something to prove?" He let out a deep sigh before he continued. "Mario was bound to be picked off anyway if that's what this is about."

The need to give in to him was so crippling my shoulders curled in from it. "It's about us putting our families first, our self-preservation and our survival, instead of this thing between us."

"Don't you know, Cleo? I survive off *you*."

He headed past me to the bar, leaving me standing there speechless. Over my shoulder, I watched the muscles in his back flex under his suit jacket. I found myself wanting to spin him around and own his mouth for saying what he did, for piercing my heart again and again. How could a man so ruthless, who took so many lives, say things like that to me?

How could I resist him?

I righted my footing and met him at the bar where Dante, Cade, and Bastian sat. A woman dressed in a sort of diamond, angel-wing suit breezed over and asked what we wanted.

Rome ordered a drink for me and a water for himself.

"I'm not drinking tonight," I mumbled as she walked away. I hadn't drunk at all since I'd been with the bratva. As much as I didn't want to admit it, I didn't trust them for one second. I couldn't risk being buzzed when more than one man wanted to kill me.

Rome ignored my comment and put his hand at the back of my bar stool. Instantly, I felt the heat of it and glared at him.

"How long do you think a partnership like this can last?" Bastian threw the question out there for any of us to answer as he stared off toward the bartender.

"I'm thinking it's a better idea to ask: How would it last in the first place?" Rome volleyed back.

"It'll last however long we want it to," I answered for them both. "Because we're all a part of each other in some twisted way and we're going to make it work because that's what we do."

"I like your drive, today, Little One." Dante's lips curved into a smile and a dimple indented the side of his cheek.

If it weren't for all the men sitting here with him, I'd have sworn he was a god. "I think we'd both like it more if I was kicking your ass at the gym."

"After this meeting, I think we need to burn off some steam." He cracked his knuckles, two black rings and a gold one drawing attention as he did. His style and his good looks had the waitress staring as she set glasses down in front of us. He held up his just as she sighed with hearts in her eyes and turned away. "To a successful first meeting today."

Before I could grab my drink, Rome swapped his with mine and winked at me. Then he barely sipped on the alcoholic beverage in his hand, like he wanted his senses, like he needed them. At this point, I needed mine too. It was the reason for not drinking.

"And to a successful funeral, considering no one was killed in a drive-by," Cade mumbled into his phone.

"What did you just say?" I nudged his shoulder so that he would look up from the damn device.

"We had a lot of visitors at that funeral," he said. "The Polish, the Armenian and the Japanese drove by. Politicians were there; leaders were there. We had targets on our backs and were barely armed. I thought for sure Rome would take a bullet."

"Your ass knows that no one is hitting me in a drive by." Rome leaned back and slid his glass out of his hand.

"You're not Neo from the Matrix. You can't dodge a damn bullet."

"I can anticipate. No one was hitting up that funeral. Too many witnesses."

"We've got the cops under wraps." Cade announced.

"Yeah, too many witnesses from other families. The Stonewoods. Another gang showed up."

Cade narrowed his eyes and then ducked his head back down, typing away quickly to check things out. "I didn't see that on the security footage—"

"Because the damn security footage won't show you everything." Rome pinched the bridge of his nose.

Dante laughed at their bickering, then clapped Cade on the shoulder. "They avoided street cameras. They're an underground gang. We got them logged. Don't worry about it."

The list of enemies had my shoulders tensing, my back muscles coiling up with nerves. I'd been under scrutiny before, been held at gunpoint by a lover, been beaten and taken advantage of. It was always by one person at a time, though. It was mostly controlled too. I knew how to warp a man's mind well enough to stay alive.

Yet I wasn't sure I could mold and sculpt a whole unit. How would I handle a gang that I knew nothing about, a mob I'd never had to deal with directly? I was ill-equipped, green, and naïve.

Rome's strong hand went to my neck and he massaged the muscles like he automatically knew where the knots were. I breathed out slow as his hand trailed down the sides of my spine, pushing pressure points and kneading out areas I didn't know existed.

While everyone talked, he leaned in and whispered in my ear. "Relax, Cleo. We've got a long way to go before you can tense up on us."

CHAPTER 10

KATIE

TWO WEEKS WENT by. I'd spent every day with Ivan going over business dealings and my inheritance. He reiterated over and over again that this was all for our family.

At his house, doctors would file in and out. He would take pill after pill and wave off my questions about his health. Sometimes, though, I'd catch a doctor's eye and they'd share a little more information than Ivan wanted.

"Sir, your bloodwork is good," one said. "Your last test was good too, but we should be taking memory tests daily with your medications. You can't continue taking these the way you are."

He'd glare them into submission. All I learned from the revolving door of doctors was that he was participating in a study and the medication was holding off the onset of his dementia for the time being.

It didn't seem to matter to him. The man was only focused on one thing and that was continuing his bloodline. He'd say over and over, one day I'd have a son, one day his great grandchildren would have all this.

All this was billions and billions of dollars. I focused on the accounts and the amount of zeros for a long second when he first showed me. "All for the family, no?" he said and chuckled like he knew I was surprised.

I didn't disclose that I never wanted kids. I didn't want to bring a life into a world so dark and cruel. He didn't need to know, though. I didn't owe him anything.

Every day, I woke up in that new penthouse and stared at the ceiling, thinking of how I would change it all. I had the contacts, I had the training, I now had the resources. I just had to implement.

One day, I called Dante and went to work out with him. We trained hard, me constantly fighting for what could be my life against Dante's hard advances. I didn't hold back with him because I knew this training had saved me once before with Boris. I'd need it again.

When I landed a kick to his side that brought him to his knees in one of the gym's rinks, he wheezed out a laugh. "Enough, Little One. You're vicious today."

I sighed and fell down beside him to rest, taking in rapid breaths. "Thanks for sparring with me."

"No skin off my back." He hesitated. "Except that your boy keeps asking about you."

"I don't have a boy." I took a large breath in, trying to center myself now he'd brought up Rome.

"You do and you always will. That guy might have buried his chain, but he also tied it around you somehow. You're linked together forever."

"Not by choice," I grumbled, picking at a small piece of plastic that had peeled off the mat.

"You fixing to put him out of his misery any time soon?"

"I don't have a way of doing that now. We can't be together, Dante."

Dante started stretching and I followed suit. Like always, he seemed to think over my words before he replied. "There's always a way to make things work if you want to."

"I don't," I shot back, probably much too fast for him to believe me. My body heated thinking about Rome, though. I felt his touch, I heard his voice, and I dreamt of his smell even when I knew I shouldn't. "I can't trust him. He'll never put me first. And I can't put him first now either. Don't you think that's necessary if you're going to be in a relationship in the mob?"

"I think it might be impossible if you're in the mob, Little One." He held his arm across his chest and his muscles flexed as he stretched. I did the same, my body completely in sync with his, as it usually was here within the gym. "You think anyone puts their untouchable first?"

"Probably not. Still, I can't do that. And I can't risk my place in the bratva for a lover. I've got bigger plans. We *all* should have bigger plans."

"To do good things?" he joked. He motioned for me to lie down and my body was so used to following his in this space that I didn't even question it.

"Something better than what we've done, at least." On my back, I stared up at him as he brought my leg to my chest slowly and stretched me. "Are you okay with just doing this?"

He chuckled, and with his chest on my leg I felt the movement through my body. "I'm okay right here, Katie." He waggled his eyebrows.

Dante had a hippy vibe to his military trained personality. Somehow, he maintained an attitude that almost came off as lazy and he joked as if there was not a worry in the world. His centered spirit calmed you and his drive to be the best pushed you. I loved that about him.

His laugh was contagious too. The man had caramel skin with tattoos snaking around it and such light green eyes that when I'd first seen him, I'd wondered if they were contacts.

To any woman, he was a sizzling, off the charts catch.

To me, he was just Dante.

We could laugh at the position we were in and call it a day without ever thinking twice about it.

Except today.

Because the laugh caught in my throat when I heard the voice I dreamt about growl, "Get the fuck off her."

The sparkle in Dante's eyes didn't die as I jumped and he turned his head toward Rome's voice.

Slowly, Dante pulled my leg back with him and tapped my other one. The sync I had with him was suddenly gone.

He tapped it again and said, "Have to stretch your other leg, Katie."

I turned to see Rome burning a hole of rage into both of us. I didn't lift my leg immediately and I could admit that it was almost in fear.

I didn't belong to him. I didn't answer to him. I wasn't with him. That was the concrete truth. I was proud that I had been able to tell him we couldn't be together and I'd stuck to it by not calling him or reaching out in any way.

But as people buzzed around the grey-toned gym, punching bags and sparring in the other rinks, I found that my body wasn't at all tired from my workout.

I had been ready to go to him immediately, ready to listen to what I knew he wanted. He didn't want Dante stretching any part of me. And I knew if I let Dante finish, there might be hell to pay.

Or maybe he'd walk away from me altogether. He could decide I wasn't worth all the fuss. And that thought sparked a fear in me that I wasn't ready for.

Still, I told myself, it would be for the best. I lifted my leg slowly, painfully, almost unwillingly. My mind had different thoughts from my body about what was right, and my body fought me tooth and nail.

Dante pushed down on my calf and brought my upper leg all the way to my chest. He leaned his body into it, watching me the whole time. "Okay, Little One?"

I took a breath as I stared at Rome, as I watched his strong jaw tick and his tattooed neck flex. His hands fisted and I knew just from the color his face was turning that we were far from over and I was far from okay. "I'll get there, Dante."

He nodded and slowly released my leg. Then he stood and walked right up to Rome. They matched each other, chest to chest. A stare down of epic proportions ensued. I knew exactly what the silent conversation was about. Rome claimed me as his, forever and always. He didn't like sharing in any sense of the word. But Dante had my back and we'd bonded over the years of training. I liked to think our friendship was valuable to him, that he would protect me if he thought I needed it.

"Dante," I murmured and put my hand to his chest. "This isn't the place."

"The place for what, Little One?" He kept his green eyes on Rome. "There's no misunderstanding, right, Rome?"

"Only if you want one, brother. We're all family here, right?"

I scoffed at his assessment and crossed my arms, ready to put him in his place. "Yes, Rome. You two are just like brothers to me."

Black fire licked across my skin as his gaze burned up my body. He let the words roll from him, slow and low. "There'll be nothing brotherly in the way I punish you for that statement, Katalina."

My body had cooled from my workout but it heated right back up again. I didn't need to goad him anymore. I was taking sick pleasure in it and I knew I wouldn't be able to indulge, that I shouldn't indulge. So I spun around and headed to my gym bag. "I'll see you later, Dante. Text me your schedule."

I heard Dante go his own way but I didn't look back. If I did, I'd stumble on the image of the monster in the gorgeous man I was trying so hard to avoid.

As I knelt to grab my bag from a hall locker, I heard Rome approach. I kept my head down, hoping he would give up and leave.

"Care to talk?"

I growled as I ripped out my top and stuffed my arms into the long sleeves. "Rome, I don't want to see you, let alone talk to you."

He hummed. "You didn't stay late at New Reign the other night. I haven't seen you since."

"Yes," I nodded, "That's the point."

"What point, woman?"

"I meant what I said. We don't have self-restraint, which means I'm restricting our relationship to a need-to-see basis, and I only need to see you when I meet with the Armanellis."

He grunted. "If you say so." He rubbed his hand over his five o'clock shadow, like was considering whether he should continue. "Fuck it. Since we're here, I have a few things to say. First and foremost, Dante and you are done training together."

My eyes bulged as I zipped up my shirt over my sports bra. I stood and glared at him, then poked him in the shoulder. "Are you kidding me right now?"

"No smile on my fucking face, Kate-Bait."

"You have some audacity, seriously," I fumed. "You think you can control who I spend my time with?"

"I can and I will. That's over." He didn't even stutter as he said it. The man was more straight to the point than even I liked and I was blunter than most.

"You're insane. That fact that you're even here right now... Are you following me?" I practically screeched, too pissed off at him to keep my voice down. "You don't get to barge into my workouts just to be a possessive asshole."

He crossed his massive arms over his chest, and I tried my best not to look but my mouth watered at his cut-off shirt, his arms flecked with droplets of sweat. "Does it look like I'm following you?"

He must have come here for a workout. I saw his tennis shoes, his gym shorts, and the outline of his abs under his shirt. He looked like a sculpted Italian god, and I wanted to lick the sweat from his skin.

I took a giant step back. "If we bump into each other, I expect you to walk the other way."

He smirked at my feet retreating, and the boyish twinkle in his eye made my heart twist. Would we have been something different had we met outside the mob? Would we have loved like a normal couple?

"I'm never going to walk away from what's mine, woman. You might be playing cat and mouse with me right now, but make no mistake: I'm going to catch you."

Then Rome ate up the space between us, fast as a streak of lightning in the dark, and his hand caught my arm. He swooped down to pick up my bag and yanked me along with him toward the exit.

"Maksim's outside." I stumbled along. "We can't go anywhere together and I don't need you two fighting."

"Then, tell him to fuck off when we see him." He continued toward the door.

I ripped my arm from his grip. I wasn't stupid enough to think I could get free of him without him letting go. "Rome, this isn't the plan."

"I've never had a plan with you. You've blown up every organized structure since the day I met you." He glared at me like I was the enemy.

In a way, to him, I was.

"So, what? You want me to follow you out of here and what? Announce we have some fucked up relationship we need to figure out?" I folded my arms across my chest, because if I didn't, I might just reach out to him.

His face was filled with anger, but also hurt. I knew he wanted me in the same way I wanted him. We couldn't ignore the fact that we'd grown up around one another, that we knew each other better than most. And my heart ached at realizing I'd probably never find another that could connect with me like he could.

I had too many issues for someone normal to deal with. Rome smoothed over the jagged pieces of me and I sanded down the rough edges of him. His monster calmed my beast. Walking away from that wasn't easy.

"I need something, Katalina. Don't give me nothing."

"It's not healthy," I whispered, all of my nonchalant act gone. I was holding on to my heart here while it gravitated toward him. I was gripping my body as it fought me to go to him. I didn't have much strength left.

"If not your address, and if not you coming with me, give me your number."

I took a deep breath as I considered his compromise. I scrunched my eyes shut, knowing I was doing the wrong thing, that I would be complicating everything, but I stuck out my hand anyway. He dropped his phone into it and I tapped in my number.

No bonds, no ties to your addiction, was how you overcame it.

Yet Rome was too strong of a drug.

I didn't know if he'd end up being fatal to me or helping me through the world.

I just knew I couldn't live without him.

I threw the phone back at him like it was a grenade, ready to explode in my hands.

His gaze licked up and down my body one last time before he took a step backward. "Answer when I contact you, Katalina."

"And if I don't?" I sucked in a breath as he strode up to me.

He wrapped his arm around my waist to pull me close and whisper in my ear. "I'll find you. And you don't want the monster to come looking."

CHAPTER 11

KATIE

O F COURSE I didn't answer his call.

It was a restricted line, so technically, it could have been anybody.

But, I knew.

My whole body tightened as I stared at my phone ringing in my hand. I considered how it would be if I did answer. Would we talk about the weather? What the forecast looked like for the next week?

We couldn't make small talk or chit chat. We had nothing to discuss. We never had. Our lives were heavy and dark, filled with things you didn't talk about over a phone call.

What would I say to a man I wanted but couldn't have? I didn't idly talk with anyone on the phone. For me to answer, for me to even consider answering, was ludicrous.

I threw the phone on the bed and went to go shower. As I let the steam engulf me, I stared at the tiling on the walls. The mosaic designs in cream colors fogged up with the heat over time. I stood in there so long thinking of the call I couldn't take that the fog turned to droplets. I slid to the ground and considered how long Rome would try, if he'd ever give up on me.

Or maybe another would grab his attention. He had a sex club after all.

The thought had me off the floor with jealousy, with frustration, but also resignation. I turned the handle and the water stopped falling. I dried off and went back to my phone.

My fingers hovered over the keys. One phone call and I could have Rome's number.

Instead, I texted Maksim, giving him our signal that I was safe and sound for the night.

I put my phone on the opposite side of where I slept, trying to forget the call that had ruined my night.

And that was singular because he only dialed my number once. He definitely hadn't left a message and I wasn't even sure he'd waited to hear the voicemail click on.

Rome was always impatient when he wanted something. He'd lived a life where efficiency was necessary and it bled over into everything he did. I didn't know if it was a product of his lifestyle or if he'd been born with it.

Still, I was more than a little surprised when the next day, as I got ready for another meeting with Ivan, Rome texted me.

Lately, the meetings with Ivan had been more heated as we brought in lawyers and allies to sign documents. We were getting close, so close I should have been focusing on that, not a text from Rome.

Still, I sat on the bed in my lingerie, about to change, and I pulled open the text. The number wasn't blocked this time, giving me a way to respond.

I shook away my excitement, reminding myself that I'd been the one to push him away. It was necessary for us both to have clear heads for our families, our line of work. We didn't need relationships. Some mob family codes actually forbade them for the very reason that they put your mob family at risk.

Emotions and ties just ended up broken apart on the floor in front of you.

And yet we were both bound to bleed out in front of one another anyway.

> **ROME:** You didn't answer.

> **ME:** You didn't leave a message. Or a number to call back.

> **ROME:** I have it on good authority you stared at me ringing your phone. You ignored the call and I know for a fact you could have got my number if you wanted it.

> **ME:** Maybe I don't want it. Ever cross your mind?

ROME: Never. I'll see you soon.

ME: What?

ROME: I'll be at the meeting.

ME: Why? You're not invited.

ROME: We will be. That meeting's bound to go to shit.

ME: I don't want to see you. Don't come.

ROME: Now, we both know I don't listen to commands well.

ME: Rome, this is business.

ROME: I'm well aware. What are you wearing to your business meeting, Katalina?

ME: Oh, get fucked.

ROME: Wear something for me, huh? If I can't have your pussy, I'd at least like to admire the view.

This was a conversation that was bound to lead to sexting if I didn't stop. This little taste of my addiction was already becoming a bigger problem. My thighs were clenching as I sat on the side of the bed, my heart racing for just a fix, my soul yearning for the place it felt most comfortable. Next to the man who put me on top of the world instead of those who constantly tried to drag me down into the depths of it.

ME: Don't you have anything better to do right now?

ROME: Yeah. I could be fucking you in your bed if you'd give me your address. I know just where to touch you to make you scream. Want me to come show you?

Jesus Christ, he could raise the heat level in seconds. We needed a cold bucket of water for the two of us.

ME: Admire someone else.

ROME: That an invitation to substitute cubic zirconium for a diamond? I'll pass.

ME: You're ridiculous, you know that?

I sent the text with a small smile on my face. Maybe he was just throwing out a compliment to keep the conversation going, or maybe he knew it was what I needed. He was the one man who never made me doubt myself in any regard. He held me to a sky-high standard.

Would my confidence ever get to where he thought I was? I didn't know, but I dressed in a black crop top that showed my tattoo. His words on my skin. His confidence in me.

It was a tribute to the monster that loved the woman he thought I was.

I hoped I could prove him right.

I headed out after pulling some ripped jeans on and smoothing my dark hair with a straightener.

"Maksim!" I said. "You brought a friend."

Maksim stood at the hood of the SUV outside my building with a tall, broody looking man that was about our age. The two of them side by side in front of a dark SUV were what nightmares turned to fantasies were made of. Maksim had the dark, Italian look with a couple small scars on his face that I knew were from his time being a bodyguard. His friend stood just as tall beside him. He had a strong jaw, an athlete's body, a good hairline. When I took him in, though, I didn't see any of it, because his eyes were almost translucent because they were so blue.

He held my gaze and smiled, putting out a hand for me to shake. "Luka, heir to the bratva out west."

I ran through my mental rolodex of people I'd seen at Mario's funeral. "You didn't come to town when Mario passed."

"No need," said Maksim. "Egor was here." He nudged his friend in the shoulder like it was an inside joke. "Can you imagine you two sitting through a plane ride together?"

Luka didn't squeeze my hand too tightly or drop his gaze at all while he measured me up. Instantly, I liked him.

"I'm just here to keep Maksim company," he said.

"Or spy for Egor?" I suggested.

"My grandfather could ask me to carry him across the street to a hospital after being shot and I wouldn't do it. You can believe me when I say I'm not here to spy. Maybe to meet you. But only because Maksim says nice things."

"Maksim does, does he?" I smirked at him and then waved off our meeting of the minds in the middle of a busy Chicago sidewalk. "Shall we all ride to this meeting and get it the fuck out of the way?"

"You think I need to be prepared?" Maksim asked as he opened the door for me. I didn't share much with Maksim, or anyone in the bratva for that matter. I couldn't trust them not to trickle down information to others.

Still, he was the only one who could help me if a situation went down. "It'll be heated."

"I swear to God..." he grumbled before he slammed the door. When he got into the front seat and Luka was situated in the passenger beside him, he glanced back at me and said, "You got to start giving me more, Katalina. I'm your guy."

"I don't have a guy." I broke eye contact and stared at the city that rolled by. Men in suits, women in heels with briefcases buzzed past. They didn't even see the men lurking behind them in the shadows, how the gangs wove in and out of society. They'd all become experts at being invisible. I caught one in a hoodie hunched over on a bench. When I met his gaze, he glanced away quickly. He was spying for another gang, surely.

Being aware was my life now, the way I lived another day. If I didn't stay alert, I'd be grabbed and end up dead and dumped down the river somewhere.

"You've got to have someone, huh? You can't take all this on alone, and the Armanellis—"

"They're not a part of this."

Maksim chuckled and nodded. "They'll always be a part of you, Katalina. Family isn't just blood, right? You're not so stupid to think that. I know you know that better than anyone."

"Maksim, aren't you only supposed to be my security?" I teased, lifting an eyebrow.

Luka spoke from his side of the car. "He can't be just that to anyone he cares for. You know we're supposed to be enemies. My dad wanted me to kill him when we were ten."

My gaze ping-ponged between the two. "Did anybody have a good parent other than me?"

Luka sighed and tapped the back of his hand against the window. "Not preparing us for much in the mob if you aren't constantly training for the worst."

"If we didn't only have the worst, maybe we'd have better." The statement was more to myself than both of them.

"I agree." Maksim looked both ways and behind us before he turned down an alley and wove through a few streets. He then veered onto the highway and we started our real drive to Ivan's. He thought mixing up his routes would help deter followers but I was sure it didn't. "It's why I believe in you. I need you to believe in me too."

"I'm doing the best I can." I dragged a hand over my face. "Let's talk about something else. Something light."

I closed my eyes as we rode and Maksim listed off things we needed to make decisions on. "Nico and his wife are most likely going into witness protection. I said we could give them a cut of my earnings for the next few years to help ease the transition. Oh, also, give Akim money for his son."

"You'll run out of money at this rate," advised Luka.

"I never had money before. What do I need it for now?"

Maksim laughed. "Got a point there."

"You weren't leading the bratva before," said Luka. "They expect a certain level of financial security."

"And they'll get it. Some will get even more because of the decisions I make. So everyone can thank me. If they don't want to, they can keep their mouth shut."

"Ah, that's the type of leadership I'm used to." He combed a hand through his thick brown hair.

"It seems to be the only leadership anyone listens to around here." The statement was petty but I was tired. This meeting was about to exhaust me more.

We pulled up to the beautiful white home and were greeted with an open door. Ivan waited for us at his dining room table, Konstantin, the head of the Miami bratva sitting there with him. Neither stood for me the last to be seated.

He didn't greet us or even mention Luka being there, he simply motioned toward me. "Begin with the logistics, Katalina."

I didn't hesitate. I dove right in like we had at the other meetings. The lawyers fanned out to hand out the contracts and then exited the room while I continued talking.

The contracts for partnerships between businesses, for security, and for making most of our income and businesses legal, which most importantly took trafficking off the table, needed to be solidified and signed off today by the one man at the table. He was a leader of the bratva in Miami, an extremely wealthy one who didn't ever want to change his way, I was told.

Maksim and Luka stared at me in shock as I finished. Maksim got up and came to stand behind me, like he knew I might need the damn security.

"I know this is the first time you're hearing this, but it has to be done," I stated while the older man across the table stared at the document in silence.

Ivan motioned toward a man standing in the corner. "I'll need a beverage. Get us some tea."

My stomach rolled at the thought. "Water for me only."

I'd been disgusted at even the thought of water or food or drink lately. I wanted to focus on this family, on moving forward. The only thing that could occupy my thoughts was Rome or talk of these contracts. Nothing else was important. My dream, our organization, our plans consumed everything in my mind.

The closer you got to a goal, to the finish line, the more you wanted it. I was so close, it felt like the sun was right up against my skin. It burned in me, shined all around me, and was ready to kill me if I didn't do something about it.

"Katalina, things like this take time." Ivan shook his head and tsked like my negotiation was too fast, frivolous, not smart.

"And every child sold takes a life."

"They aren't our children," the man from Miami, Konstantin, stated. He smiled and the hairs on his face folded into his wrinkles. I wanted to burn each one off slowly, hold a lighter to them and watch them flare. That man had stared at me from the second I'd arrived at the funeral and watched me like I was a piece of meat. He didn't want to end sex trafficking, because he was a part of it, because he didn't see where he could earn just as much money, and he probably enjoyed it.

"Do you have children?"

His beady eyes narrowed, the blue in them as cold as ice. "Do you?"

"Yes." My heart swelled, thinking of the girl that I had met so long ago at Marvin's, how her eyes looked dead inside and mirrored my own. "They are my children. They are my sisters and my brothers. They're mothers and daughters. This isn't a plantation from years ago. We aren't selling slaves or humans or sex trafficking them. We find another way."

His hand slammed down on the table. "You don't get to come in here and change everything." Spit flew from his mouth while he talked. "Ivan! This is ridiculous."

147

Ivan waited as a man brought out our tea. It steamed from the cup and he let the aroma fill the room before answering. His eyes bounced from me to the window where I knew men stood outside waiting for our visitor. "What's all this about?"

His eyes appeared empty when he looked at me for a second and he shook his head.

The display was out of character. It wasn't Ivan at all.

It was his disease.

We'd made deals with pharmaceutical companies and colleges to get him care, to get him medication to control the onset of his Alzheimer's. Some of the studies and trials were working on him.

Still, there were moments.

He shook his head and shut his eyes. When they opened, the clarity was there again.

"This isn't for me to decide anymore, Konstantin," said Ivan. "My memory, my health, it comes first."

"No. The bratva comes first." Konstantin stood up, his deep voice guttural and full of fury. He dove into his navy suit jacket, the lapels much bigger than Ivan's to accommodate his bulk.

Ivan rolled his eyes when Konstantin pointed a gun at him.

I didn't even flinch when the gun swung my way. I'd done the dance one too many times with men I'd been with, with Ivan over the last few weeks training me. I could see in his eyes that he wouldn't pull the trigger.

"Don't point a gun at me if you don't intend to shoot it," I said and leaned back in my chair. "Ivan needs rest. I need a drink. You need to agree to all of this or your bratva can go to hell."

"You go to hell," he said, jerking the gun that pointed at my head.

"Send me, then." I shrugged. "See how it works out for you."

He glanced around and the man in the corner had a gun on him. The two men outside most likely did too. Maksim's gun had most surely been pulled and aimed above my head also. Snipers were set up all over this house. They always would be and they knew to protect the family that owned it, that paid their bills.

My bratva knew. I held the key.

"The Stonewoods and the Armanellis are my family too," I said. "They've already agreed. You don't want to, we deal you out. Sign where the lawyers have said to and do as you're told."

"My earnings will be cut in half," he ground out.

"You'll only lose an eighth of your earnings. And that will grow back with the other contracts." I combed a finger through my straightened dark hair. I pulled on the collar of my crop top. "You don't have to trust me. Trust the process."

"Where's the process, huh? You come in and take all our money. Some woman we don't even know." He swung his gun toward Ivan. "You did this."

"I should have you killed." Ivan was growing tired. I could see by the way his shoulders slumped, by the way he'd forgotten where he was before.

"You should kill yourself," said Konstantin. "After all this, you pretty much have. Giving the bratva over to her, leaving us to rot under the influence of Italians and CEOs."

"Maybe we need to call them here then." Ivan rubbed his temple.

Like dominos being perfectly aligned, I saw now that Rome would come. He'd arrive with them all and they'd make a statement with one of the last contracts we needed signed. The man had known even before I had how this world turned. It was a solid reminder of what I needed to learn.

"Call who?" asked Konstantin. Then he sneered at me. "Bastian? The man who fucks this girl when we aren't looking, or is that Rome? They just agreed to this because they're pussy whipped and I'm not about to be."

I almost stood up and reacted. He did deserve to die. I needed to be bigger than my pride though. I needed to prove I was better than all of them by not killing the man immediately even though they thought a woman would be the first to indulge her emotions.

"Yes, I think we will call Bastian." I took a deep, calming breath. I kept the show moving. This was one in a long line of many to come. We'd set an example with him, though.

"Bastian," I purred into the phone while glaring at Konstantin. He could believe what he wanted about me at this point; he could roll in his hatred for me for all I cared. I wanted to make him squirm with discomfort and have the hate ooze from him. He'd still sign on the dotted line. "Ivan would like to have you over for tea."

"Yeah, we figured that was going down. I'm bringing the crew. He's trouble and I won't be there without them." Bastian said calmly to me.

I wouldn't argue that. I responded, "If they are with you and would like to attend, that's fine too."

I hung up and stared at the old man. Konstantin holstered his weapon and sat down while he grumbled, "I guess we wait and drink tea."

The clock ticked. The birds chirped outside. Time passed with only tension making noise in the room. It didn't take long, an indication that Cade was tracking me and that they were in the area, prepared for all of this. I didn't care.

This was the first step of legalizing the bratva. We did this my way if I ruled and we did it by making allies, by weeding out illegal trafficking, by saving lives instead of ruining them. The men would have to fall in line. We did what I said, what I believed in, what I knew would ultimately benefit us.

Bastian, Rome, and Dante walked in after half an hour of the two men sipping tea and me water. They all stood tall in their black Armani suits. I knew the brand because I'd been with them and Mario at the boutiques in the past. Rome, though, even in the relaxed way he walked, overpowered their presence in the room.

Or maybe I just felt it. This was the first time he'd attended a meeting since the funeral with Bastian. I should have been focused on the contract, on getting that signature, and making all this work. Instead, that man's presence suffocated my thoughts of anything else. It was like his grip on my neck. The shivers down my back weren't from the cold. The darkness in his eyes penetrated even the deepest parts of my soul.

His jawline was flexed and when he made eye contact with me, it popped.

"Glad you could all make it," I murmured.

Bastian and Dante smiled and took a seat at the table as Ivan waved them in. Dante unbuttoned his suit jacket and Bastian nodded when the corner man offered tea.

Rome stood behind them both, arms crossed.

"Would you like to sit?" Ivan motioned toward the empty chair near me.

"I'll stand," he said and didn't glance my way again.

My mind should have been focused on the contract, focused on making each partner accountable. Instead, I willed him to look my way again. I wanted to peel back his hard exterior, figure out why he wouldn't turn his face toward me.

"Suit yourself," Ivan replied and stood. "This isn't my choice. I'm tired. You all figure it out. I'll be retiring now."

The room stilled. No one said a word as Ivan's chair scraped loudly on the wooden floor. We all stared at him in disbelief.

Ivan had sat with me for every meeting from the beginning. Now, he appeared worn out, sunken in and deflated.

He didn't say another word, just turned on his leather loafers and disappeared down the hall.

"Well, I guess you'll lead the bratva to hell without him then," Konstantin mumbled.

"If you'll sign on the dotted line, we won't go anywhere

near hell," I said. "If you won't, I'll drag you there and watch you burn."

"You warn me like you can do a thing." He smiled at the men who sat there. "I'm not scared of any of you."

"We don't want you scared, Konstantin. We want you willing. This partnership will work better with everyone fully involved."

"I don't work well with pussies." He motioned toward me.

The low hum that rolled through the room made me clench my thighs. Rome's anger affected me in a way that it shouldn't have. I stared at him, hoping to see some emotion other than fury cross his face.

"Are you calling me a pussy or these men?" I was taunting him, knowing he would never refer to the Armanellis like that.

"I swear to God, I am going to kill you," Konstantin whispered, but it was loud enough for us all to hear.

Maybe we should've known that Rome wasn't in the right mindset. His monster was clamoring to get out. The rage had consumed him, rage over something I wasn't exactly sure of.

He pulled his gun and shoved it into Konstantin's head. The man's eyes bulged and his hand flew to his own gun. He never got to it though because Rome was too fast. He took the man's hand and twisted it until we saw his wrist break. The pop of the bone was loud but even Ivan must have heard Konstantin's blood curdling scream from the other side of the house.

"I'm not here to play games or to waste my time," Rome said, his face devoid of emotion. "Sign the papers."

"They won't be legally binding," whimpered Konstantin, "considering that I am being forced into putting my signature on paper. "

"Would you like me to give you a choice?"

"I deserve a choice, don't I?"

"You deserve a choice. Of course. Choose death or signing the paper," Rome said pointedly.

"You've got some evil in you, huh? I like to see that. Maybe it *is* you that's fucking—"

Rome lost it. He didn't wait. He didn't look at me for a signal, or Bastian for that matter. The gun flew from the man's head to his leg where Rome pulled the trigger.

I jumped at the sound, before Konstantin wailed.

Blood had splattered across the contracts and onto our shirts and faces.

"I hit your artery. If you don't get to a hospital in the next five minutes, you *will* bleed out and die." Rome had his hands on the man's shoulders holding him to his chair.

The man screamed and screamed, but he dropped his own gun from his hands like he knew he couldn't shoot anyone in the room, like he didn't really hold any of the power.

What a sad feeling to know your place and realize you can't save your own life because of the hierarchy you agreed to. What an even sadder thought to realize many didn't agree to it at all.

"This is your world," I whispered to him. "Not mine."

He didn't respond to my comment, he just begged for his life, for us to let his men in. He screamed their names, but our men were certainly holding his men back outside.

I stared at the man who had wanted to send me to hell. I remembered how he downplayed my power, how he called me a pussy, how he insinuated that I was a whore who worked my way to the top.

I contemplated his words and wondered if he was right. And laughed to myself because, it would be ironic, right? The men that had sex trafficked women would be picked off one by one by a woman who had been sex trafficked herself. Did these men not realize that they'd created this beast, that I fed off the power they'd once stolen from me? That after they'd put her pussy up on a pedestal for so long, she'd learn she deserved to use her body in any way she so chose to get what she wanted?

All he had to do was sign on a line; all he had to do was look up at me and beg for his life. He did none of those things. His cold blue eyes never looked my way. He could not bring himself to see me as an equal. A woman in power was beyond what he could accept.

Bastian watched and Rome held him down as he struggled.

They were waiting for him to do the same thing as I was because, at the end of the day, these men were my family. They knew what I needed from him. And they were still mafia men. They would let him die.

I had to be stronger. I had to be the woman of the mafia.

The queen that reigned with love for life instead of with wrath.

I turned to the corner man. "Get someone to take him to the hospital. Drop him there. Make sure he survives."

155

Konstantin heard my words. His screaming and begging stopped. The room held silence as blood from his wound poured out onto the wood floors. We watched the red seep into the cracks and I knew the cleaning up afterward would be difficult.

"I'll sign." He stared at me; his blue eyes genuinely full of a remorse I couldn't have fathomed just seconds before.

"If you sign, you sign it of your own will when you finish your hospital stay." I wouldn't put our partnership in jeopardy. I wanted clean signatures.

His men rushed in and dragged him out and we were left with red smears across the floor.

Bastian stood and came over to give me a hug. "I guess you did the right thing. I would have let him go."

"You'd let all bratva go if you could."

"That's very true." He patted my back and kissed my cheek. As he walked out, he said to Rome and Dante, "I'm not in the mood for clean-up. You need to rein it in, Rome."

Dante followed him, leaving Rome staring at the floor. I lifted my chin for Maksim to leave the room. He hesitated until I wide-eyed him to leave. Luka smiled on his way out and said, "Nice to meet you."

Nothing about this meeting had been nice, but I didn't respond as they left.

Instead, I waited. I wouldn't break the silence between Rome and me at this point. He could do the honors. He could defend his actions this time. If it was because of how we'd left things, he could admit that. I didn't owe him anything now, not when he'd acted out without consent from any of us.

"His gun was lying on the table pointed at you when I walked in," said Rome, his voice quiet. "Did he hold you at gunpoint?"

"A lot of men have held me at gunpoint, Rome."

"You're baiting with your life now?" He almost whispered the words. The question was ominous and I knew he wouldn't like my answer.

"Haven't I always baited with my life? And anyway, it's my life to bait with, right?" He had to learn, we both had to. Our lives couldn't be intertwined the way we wanted.

He growled and ran his fingers through his hair before he pulled on the back of his neck and looked toward the ceiling. "No!" he screamed and slammed his hand down on the table. He reared back and then crashed his knuckles into the table.

Over and over again.

I had to walk up and grip his arm. "Stop."

The wild in his eyes as he glared at me was a reminder at how close this man was to complete oblivion and chaos. The blood dripped from his knuckles into the table where he ground his fist in hard, trying to shake whatever he was feeling.

"Please stop, Rome." I said again because his knuckles were raw against the wood and the pain he was causing himself was too much.

"It's my soul, my monster, my *life* that is fed by yours, Katalina. You're mine and you keep me living. So I keep you living. You're fucking mine. This life, this heart"—he shoved his bloodstained finger into my chest—"that's mine. No one fucks with what's mine. I should have shot him in the motherfucking head. Next time, I will."

He was shaking with rage, and most days, I would have let him have at it. He needed to learn that this would be us forever and ever now. But like I was his, his monster was mine. It wasn't used to not being able to protect. I saw the anguish rolling around deep down inside him and making him crazy.

Was I crazy to sit through what I just had with Konstantin, to be held at gunpoint without batting an eyelash? To not feel anything truly until now?

A heart crumbling and screaming for it's soulmate was the worst pain and the scariest.

All I wanted was to soothe him, to make our relationship okay.

He wasn't made to be helpless, Rome was made to fight, to protect, to worry about his family so much that he didn't stop to think that the bratva could have shot *him* through the window. He didn't think twice.

I saw all the steps now; I knew they had guns trained on him. His life had been on the line. My heart beat for that life as much as his heart beat for mine.

I stepped into that expansive chest and hugged him. I didn't kiss him or rub my hands over him like I usually did. I enveloped the body that was twice my size in my arms and sighed into him. "We're okay, huh?"

"What?" He whispered into my hair and then he breathed me in.

"We're okay. It's all okay."

"You're going to kill me, Kate-Bait."

"Remember, you said once, you'll survive..."

His arm wrapped around me and his hand rubbed over my tattoo. "Because if you don't, you die. You trying to say that the same goes for me?"

I shrugged. "I was a little nervous you were going to get yourself killed today by shooting Konstantin. None of them trust you, or me for that matter. They could have shot you today."

"I'd have lived," he said into my hair.

"You could have died just as easily as I could have."

His hand rubbed my back as he said, "I need you to have better security. I'll split time between you and Bastian."

"No." I shook my head on his chest. "We're not even sup-posed to be here together now. Maksim does well and I need them to trust—"

"Don't say it. I could care less about their trust."

"I earned Konstantin's today." I smiled into his shirt and took my own whiff of him.

"That you did, Cleo. That you did."

"We only have a few more signatures to go. If we implement without hitches, the trafficking will dramatically decrease in the next year."

"There'll be hitches, babe." He pulled back to look down at my eyes. The chocolate brown there oozed a love for me that was so tempting I could wanted to melt into it. "There's going to be a lot more."

I took a step back, but he just stepped with me and kept his arm locked on my waist. I smirked. "Let go, monster. You can't have me here or anywhere. We have to be done."

"We're never done. I want your address."

"You can't have it. We can't…" I sighed because my body and heart were running toward him and leaving my mind behind. I had to reign them all in and stay the course. "We can't be anything, Rome. Not for a long time."

"We are something. I'll take your address when you're ready to give it."

"I won't be."

He stepped back and I chilled immediately. "I guess you're leaving me to my own devices."

The warning in his voice didn't scare me. The animal in him wasn't going to leave me alone. And the fiend in me was about to give in. It wouldn't be smart. Some would even say we were heading toward our own demise. The fact that I was looking forward to it was what truly scared me most.

CHAPTER 12
ROME

I GAVE HER ANOTHER two weeks. In that time, I knew that Ivan had been training her. I knew she still went to see Dante at the gym, even when I'd forbade her to. She wanted a damn punishment, I swear. I also knew she met with Cade and Bastian. They even invited me to sit in on their meetings.

I didn't. That woman was about as malleable as a rock. She wouldn't give in to my request for her address at all.

She hadn't reached out again by texting or calling. I tried to give her time. I even got to the point where I hoped she'd send a message via Cade, Bastian, or Dante.

That shit hurt my pride. It enraged me. Why the hell was I the one she had to avoid when she'd been in my bed, slept in my damn panic room, and wanted me most? I saw the look in her eyes even when I was putting a bullet in someone. That woman wanted me.

I could have hassled Cade for her address. I could have got it, but I was trying not to give in to the rage that normally consumed me. She had me and us all looking at ourselves in the mirror and questioning our own existence. We'd lived powerful lives based on what the mafia had given us. It was easy to take, to enforce, to get what we wanted. I wanted her to come willingly.

That was one of the hardest things to admit to myself over the past few weeks.

We needed to change.

It started with me asking for something. At least I'd given her a head's up this time. That was more than we normally did.

I was the enforcer of the family. She had to know that, from me, she only got change to a certain point.

If she didn't want me to show up in the dead of the night, she should have given me the damn address.

Instead, I was sitting on the loveseat in her new penthouse suite, the coils of tension that had been wrapped around every muscle in my body finally relaxing at being near her. We belonged together in the shadows and darkness. It was where we thrived.

I breathed in deep and watched her chest rise like we were in sync. She'd kept her hair bone-straight over the past couple weeks and as black as ink. She appeared lethal despite how small she was.

I left without waking her and walked down a flight of stairs to the apartment I'd bought out from another resident. Ivan's team wasn't doing enough to protect her. The fact that this was even doable showed that.

They had men outside the building and thought their checks inside the building were enough. Not now that I lived there. Not now that I could sneak in and out after each of their checks.

I broke into her penthouse the next night and the night after. No man at her door made it that easy.

I'd been about to leave when a whimper escaped her lips. She clutched the sheets over her and twisted in them. Her face scrunched in pain as she whispered "no" over and over again. There was a monster in me that usually controlled my biggest emotions, and the one I had in that moment was fucking love. My mind tried to pull me toward the door, but the beast loved Katalina more than it loved me. He dragged me to her, and I knelt down.

"Kate-Bait," I whispered and put a hand to her cheek. "You're okay, huh? You're okay."

She jolted awake and the hand that was at her sheet went under her pillow and drew a knife. It was at my throat so fast, another man would have been left at her mercy. My hand moved quick though. I caught her wrist just far enough away from me that the knife didn't break skin.

She sucked in small breaths, each of them rapid with adrenaline. Our gazes held in the moonlight.

"No weapon is going to save you from me," I said.

"What the fuck are you doing in my room?" Instead of taking the knife from my neck, she shoved it harder into me. I smiled at her fight, at the part of her that didn't ever back down.

"I'm making sure you're safe from your nightmares, no?"

"You are my nightmare." She snatched her hand away from me and threw her knife onto the nightstand before ripping the sheets from her legs and leaping from her bed. "Go home."

"What are you doing?"

She ran to the bathroom and slammed the door. I heard her vomiting in there so loud I wasn't going to stay on the other side.

I barged in. "What the hell is wrong with you?"

She glared up, her cheeks hollowing in and out from her labored breathing. She held up one finger and barfed again into the toilet.

"Jesus Christ," I grumbled as I strode forward and scooped up her dark hair into my hands. The smooth strands fell from my fingertips. "Why you keep straightening your hair is beyond me."

"This hair makes me look like I take no shit."

"Gives me barely anything to grab on to, woman." The remark was more for myself than for her. I missed the way she'd looked in my panic room. Relaxed and at home, like we hadn't tightened her so much that all the wild in her was gone.

"My hair isn't styled for you." She wiped her mouth and then sighed before flushing the toilet. "I'm good."

"Sure?" I kept my fingers threaded through her hair as she stood and faced me, wanting an extra second here before she went back to pretending there was nothing between us. My grip tightened when she nodded. I wasn't ready to let her go.

She felt it as she smiled and tilted her head into my wrist. "You can't hold me forever, Rome."

"I might try."

She laughed and then bit her lip before she whispered, "Let go, monster."

It was like prying my hands from the edge of a cliff. This girl didn't know I was hanging on by a thread, that I wasn't sleeping without staring at her in the middle of the night, that when I did sleep, I dreamt of her, that my body was being controlled by a desolate beast that only wanted to be with her.

She turned toward the marble vanity and started the faucet. Cupping her palms together, she caught enough water to wash out her mouth.

"You sick, or is this a result of the nightmares?" I motioned toward the toilet.

"Maybe the nightmare." She shrugged. "Maybe a little of everything."

"Have you been to the doctor?" I lifted an eyebrow.

"For what?" She bent to grab mouthwash from under the sink and I stared at her ass the whole time. She cleared her throat and I snapped my gaze to hers in the mirror. "Rome, I'm not sleeping with you. So you can go home now."

I sighed and pulled at my neck as I looked toward the high ceilings. "I'm not here to fuck you."

She shimmied her ass and my dick jumped. "Sure about that?"

"Don't tempt me, Kate-Bait. You're changing the subject. Get a doctor's appointment."

"There's no need. I have issues when I sleep. The nightmares are...I didn't use to have them. It's just stress."

"Probably best not to take a chance. You could have the flu or something."

"Do you ever not map out the 'what ifs?' I'm not your concern anymore."

I swear to God, she wanted to taunt me or wanted a reaction. My feet ate up the tiled floors to cage her into that vanity, my arms on either side of her. "What makes you my concern, huh? You want me to drag you out of here and lock you up in a room again? I'm happy to."

Her eyes narrowed to slits. "You'd start a war."

Her words held weight. She wanted me to back off, to cower from her. Yet her pulse jumped on her neck and her breaths came faster. I watched her breasts rise and fall against the thin fabric. Her nipples hardened, dark and pointed under the smooth cream of her shirt.

My dick hardened against her ass. "If you want me to start a war for you, I will. It'd be one I would win because I'm not afraid to spill blood for you. The whole city could bathe in red for all I care. We both know that. The bratva is no match for us. And maybe it's best that way. If I lock you up with me and take away this new bloodline of yours, there are no complications."

"Except that you'd have stripped me of my freedom, Rome. And that's all I ever wanted."

"You were always free with me, Cleo."

"Not free from tradition, not free to have a say and a voice. Not free from where the family thought I belonged. And even still, what worth would I have?"

"The worth of being with me. Us together. Is that not enough?"

"You love me when I'm yours, but can you love me when I'm not too?"

"Unfortunately, that seems to be the case, doesn't it? I'm hovering over you like a lovesick puppy in the middle of the night. And keeping tabs on things I never would have before. All because you wouldn't give me a damn address so I could see you, so I could know you were safe."

"Don't do that. Don't make me out to be the bad guy." Her voice strained, trying to hold back her anger. "You couldn't pick forgiveness or love in that moment with Mario. You chose hate and the family way instead. And I chose to walk away from the family that did that time and time again. I chose to create a different family here with them."

"I'm going to follow you wherever you go, woman. You're not walking very far without me." I gripped the counter on either side of her, trying my best not to grab her hips and bend her over to remind her that I had some power here, some control, at least in our relationship.

She sighed and combed her fingers through her inky black hair. "Go home, Rome."

My grip turned to a white-knuckled one as I ground my teeth together at her trying to make me leave. I tilted my head just close enough to her neck that I could breathe her in. The smell of her, the way goosebumps skittered across her collarbone, and the soft gasp that escaped from her lips emboldened me. "Home is up against your ass. I live where you are."

"No. I live with the bratva now. There's men out there that will come if I call them."

"You intending to call them up? You want me to lay bodies down for you tonight? I'm at the point that I will."

She bit her bottom lip and arched her ass into my cock. It was enough of an answer, even if she didn't speak. I let go of the counter so I could lift her shirt, knowing I'd find nothing under it.

"Rome, we shouldn't be doing this," she whispered, but she was letting the fabric inch higher and higher.

When the fabric skimmed her ass, she shuddered and I smiled like a wolf about to eat his meal. I hummed at her statement, not giving it much attention. I was focused on those two round globes. With her back arched, they were just the right size for me to squeeze. My hand latched on and I watched my fingers press into her soft skin, my thumb dangerously close to that asshole that I wanted to fuck.

"You like being in power in the bratva, Katalina?" I whispered as I massaged her cheek. Her body moved in rhythm with my touch, like she couldn't help herself. She panted and I saw how her arms had moved in over her breasts like she was trying to feel them up herself.

"Power's a loose term, Rome. I'm learning and it's still Ivan's say over mine."

I smacked her ass hard and she yelped, but before she could pull away I was massaging it again. "I'll punish you for downplaying your power. Remember you've always been ready for this."

Her gaze on me softened. "I'm only me, Rome."

"It's not *only* you. It's Katalina, Cleo, Kate-Bait that rose to the queen of the bratva. You're everything and you handle anything." I brushed my thumb over the tight ring I'd yet to enter.

She gasped and pulled her back up a little.

Retreating from one another wasn't an option at this point. I tangled my other hand in her hair and pulled her back. "Don't think we aren't going here, Cleo."

"It won't be tonight," she panted, trying her best to keep it together. "You're going home."

"You think you're kicking me out without letting me taste you? I've been starved of my favorite meal for far too long." I dipped my finger far into her pussy so that she'd gasp for me before I slid it out and sucked the juices off. "I'm going to show you why I need to stay."

"You can't show me because there's no good reason for you t—"

"Watch yourself in the mirror while I eat my meal, woman." I kneeled on a knee and smelled exactly what I'd been missing for weeks.

She didn't say yes or no, nor did she move. I brushed my finger over her clit, and her nipples tightened under the shirt instantly. "Bend forward. A ruler knows when to take the gift they've been offered."

She shook her head like I was being ridiculous, but her pussy was open to me now. I dragged my tongue across her pink lips and licked slowly. I took my time. I enjoyed my feast.

She moaned my name like she was mine, she rolled her hips over my face like she was mine, and she definitely tasted like she was mine.

I ate her out like a ravenous animal.

It didn't take long for her to scream out and clench around my tongue as I thrust it into her center while still rolling my fingers over her clit.

I pulled away and stood, but held her hips up so she could steady herself and come back from her orgasm. When the muscles in her shoulders relaxed and she opened her gray eyes, I saw the smoky haze of a woman satiated.

I licked my lips as we stared at one another. "Best meal I've tasted in a long time."

She nudged up against my dick that was standing to attention. "I want the rest of you, I can't deny that," she murmured. "But if they find out about us, I've lost them all because of you."

"No. You can handle them all and that's what you need to understand."

She didn't say anything and it reminded me that still somewhere in her was someone small and completely vulnerable.

"Look at yourself in that mirror, Katalina. Hold your head high."

We stared at one another, finally alone in a place where we could. Under the bathroom lights in her new penthouse that cost millions of bratva dollars, we exchanged something. I was the killer of her enemy and she was a leader choosing to lead or to love.

"I can't have you and them, Rome."

"You can and you will. You've made a damn bed with me, you gave me access to the most precious thing you own, and it's not your pussy. You gave me your heart. If not me, then the monster in me. You going to lead without a heart? Most of those before you have done it, but it wouldn't be the smart thing to do."

"Why is it that you always come to me speaking of leading when you don't?"

At that point, I didn't want to talk. My dick was resting just between her ass cheeks, my hand was wet with her orgasm, and my mouth still tasted like her pussy. "I lead here." I tensed my cock against her and she shuddered. I grabbed her neck and she lifted her chin automatically. "Do I not?"

"Fucking a woman doesn't take a lot of leading. It takes a good dick and some rhythm. I have to lead a disorganized group of heartless men who don't trust me."

"So, build trust."

She squinted at me. "I don't—"

My hand squeezed her windpipe closed. Her eyes flared along with her temper. She didn't like being cut off, but I didn't like her doubting herself. She needed to learn to have the confidence in herself that I had in her. Tonight, I would show her what it meant to rule.

"Who took your virginity?"

"Why does it matter?"

"Answer the question, Katie." It was a command because she didn't need to know the reason at that moment.

"Jimmy's son. I don't know if you remember—"

"I remember." Her description stung, but I didn't focus on it. This wasn't about me or my jealousy of any man who slept with her.

"Did you trust him?"

"Obviously." She rolled her eyes and shrugged at me like my questioning was going nowhere. Her ass pushed into my dick, and it reminded me how impatient she could be. "I wouldn't have slept with him if I didn't."

"You gave him a prized possession because you trusted him. How did he earn that trust?"

"I don't know, Rome. It was a long time ago. "

"Let me show you." My hand snaked down to grab her breast and my other hand snaked down her spine.

The hole that no one had entered, the hole that she felt was too sacred to give anybody access to, would be mine. My fingers slid down into her crack and she eyed me curiously.

"Bend forward for me, Katalina."

She bit her bottom lip. We both knew what I was about to do. She took her time, chewed those supple lips for a few seconds too long.

I had been waiting, my dick had been throbbing, the monster in me was shaking to get to her. I smacked her ass hard, harder than I had intended. She gasped, biting her lip to keep from moaning at how she liked it. It would leave a hand mark, but I saw that she was finally going to comply. She bent slowly at her waist, arching her back so that her ass popped out further, her cheeks spreading so that I could see her puckered hole, the one place no one had ever had the pleasure of fucking, the place I would own. Me, and me alone.

I'd get to take that innocence, dirty it, destroy what made it virgin, and my cock pulsed at the thought.

My fingers moved back and forth over it. "How do you earn trust, Katalina, from someone who has had their trust broken again and again?"

Her breaths were coming more quickly. She shrugged, and I nodded because it wasn't an easy answer.

"You have to learn what they like." I smacked her ass again hard, and this time she moaned.

My other hand was at her pussy, and as I slid a finger in, I got the lubrication I needed. "What they like is their weakness, it's what makes them open up to you, gives you what you need to get the job done. You know all this. You've found a man's weakness time and time again and earned their trust."

I slid my finger from her pussy and up to her ass. I didn't wait for permission. I shoved my dick home into her pussy and pushed my middle finger up her ass. She screamed, slamming a hand into the mirror as I rammed her hard enough to give her bruises where the front of her thighs pressed against the counter.

"You feel that? It's what you like. It's how you'll end up giving me the last virgin piece of you," I whispered in her ear as my dick fucked her to a place where she'd beg for it over and over.

"Rome, it's too much."

"Or is it not enough?"

She bent further down, her forearms resting on the counter, and let me lean over her.

She clenched around my finger and I pulled it from her ass before she hit her high. "What the—"

"Trust takes time, Katalina. We have all the time in the world." I leaned farther over her, placed my hands on the mirror to position myself at a better angle.

"No." She shook her head furiously. "We have no time left, Rome."

When she said the words, something overcame me. Fury that she didn't think we could conquer them, passion to own her like I knew I could, and rage at thinking anyone would try to stop me.

Shoving into her fast again, I hit her G-spot, using the mirror as leverage. I fucked her hard to remind her where I belonged.

She yelled my name every time my dick pumped into her. Her straight hair swung back and forth in rhythm, fast and smooth, her mouth open to pant.

One hand went to her hair, and I bunched it up, pulled her face high. "Say you're mine. Say I can have you as long as I want."

"Time's not up to me."

"The fuck it isn't." My other hand fisted and pounded into the mirror. The force cracked the glass and my blood stained the edges of it. "Say it."

"You bleed for something that's not doable."

"We can do anything. You can do anything," I whispered. She could rule these men; she could rip them apart too. She could bring down the whole city if she wanted or put it back together.

She was Cleopatra and I just had to make her see. I had to remind her that she'd survived the worst already, that the bratva were malleable, didn't have a hold on someone like her.

I slid my dick from her, slow this time, let her feel each inch of it come out. I stepped away from her. "Turn around. Look at what you do to the man who is supposed to kill you. To kill anyone who's a threat to the Armanelli Family."

She turned slowly and glanced down at me stroking my cock for her. Her gaze lingered before she hopped up onto the counter and spread her legs. I walked to the edge and tilted the head of my cock toward her entrance. I let the wetness drip onto it before I ran it over her clit. She immediately shuddered, and I saw those nipples tighten like I'd pinched them.

"You better fuck me like you mean it, Rome."

"You better rule the bratva and this city like you mean it. Show them what we're made of, huh?"

Her jaw tightened, her mouth thinned, and her grey eyes turned as cold as a stone in the middle of a Chicago winter storm.

There was that fighter, that survivor, that queen. She'd have them kneel before her. Anyone would bow.

She wrapped one leg around me and then the other before she lowered her body down where it belonged.

Hard.

Here we were, remembering what we wanted.

What we deserved.

What we were.

Together.

I met her thrust for thrust and our stares stayed glued on one another. "You'll do it. You know how I know?"

"How?"

I dragged my hand along her ribcage where she had my words written. "Because if you don't, you'll die. I will too. My blood is still your blood, Katalina."

I pushed into her again and her eyes changed. From prey to predator, I saw Katie transform to Katalina, to Cleo, to the woman I knew she was. A tear streamed down her face in recognition.

The weight of the city had just borne down upon us.

CHAPTER 13

KATIE

I CHECKED MY WINDOW shades to make sure none of the bratva would see us. I checked my last text to the security team that I was going to bed.

No updates.

So, I let him stay in my bed.

I should have asked him to go, but something changed when I looked at myself in that mirror, when I looked at him and saw something like love in his eyes. Rome pushed me to be something I knew I could be but was scared to be. I'd walked a thin rope for the last few weeks, trying to listen to everything Ivan explained, trying to implement where I could with the bratva, and trying to remain calm when their eyes were on me, shooting daggers my way.

Those men didn't trust me. They didn't trust anyone really. I expected that, and I expected the hate too. A woman whom they felt was an Italian whore had just come to rule their empire.

I could have rolled my eyes at the notion, though, at calling what the bratva had an empire. The men had been disorganized, acting on emotion, and killing on a whim.

Just the night before I had to call off a murder based on a food choice. One of the leaders wanted another dead because he hadn't remembered how much the man didn't like shellfish. It was blatant disrespect and that would cost him his life.

I'd shot it down and been met with fury. Ivan had to quiet the room and I had to live with the threatening stares.

It wasn't what I feared when I went to sleep. My life had always been in some kind of danger and it always would be. I was accustomed to that fear.

Now, though, I had the weight of this city on me. And I wasn't sure I was good enough to take that on.

I could let so many down even if they never knew I was going to bat for them in the first place.

And that was the expectation. I could see it in Ivan's eyes, even. He thought that in the end I would fail, that I wouldn't be able to change or lead the bratva. No one really believed in me and most days I barely believed in myself. I just went through the motions.

Except when Rome stood behind me, except when he made me stare into my own eyes and see my power. I let the man kneel before me. He was a monster, a ruthless killer, a demon to most who encountered him and still he saw the best in me.

He was the only one who kept me safe from the doubts that flew around in my head at night.

So I let him stay.

He lay down next to me, but I didn't cuddle up to him. We'd only done that in the panic room and we were in a different place now.

He let out a sigh and then pulled me up against his chest. "We're not going backwards, Kate-Bait. If we're in the same bed, every part of your body is going to be up against mine."

"It's amazing that you're the killer in the family and yet you want to cuddle."

"Got to know if I have to do some killing tonight. I'll make sure to kill another nightmare if you have one."

I smiled to myself and squeezed the arm he tightened around my waist. "Goodnight, monster."

I slept deeply, like a beaten animal in a safe, warm home for the first time in ages.

When I woke, it wasn't from a bad dream but the immediate need to empty my stomach. I ran for the toilet and heaved up nothing really, just spit. I hadn't eaten much at all that day.

The tile under my knees looked expensive. I wasn't an interior designer but I knew everything in my penthouse came at a hefty price. I didn't pay for the look of it. We'd decided on this place for the safety. We knew the bratva had ties to the building, that Ivan was within driving distance, and that our security could idle outside without issue.

The penthouse was safe but the tile, the rooms, the aesthetic was cold. Stark white interior and tiling that was so white I was sure the rock would stain if I bled on it.

And still, I hoped for any blood to come from me now. Without it, I knew I was fucked.

I kept telling myself that the sickness was from stress but without red, I knew it was from a baby inside me.

I just didn't know how long I could keep Rome and my baby a secret.

My baby.

The thought echoed around in my head so loud nothing else could be heard. Not one thought but the worry of what was growing inside me.

I wasn't mother material. I'd lived without a mother since I was born. And since my father committed suicide, I wasn't a shining example of what a woman should be.

"You're pregnant."

I jumped at his voice. The man who had most likely made it happen was a killer. If I was pregnant, I'd chosen a killer as the father. I had blood on my hands too, stained with criminals' lives.

I closed my eyes for a moment before responding. "We don't know that for a fact."

"Have you had your period?"

"I don't have it half the time. Symptom of PCOS."

"What's that?"

"Polycystic ovarian syndrome. My body doesn't produce just one good egg but tons of little ones that sometimes don't mature enough for a period." I waved off the whole explanation and his brows shot down in concern. "It doesn't really affect me much if I'm on birth control but with the mini pill sometimes I don't get a period. It's never been a problem before. I take the pill on time, I do all the right—"

"You've been sleeping with the wrong men."

"What?" I asked, baffled.

"Strong sperm count." He smirked to himself.

"Are you seriously making a joke right now?" I wanted to throttle him.

He chuckled like he wasn't at all concerned. "Right now? As if there would have been a better time for that joke."

He didn't see the gravity of the situation. I was sure of it. He was probably thinking this wouldn't be a big deal: just get rid of the baby. That's what he knew I would choose immediately. And that hurt my heart in a way I never thought it would.

"It's a little early for jokes about your sperm considering we don't even know if I'm—"

"You are."

I glared at him. "Do you have a freaking sensor? Are you a doctor?"

"No. That's why we'll call the doc to come run some tests this morning. Or you go in. You're not going to sacrifice the health of our child by avoiding going, Katalina."

"The health? It doesn't matter," I said more to myself than him. Then I shook myself from my own thoughts.

"It matters," he whispered back to me. He wasn't supposed to be this close; this wouldn't be his and mine to deal with.

It would be me, it would be my body, my life, and this new immediate love that I would have to extinguish if I wanted to rule.

Is this what women had to choose? How did we make that decision? How could we do it all or end it all like that?

He couldn't understand the fear, the immediate turmoil I felt. So I pushed him away, acted like a child who didn't want any help. "And how do you know it's yours?"

He ate up the ground between us fast. He must have woken up way before me because he was completely dressed, even had his shoes on. They came into my view as I stared down at the floor. His loafers shone like nothing had ever touched them, like he walked on clean carpets all day long.

Surely, he would get blood on his shoes. Where did it go? Wiped away like a clean slate, no memory of the mess.

"Don't be petty with me this morning." His words were punctuated, firm, and low as they rolled from his lips.

"I feel petty." I sighed and dragged my hand along the tile line, felt the grout in between the beautiful smooth tiles. It was rough, jagged, and definitely imperfect. I closed my eyes and whispered, "And I feel…a lot right now. Just a lot."

"You're entitled to that. You'll be fine, huh? You've just been pushed to do this whole reigning of a kingdom quicker than you originally anticipated."

"What do you mean?"

"You got our little minion in there. We're working double time to make sure the bratva, the Italian families, the Stonewoods, and every rival family out there know they're going to be on their best behavior until the end of time for our next generation."

"You can't think this is a good idea. We could wipe the slate clean quickly—"

"It's not an idea, woman. It's a fact. Let's go to the doctor and confirm it." He didn't acknowledge my other comment.

"We should have one come here. Discreetly."

"The sooner everyone knows..."

"We don't have to keep it, Rome." My heartbeat stuttered at the words and my gut clenched. I sounded deflated, like a balloon that'd lost all its air. "We weren't careful enough, but we can be now."

"When have we ever cowered?"

"It'll blow up everything."

"I'm ready to go nuclear if you are, babe." The man was smiling one of the biggest smiles I'd ever seen from him.

"This doesn't solve any of our problems. It just amplifies them." I said, my voice rising at the fact that he didn't think this was a big deal. "I can't put you first and you can't put me first. It's always just been about the family. It's not fair to bring a baby into that."

"That baby will be a part of both our families."

"That doesn't make any sense!" I threw my hands up.

He sighed and ran his hands through his thick head of hair. "One step at a time, Katalina. One step at a time."

CHAPTER 14

ROME

WHILE SHE SHOWERED, I called the damn doctor, the family, and the Stonewoods.

I didn't give a fuck about the bratva. They could wait.

"What did you just say?" Bastian whispered when I relayed the news.

"You heard me the first time."

"I swear to God, my dad would have killed you both at this point."

"Or just me and announced you and Katie were having a baby together."

"Not a terrible idea," Bastian said, his tone thoughtful.

"Don't piss me off right now," I warned.

"Don't piss you off?" The pitch of his voice rose. "If anyone else said that to me, they'd be dead."

185

"I'd be the one taking their head off," I agreed.

He sighed and then he started chuckling. "We've managed to join the families without formalities, I guess."

"If she keeps the baby."

"Of course she's keeping the baby." He scoffed.

Bastian never failed to amaze me with his loyalty to his family. He'd never wanted to be a mafia king but he stepped up to the plate and swung a home run, making the call to end his father's life when he needed to. He could have us eliminated too, or at least the baby, to save the family the drama that would ensue. Yet he didn't even consider it.

My throat tightened when I heard the conviction in his voice. He'd protect that baby just like I would.

"It's her choice, Bastian."

"That's our blood in her now, brother," he shot back.

"I'm not arguing that."

He sighed, because he knew I was right. "The only reason she wouldn't want that baby is because she wants the bratva to trust her and she needs to make sure she can trust us. So let's make sure none of it is a problem."

"The bratva will always be a problem."

"Then, we make sure it's one she can handle. Meet us at the club. The family will be there in about an hour."

Neither of us said goodbye before we hung up.

I paced her penthouse, careful not to go near the window she'd said the bratva checked.

I went and sat in the bathroom, letting the steam swirl around me as I watched her rinse off. "Your belly is going to grow."

"If we decide to keep it."

"Already have," I grumbled. Then I winced. "I know it's your choice ultimately."

She turned the water off and stuck out her hand for me to give her a towel. I waited a beat and she smirked. "Don't get distracted, Rome. It's how we ended up here in the first place."

I shrugged, handing over the soft cloth. She had always pulled my attention from everything else. It could have been the end of the world and I would still have been drawn to her like a magnet.

"I wonder if you know what a mindfuck you are, Kate Bait."

She'd caught up her hair with a clip so that it wouldn't get wet and now she let it fall over the column of her neck and down her shoulders as she dried off. She wrapped the towel around herself and turned to look in the mirror. "If you mean that I'm attractive and men can't control their urges, then, I guess I've known that since Marvin and Jimmy. It's not a blessing in this world unless you make it one."

"I think some are dealt a better hand and it's the other way around for them. Beauty is icing on top of their cake."

"Yeah, girls born into a good family with a good face get a lot of good things. I had it for a small time with my father."

"He was a good man."

"He was a hard worker and a great father. Maybe it was him immigrating from Jamaica but he never gave up. Not until the end."

"Maybe him giving up was for the one thing he loved more than his pride, huh?"

She shrugged like she didn't know what to do with that. I knew she'd forgiven him for leaving her in this world. But I knew her heart missed him too, that it always would. "All I know is I don't think you could ask for a better man than he was." She murmured, her voice far off. "I got lucky even if it was just for a short time. Some people don't even get that."

I leaned back on the counter and watched her get ready. She moved lightly but always with purpose.

Katie never enjoyed the luxuries, I didn't think. She hadn't had them until she was with men like Jimmy and maybe she didn't want to indulge. Or maybe she just didn't know how. She'd been surviving for a very long time.

She didn't move in this penthouse like she owned it or like she wanted anything to do with it at all. She only pulled items from one drawer which made it clear to me that she only used one. She didn't take up all the counter space but stood at the very end of it in front of that drawer as she brushed her hair quickly and flipped it back out of her face. She applied a touch of lip gloss. "Life is the luck of the draw from the very beginning."

"I intend to make it less about luck for our kid." The words flew out of me before I could stop them. Was I right to think I would? Could I control our places in the bratva and mafia enough that my offspring wouldn't live the life I did?

"No one has that power, Rome. Not even the monster in you can make that happen." She let what she said hang in the air, and it filled the bathroom with a heavy scent, one of fear and despair.

"If I can protect the Armanellis from others, I can damn sure protect our kid, Katalina."

The hum that rolled from her had me questioning everything. "Can you protect them from us? Me and you? We've been raised by this mob, molded by blood and pain and a ruthless struggle for power. I don't know any better. Do you?"

"Your dad taught you better. You know more than every single one of us here."

"I hope you're right." She brushed past me to go to her closet and get dressed. She threw on a black jean skirt that was frayed at her thigh and a loose white top before we headed out. "How did you get in without the bratva seeing you?"

"You want me to give up my secret after you wouldn't give up your address?" I let her scope out the hall before I exited and closed her door.

"My address is on a need-to-know basis. I'm supposed to be keeping a low profile and myself safe."

I waved my hand around the hallway of the building. "This is safe? You've got no security where there should be."

She sighed and slid her phone from her pocket. "You're changing the subject. How did you get in? If you want, I can call and ask Cade. I'm sure he knows."

I ignored her threat. Cade had ended up giving me her address, but no one knew what the fuck I was doing in the dead of the night. "He's not going to give you the answer you want. It doesn't matter anyway. I'm here now."

She narrowed those moon eyes at me. She looked tiny in the hallway, about to slide the phone back into her skirt's pocket, young with almost no makeup on. Her t-shirt was baggy, dwarfing her even more.

"You need to add my number." I pointed to her phone.

"I don't know why." She didn't fight me, just handed it over so I could enter my cell number.

"Because you might need me." I waited a beat. "Especially now that you're carrying my child."

"We don't know that for a fact," she hissed and the laugh that burst out of me caught me off guard. She was so damn quick to lash out. We were both that way with each other and I was already imagining the time we'd have with a kid.

Imagining and looking forward to it. It was a dangerous amount of feelings to have at once for something that might not even come to fruition. "Don't you think they should start seeing us together?" I walked toward the elevators.

She grabbed my bicep and yanked me back. "Absolutely not, Rome. Maksim is just beginning to give me a little breathing space."

"They don't give you shit, woman. You take it. This is your domain, your bratva. Remind them if you need to."

"I don't need to. I want their trust and I want to trust them too."

"So call them." I crossed my arms in front of me.

"What?" She stepped back like I was insane. I walked up to her and pulled her phone back out.

"Call them and tell them I'm here. Tell them first and build their trust. Give them something to hold onto."

She rolled her lips between her teeth, so I knew she was thinking about it. We stood there with the air conditioning blasting loudly for maybe a whole minute before she snatched the phone from me and dialed.

"Maksim?" She paused and then whirled away from me, pacing up the carpeted hallway and back toward me as she talked fast. "I'm with Rome. I don't know how he got in and I don't care. That's not the reason I'm calling... Yes, I still think you can handle security for me. Rome knows the ins and outs of every building in the city. He was bound to get in."

She rolled her eyes and sighed.

"No, I'm not calling about that. I appreciate the job you're doing. I realize this is a big deal for you and I trust both you and Luka. I'm calling because I need you to let me leave with him and not tell anyone. I'll disclose more information later."

She waited and chewed a nail as she nodded at whatever he was saying.

"I do understand. You're one of the very few I trust at this point and I promise you we won't jeopardize anything, okay?"

She hung up and shrugged at me, one palm swung up to the ceiling. "I guess we're good to go. He's covering."

With her dark eyebrows raised and her gray eyes wide, I knew she was surprised. She didn't realize her sway, how much power she had, but also how much she appealed to people. They wanted to be a part of Katalina's inner circle, she just had to have the confidence to ask them. This was going to be bad but it was going to be fixed. I knew deep in my bones, I wasn't getting rid of something we'd made together.

When we got to the club, two of the doormen held New Reign's doors open for us.

Katie walked in but her footing faltered when she saw Dante, Cade, and Bastian in a room with Jett and Jax.

"You called everyone, didn't you?" she grumbled under her breath.

"All your boys that matter."

She sighed and her hand shook as she wiped it across her forehead. "I'll be calling Ivan tonight, then, I guess. We need a plan with my family too."

"The bratva isn't your family. I am." I wove my hand through hers. Katie put on a good show, but her heart was beating fast. Mine was too. My skin against hers seemed to soothe her shaking, and the beast in me calmed.

The queen and her monster.

We were power and chaos bound together. Our dark pasts drove us to darker futures, and we were going to have to fight through the dead of the night to come out on the other side. Or maybe it'd swallow us up and that's where we'd remain: her ruling and me ripping apart those who threatened us.

Bastian sat at the head of the table and this time I hesitated to go stand behind him. Suddenly, I was pulled in two directions. Katie had always been someone who could take care of herself. Our relationship had been volatile, but I knew my loyalty lay next to Bastian and that she was protected under his rule. In all our hearts, she was still one of us even if she was part of the bratva too.

Now, though, there was an innocent bystander. A baby in her belly. In the belly of a woman Bastian wasn't exactly sure he could trust. He wanted to. I saw how badly he wanted to, but they weren't connected. Not like I was to her. No one felt Katalina's claws and how she hooked them in quite like I did.

"Rome?" Bastian tilted his head at me, not sure why I stood there frozen.

The frigid night wind bit into each of us as we stood in the rain near the loading docks. Storage crates the size of small homes surrounded us, the city traffic noise in the distance.

My father had been jittery all day and when he jumped at a car honking in the distance, I eyed him curiously.

"It'll be time soon," Mario murmured.

He was talking about a drug shipment coming in. It was the last of many that month, but we were slowing pulling out. The FBI had been tracking us too closely to continue and we'd embedded ourselves in other businesses. We had hackers controlling gas valves and security for nuclear bombs. We had access to laundering money, deals with big companies, casinos, and we had completely legal dealings with the Stonewoods. There was no reason to continue with the drugs.

"Yes, it'll be time very soon." My father said the words with venom and he moved quicker than most everyone.

Except my father's every thought was one I could see coming. He'd trained me.

But I'd gone beyond what he'd taught. I'd lived with him since birth. I'd endured beatings and whippings and burnings at his hand. I'd been left locked in closets for days. I'd moved just the way he wanted me to and learned his emotions to save myself.

When he found me too old to punish, he immersed me in this life. His praise for the way I killed drove me to kill even better. I avoided his punishment by inflicting my own.

At this point in my life, I met his cruelty with strategy and outmaneuvered him most of the time.

I saw his plan before he could implement and strike.

Before he could pull the trigger, I'd pulled mine.

He fell to the ground, the white in his eyes so bright in the night with surprise. "You shot me."

"You betrayed the family."

"I am your family," he whispered, clutching his chest with one hand and looking down at the gun in his other hand. He gazed up at me and then back down at the weapon, as if measuring the time it would take to bring his own son down to death with him.

Mario swore fluently in Italian behind me, but the whole world was muted as I stared at my father bleeding out.

"What's family anyway?" I ground out. "You were never a father to me."

"I've created someone even more evil than myself." He choked on a laugh and looked at the blood on his hands. "To empty your father of his own life. I never would have imagined it'd be you."

"Who else then?"

"I brought on my own demise. And still I wonder if you realize that you'll always be bound to them as their monster now. You'll never be anything more. You'll never know more. You've trapped yourself."

"Or freed myself from you."

"But boy, without me, you'd already have been dead." His eyes slowly closed.

I dropped down beside him, but Mario's hand went to my shoulder.

"You were more my son than his, no? I'm grateful tonight that you chose the family." Mario was choking up. He put a fist over his mouth as he looked at his brother. He patted me so roughly, my body swayed from the force. "Remember, we're always the right choice."

"Go to Bastian," Katie whispered and yanked her hand from my grip. She walked away from me before I could disagree with her.

The Stonewoods and Armanellis had already seated themselves around the large table but Katie circled us instead of sitting down in any of the empty chairs. I grabbed the one next to Bastian, unsure of what the fuck the woman was doing anyway.

We all followed her path like a group of lost boys. No one questioned her circling. We waited with some fucked up baited breath.

Finally, after three whole circles, she stopped at the middle of the table and lifted a tiny leg so she could step onto a chair and then onto the table. She crawled to the middle of it and then stood. Hands on her hips, she looked down at us all. "I'm the center of attention and the topic of conversation, I might as well put myself there literally."

"Jesus Christ," Jax grumbled and knocked on the table twice before he continued. "You have to be ridiculous about it, Katie?"

"Go to hell, Jax. You know how messed in the head Brey was when she was pregnant? She called me all the time with the most jacked up anxieties and I was there for every single one of them. You think I'm not going to have those if I'm really pregnant and decide to keep the baby? I will… I'll have them and worse, I'll deal with them while dealing with a bunch of fuckers that don't trust a goddamn thing I'm doing."

"I'm here to do whatever you want. I know the shit Brey went through. Hormones, pregnancy, giving birth." He shuddered like they were the things of nightmares. "Brey did it with grace. She's about the only person in the world I think can do it like that."

"Exactly," Katie agreed and pointed at herself. "You think I'll handle it with grace?"

Jax looked her up and down so long, a sound escaped from deep within me.

"Don't be stupid," Jax tossed my way. Then he said to Katie, "I've known you a long time, Katie. You can't do it with grace. But you'll do it."

"That's not good enough."

I cut off the conversation. "You'll do it with fury and vengeance, Cleo. But most of all, you'll do it with love."

"Ivan won't agree." She spun to Bastian at the head of the table and crouched before him. "The bratva don't want

196

Italian blood flowing through their bloodline, Bast. We could end it easily."

"Is that what you want?" he asked.

"I want to bring her into this world protected by all of you. If I can't protect her, I don't want her."

"Protect her from me?" We all heard the hitch in his voice, loud and clear. Bastian cared for Katalina, loved her in a way I didn't think we'd ever be able to rid him of. "You lived in my house, Katalina. I would have fought for you, would have married you. You think I would really be capable of hurting you?"

Everyone's eyes ping-ponged between Bastian and me. I watched as Katie lowered herself onto the edge of the table and let one leg dangle on either side of Bastian.

She turned to me. "Monster, stay," she whispered and I knew she was about to do something that would infuriate me. Then she turned back to Bastian and grabbed his hand.

She brought it to her stomach and said softly to the room, "Someone call the doctor. I want you all to hear her heartbeat."

Cade got up immediately and dialed a number. I didn't move. I stared at the two of them. They were connected like family and he looked at her like a lover.

She was tempting a ferocious animal. I didn't control him. I couldn't. The jealousy in me did.

CHAPTER 15
KATIE

"STAY, ROME," I repeated, this time calling out his name, not looking back at him. "This is between me and Bastian."

"There should never be anything between you and another man."

I shook my head, Bastian's dark eyes holding mine, swallowing me up in a dark maze of power.

He pressed his fingers into my stomach one by one, like he was playing a slow song on the piano. "There will always be something between a king and a queen, Rome," Bastian murmured.

This close, where I could smell his aftershave, where I could feel his skin on mine, where I could grab his throat if I wanted to, I trusted him. I trusted everything about the man because I witnessed him grow into it.

"Mario would be proud of us, no?" I asked.

"He'd be proud of you. I don't know about me." He shook his head and his breath blew out onto my lips.

I leaned even farther forward and slid my hand to the Glock in the back of his waistband. "This one's loaded, I presume?"

"Always is." Bastian nodded as I turned it over in my hand.

"You trust me?" I whispered, letting the question fall from my lips.

He didn't even glance at the gun. He kept playing that song, whatever it was, on my stomach. The silence of it, the fact that I was the only one who knew he played it for my daughter or for me, it did something to me.

"I'll always trust you, Katalina. We all trust you. Even if we shouldn't."

"You've thought of killing me, though?" I asked because he must have. I didn't become the enemy without him thinking about how easy it would be to end my life.

"I was built to consider ending everyone's life."

"You ended your father's," I pointed out. "With the nod of a head, you let it happen."

"He'd wronged us. Wronged *you.*"

"What if I do the same?"

He shook his head and his hands stopped the song. He slid both to my hips, and instead of pulling me forward, he shoved me back and glanced at Rome. "You won't because you're in love with him, tied to him, carrying his baby. You won't because you're family. Our blood does run through you now. My blood is your blood."

"Is blood all that matters?" I curled my legs away from him, tucked them under myself, and stood up again. I walked that table like a catwalk; I measured each step, took my time. "Alliances cannot be just blood anymore. That's not what binds us all. If it's just blood, if it's just lineage you care about, you better shoot me now. One of you better take my life. I'm up here, offering myself for that very reason."

"Are you fucking kidding me, woman?" Rome finally raged. He'd held it in too long and the voice that burst from him was vicious. "I'm going to kill you myself."

My hand went to my hip and then I sat down on the table, crossing my legs and looking at my nails just to add more fuel to his fire. "Are you now? "

"Get your ass over here." The fire in his eyes burned wicked, dark, like all the light had been extinguished and it was ready to burn out everyone else's light too.

I smiled at the devil that had taken over him. Rome protected what was his. He didn't like it if I threatened his property, even if the property was me. "Monster, you know I don't listen—"

He stood abruptly and lunged across the table. His massive height and strong arms didn't give me much of a chance. His arm was around my waist and he yanked me across the mahogany. I slid right into his lap, where he rearranged me and spread his hand over my belly.

"I don't give a fuck if you don't listen." He stared at me like I was deranged. "Everyone, get out. I need a moment to teach my insane girlfriend a lesson."

Jett chuckled and Dante outright laughed, but everyone moved to leave the room.

As they exited, I narrowed my eyes at the man I knew I loved. "Girlfriend?"

"What the hell else do you call this? You're mine," he bellowed.

"What if I don't want to be alone with you?"

"Too damn bad. You think I want to be alone with you after the stunt you just pulled?" He hissed out the words and they were filled with anger.

"I have to make sure," I explained. I scrambled around so that I could look directly in his eyes while straddling him.

"You don't make sure with your life, Katalina." He punctu-ated the words like my life was truly precious. "Bastian is—"

"Bastian is an ally first and always." I dragged a finger across his jaw, followed the strong line of it, and pondered if he'd ever had it broken. "No man wants to go up against me and you, Rome. Especially Bastian. He's seen all you've done and he's a team player by nature."

"He can do whatever the fuck he wants, woman. He doesn't have to play nice with others if he doesn't want to."

"But he does. He always will. He thinks the world is a better place that way."

His forehead fell to mine and he sighed. I felt his muscles relaxing and I dragged my hands up to his shoulders. "I want to fucking kill you for offering yourself up. You don't belong to *you* anymore. You belong to *me*."

He gripped my ass and ground my body into his dick. I felt the strain through our clothing.

"Jesus, Rome," I whispered. "We're not doing anything here."

"We aren't?" He smiled, but it was lazy, relaxed suddenly, like he had all the power in the room, in the world. "Why is your pussy so close to the cock that fucks it into submission, then?"

I started to inch away, but his fingers lodged in my ass cheeks. His head dipped down so he could drag his tongue across my collarbone. I moaned immediately, my nerves on high alert.

"She moans like a fucking whore but says no like a tease." The devil was in his eyes.

Mad.

Rome was livid, furious. He wanted to teach me a lesson. My core clenched because I knew it wasn't right, but I belonged in the wrong corners of our darkness. I thrived in them. I knew we should stop with the freaking leaders of the damn world outside of those doors.

But I was in a sex club.

His sex club.

I wanted to push him. The queen and her monster. We would war over and over again before we found any semblance of balance.

"Maybe I like being the whore and the tease. You let Bastian touch me and I let him too. Maybe you're okay with another man on me as long as it's not him hurting me, huh?"

He growled into my neck and every hair on the back of it stood up. "I don't know whether to call you a bitch or a mastermind for that comment, Cleo. You and I both know I'm not going to stop now. You deserve punishment."

With an abrupt, rough shove he got me on the table again. His hands immediately snaked up my skirt.

"Rome, everyone's outside those doors."

"You going to be shy about us now? You were just on the table about ready to fuck another man."

"Fuck?" I laughed at his ridiculous assessment, but it caught in my throat when he swept my underwear to the side. I heard one of the Stonewoods say something on the other side of the large doors and then glasses clinking like they were all having a drink without us. If one of them stepped back in here...we couldn't. "Rome, we should wait—"

My protest died a quick death as he slid two fingers into me and rolled a thumb over that ball of nerve endings he knew how to work just right.

This was my punishment?

This was how he'd put me in my place? I arched back on the table and moaned way louder than I should have. I slapped a hand over my mouth.

"That doesn't sound like an argument, Kate Bait. It sounds like an invitation," he murmured as he stood but kept his fingers on my pussy. His shadow engulfed me as he leaned over to whisper in my ear, "Tell me to stop."

I bit down on the inside of my cheek to try to keep from screaming as his other hand inched up to my breast where he worked to get under my bra and pinch my nipple.

"Fuck, Rome." A hum from deep down in my gut escaped. I couldn't tell him to stop, couldn't even get the word out. It got lodged in my throat. "You're too possessive. You're—"

"I'm the one making you wet. I'm the one who has you on your back, legs spread on this table."

"Please..." I moaned, not sure what I was begging for at this point, just sure I wanted more of it. More of him. His fingers worked on me faster and faster while his other hand went to my throat.

"Begging already? For the man who's too possessive of you?"

"Maybe I'm just begging for any man," I shot back.

"Goddamn you and that mouth," he murmured. He pushed himself away abruptly and I gasped at the loss of his fingers in me. I lifted my head up off the table to see him pulling out his length, long, rigid and ready for me.

His hand shot to my neck, and he slammed me back down on the table, then pounded into me. There wasn't any gentle touch, no proclamations of me being a queen or beautiful.

Rome was lost in his fury.

I got lost in it with him.

He pounded into me like he wanted to leave scars where he was marking his territory.

I met him thrust for thrust, clawing at his back, biting at his ear, ravaging his mouth, and wrapping my legs around his waist.

Obscenities flew from his mouth, and I learned on the table there that day, Rome was a madman for me and for that baby.

He wasn't capable of caging the rage and the jealousy in him either.

More than that, though, I learned I was a fiend for it. I hit a high so far into space that I came in contact with stars, probably touched the sun, and the burn of it felt good as hell.

CHAPTER 16

ROME

I LOST MY PATIENCE, my thoughts, my damn mind when it came to her. None of my actions were justified. They were uncontrollable at this point, though.

She'd got on the damn table like a meal and offered her life to him. It felt like her motive was just to piss me off. I knew it wasn't. I knew she was pushing their trust in her own way, building the connections she needed to confirm in her own mind how she would protect her baby.

Still, the jealous monster in me and the overprotective side I couldn't turn off wanted to war with her for it, to blame her and act like she was being frivolous with her life.

We finally left the room after she'd righted her clothing and I'd tucked my dick back in my pants.

Cade had drivers lining up for us outside the large club doors.

"We fall back on our contracts and stand by them," Jett said as he walked to his vehicle. "I don't care what happens with the child. My wife and my sister-in-law will have another viewpoint, I'm sure."

"Brey will be calling you." Jax nodded. "Take care of yourself...and that baby, Katie."

Jax folded into the SUV. He said the words everyone who loved her would. They wanted that baby to see the light of day.

I was going to make sure it did.

She had to know a mini version of her was going to be a damn gift to this world. Or I had to make her see that.

We filtered into tinted-out SUVs, and I informed Katie I'd be going home with her again. She didn't agree that it was a good idea, just told me I was hiding the whole time then. We stopped at a drugstore to get pregnancy tests.

Every single one showed up positive.

I smiled the whole time, couldn't stop it if I tried. She was having our baby and the thought blossomed to a reality, one that I found I really wanted. By the third test, she rolled her eyes. "It could still be something that's off with my hormones."

I laughed at her denial, but left it alone. The next morning we would see. Cade had found a doctor that we'd be going to see.

We dressed in silence the next morning, her nerves palpable in the penthouse. She asked Maksim to cover again as we loaded up and drove to a small practice on the outskirts of town.

We filed into the small brick building. The bushes and foliage around it made it appear like a little house. The lawn was well kept and the porch had baskets of petunias of all colors hanging from hooks in the roof.

The man that answered the door wasn't the regular doc we saw. "You must be Katalina." He held his hand out to her.

She stepped in and shook it. "You must be my OBGYN."

"For now." He chuckled. "I'm retired so I'm not technically going to deliver any baby you might have in there."

"Let's make sure there's a baby first, no?" She raised her eyebrows and motioned at all of us. "They're a little presumptuous."

"Ah. I see. Can I get any of you a drink, and can I ask who you'd like in the room with you?"

She turned to look at Dante standing there with his arms crossed, Cade with a small smile on his face and a phone in his hand. Bastian leaned against the doorframe, one side of his mouth lifted like he was enjoying the show.

The woman, she smiled too like she knew just what button to press. "They can all come in if they want."

"You are out of your fucking mind," I growled.

"What? Don't you all want to see the little thing?"

The doctor backed away, hands up, and said, "I'll grab everyone waters and leave you to discuss. Cade, I assume this goes on the books as a visit and there's insurance if anything happens."

"As always, Doc."

"No one's going in that room with you except me." I grabbed her elbow and steered her toward the couch so I could shove her down into the seat. I sat next to her and pulled her up against my side where she belonged.

"Oh, don't be so damn conservative. It's not like they haven't seen a woman before." She held a finger to her chin. "Well, actually, I'm pretty sure he has to stick a pretty big wand up me to figure this out."

"I'm there," Dante joked and Cade laughed.

"I'll pass." Bastian suddenly looked a little queasy.

"You?" I laughed at his squirming. "Of all people, I thought you'd be fine with it."

"With an old man sticking something up you?" His nose scrunched up. "I'm good."

"If it was a young man, would you feel better about it?"

"For fuck's sake," I said to myself. This was the shit I would be dealing with for the rest of my life. I knew it. "We're trying to have a damn baby together. Me and her. You think that shit is something you say?"

"Rome, if you think for a second all these guys aren't going to be privy to the shit I'm going through during this pregnancy, you got another thing coming."

"We need to figure out how long you can keep working out," said Dante.

"She can't work out starting today," I answered for everyone. The doctor didn't need to give an answer to that.

"I can work out all the way through my pregnancy." Katie rolled her eyes and completely ignored me.

The doctor walked in carrying a large ceramic tray of waters in his wrinkled hands. "I'm happy you're optimistic about this, Katalina."

He passed the glasses out, and we all mumbled thank yous, but none of us took sips. We weren't easily trusting. He looked like Santa Claus, big and burly with rosy cheeks and a white beard. He could have looked like Jesus for all I cared. I didn't trust anyone outside the family. It was a necessity to have him, and Cade had vetted him. I didn't care. Even though I had to trust him to stick whatever the fuck he was going to into my girl's body.

"You can potentially work out if there are no complications," Dr. Santa Claus continued. "I'll need blood work from each of you to test for any genetic complications, and we should figure out if you will want genetic testing which can identify abnormalities quickly."

"Supposedly that gives us the sex of the baby too?" Katie asked, taking a big gulp of her water. She waggled her eyebrows at me as she did. That woman knew we were all treading lightly but she was throwing it in my face like she could read the man better than each and every one of us.

Maybe she could.

I wasn't sure anymore.

"Alright, where should we go to get this over with?" Katie asked. "No heartbeat today right?"

"It depends on how far along you are. When's the last time it was your time of the month?" he inquired as he waved at us to follow.

When Dante and Cade stood, I pulled at my neck. "You both better sit the fuck down. I'm not playing. Don't you dare follow us."

"Guessing he's the father," the doc whispered to Katie, and she giggled as she walked through the door he'd opened.

I followed close behind. I didn't say a word to him, just sat down on the plush loveseat set up in the stark white room. A small square screen was attached to devices I knew nothing about.

The doc washed his hands in the sink in the corner of the room and slipped on latex gloves. "We can start with an abdominal scan if you'd like. Or go right to the transvaginal scan. I recommend the abdominal scan first if you haven't emptied your bladder lately, Katalina."

She shrugged. "Okay, abdominal scan first. You need me to strip?"

Katie was never shy with her body. I had to chuckle at her boldness. I hated and loved it about her.

"You can keep the clothes on for now," the doctor said as he motioned for her to lie down on the long medical chair near the screen and devices.

She looked at me while she did, an uncertainty suddenly there in her eyes. "Maybe it's nothing."

"Or maybe it's something," I said and snaked my hand into hers. She fisted it unconsciously, like a nervousness had wrapped her up and tensed her body.

"I have here a conductive gel that allows for me to rub the scanner over your stomach. It uses sound waves—"

I stopped him. "That going to be a health hazard to her or the baby?"

She sighed. "Rome, he's the doc. He's not going to put me at risk."

212

I didn't even glance down at her. I kept my stare on him, the stare that most of the time had grown men begging me for mercy.

The doctor's eyes darted toward the door and his hand shook a little. "Of course it's safe. I stake my profession on doing what's best for the patient and the baby."

We all sat in silence, like Katie and the doctor knew I needed a moment to process the information, process how much I trusted him. His degrees were on the wall of the room, I'd seen a few pictures of family in his home, and Cade had run background checks.

Beyond that, my gut leaned toward trusting him. He didn't sweat with fear. The man was old and maybe a little jumpy because of who we were, but not leaping from the ground at the slightest sound. He didn't hold any guilt in his eyes.

"Go ahead." I nodded toward the scanner he held in one hand and the gel in the other.

He explained it would be warm and that there would only be a little bit of pressure.

Katie nodded, her voice gone. She was holding her breath as he put the scanner onto her body for the first time.

"It's okay to breathe, Katalina," I murmured, then wondered if that was true. "Right, Doc?"

"Yup. Breathe away." He rolled the scanner up and down her body and explained, "Sometimes, if we're too early in the pregnancy, we can't find a heartbeat this way and will have to go the transvaginal route."

"Or maybe we just didn't think it through," she told him.

"Well, of course you did. You took pregnancy tests, right?" he asked.

"Yes, but I know there are false positives." She glared at me. "He's making this out to be something it probably isn't... This is probably..."

"Ah, a father's intuition." The doc stopped Katie from saying anything further. "You see that star on my screen right now?"

The doctor turned his 12-inch standing screen toward us. We saw the small-ass shape of a bean-like body. In the middle of it, a small star twinkled brighter than all the darkness around it.

I rubbed my thumb in Katie's palm as she gasped and asked, "What is that?"

"A father's intuition proved right." The doc smiled at me. "Looks like you're indeed pregnant and that little star is the heart, beating pretty strongly. I'm going to take some measurements here."

He pressed a few buttons that seemed to capture the fetus from different angles. Then he was on the screen, drawing lines across.

We let him work as we absorbed the news. News of new life, of change, of complete pivots that would have to happen.

My heart probably beat as fast as that little star was going.

"She's going to be fierce," Katie whispered, looking down at our intertwined hands. Her eyes jumped up to meet my gaze like she'd realized she said it out loud. "If we keep her, of course."

"She'll be a monster and a queen, Kate Bait." It rumbled out of me before I could contemplate anything else.

The doc's head snapped up when he heard a noise outside. He squinted out the window and I turned fast enough to see an SUV rolling slowly up his drive.

"Get behind the counter now," he ordered.

The doc's command didn't fall on deaf ears. I was used to moving quick, had to with my job, and I knew that SUV wasn't ours.

The ticking of the clock was slow, loud, ominous as I swooped my arms around Katie and lunged behind the counter across the room, carrying her like a baby.

The doctor ducked behind it too, just as the first bullet broke the window pane.

The shattering of glass had her jumping in my arms and covering her ears. She hadn't expected it, not like the doc and me had.

As bullets flew in and hit the counter, the doc said, "I was never sure a day like this would come, but I got a bulletproof wall installed here just in case. We're safe behind this counter."

I set Katie down, and her gaze burned bright, not with fear but with rage. She said, "I didn't bring a gun. I can't protect her."

"We've got eyes. It'll be over soon," I told her, but my hand hovered over my own gun, ready to pop off a shot and bring one of them down at least. I wanted one of their heads.

All of them.

On a damn platter.

As I was about to take a peek to see where I could get a clean shot, return fire began and bullets ceased to fly into our room.

We heard Bastian screaming obscenities, and Dante burst in to see us huddled there. "We've got them. Underground gang. Katie needs to go now. Her location is about to be made which means everyone is about to know she's having a baby."

My hand flew to the man who sat beside me, a doctor who was supposed to be a secret. I crushed his windpipe as I asked the one question he had better answer correctly "You leak this location?"

Katie's hand was at my wrist immediately. "He has a family, Rome. Fucking pictures of them out there on the mantle. He just saved our asses. It wasn't him. Let him go."

The man sat there, eyes bulging but not fighting back whatsoever. "I wouldn't. She's pregnant. She's got a nine-week-old baby in there." His eyes filled with tears, but not at the thought of losing his life. And I saw no guilt in his eyes.

I let go. "If I find out you had anything to do with this, I'll reign hell down on you, Doc." I got up and pulled Katie up with me.

The doc stayed sitting there, as if fear had overcome him and he couldn't move.

Dante called out, "We'll send payment for the damages, Doc. Have a good day."

No one said a word as we exited the room and filed through the living room to our cars. Bastian eyed my arm around

Katie's neck, and when we got to our SUV, he followed us to the door. "You carrying the Armanelli bloodline, Katalina?"

She stared at him. Then her gaze swung to the enemy SUV that had been riddled with bullets. Two men still in their seats were mutilated with bullets and completely lifeless. One car door was open where our men must have pulled out a hostage for intel.

"I've got my bloodline in me, Bastian," she said. "No one else's. And that means I'll decide what to do with the baby."

Bastian took a small step toward her which she met with a step forward of her own. She didn't back down, nor did she cower.

Katalina became a mother in that moment. I saw it in her eyes, saw how her vision changed. Her stance to protect was stronger and more vicious now.

Bastian backed away, willing in the end to have Katalina as an ally and let her make her own decision rather than turn her into a full-blown enemy.

"Rome should provide some type of security for you." Bastian sighed. "We need you safe as a partner if nothing else."

She turned to me to protest but I shook my head before she even opened her mouth. "I go where you go now, baby."

"Rome, I still have to talk with Ivan—"

"Do whatever you want. I'll be next to you the whole time."

She stomped her foot. "This is fucking ridiculous."

"This is real. There was just a drive-by because someone's tapping our shit and has figured out our partnership is solidified now."

217

Katie threw her hands up. "It was because of the contracts!"

Bastian and I both hmphed, and that lit a fire in her blood that turned her cheeks red.

"Baby, you got a light in you that is going to snuff out all the darkness, huh?" I said.

"What if it's an explosion rather than a lighthouse that leads to safety?"

"We'll wear our bomb gear, no? Now, figure out who you're calling on the way home so we can get it out of the way and start celebrating the baby in you." I wasn't backing down.

She damn well knew it too because she stormed past me and swung her car door open to get in. She left it open and screamed, "Let's go, you fucking animal."

CHAPTER 17
KATIE

I CALLED IVAN TO set up a meeting. Ivan didn't ask questions, but I was sure he knew already. He would want to hear it from my lips, want me to disrespect him to his face. So I agreed to see him later.

Then I proceeded to tell Rome to leave my penthouse. He'd walked me to the door while I continued my conversation with Ivan. He followed me in, not at all concerned that he was overstaying his welcome.

When I hung up the call, I told him to leave.

He didn't. He stayed the night.

He wouldn't go.

He wouldn't even try to hide himself anymore either. The smell of him teased my brain before I even opened my eyes that morning. I woke up in a haze. I had just gotten used to sleeping in my penthouse alone. But now, I'd never sleep alone again.

At least not for the next 9 months.

The last day's events came flying back.

Rome's home would be mine now. There was no way he was letting the baby in me out of his sight.

Or me for that matter.

And maybe I wasn't letting him out of my sight either. I wanted him close enough to aggravate, close enough to infuriate, and close enough for me to tempt his monster. It was the thing I loved about him, knowing a man would tear apart a city for us instead of inflicting pain for power.

Some instinct in me overruled everything else too. I was pulled to his protection because I wanted it now more than ever. I hadn't cared before about my wellbeing, probably still didn't really. I cared about the change in the city. I cared about making a difference. I would have died for that difference without hesitation before.

Now, for the first time in a long time, I was willing to put something else before my reign.

"My stomach's going to grow."

"Huh?" Rome looked up from his breakfast with a coffee mug in hand.

I sat down at the table, across from him. "She's going to grow in here and stretch me to twice my size. I won't be able to move. Definitely won't be able to defend myself."

"You keep saying 'she.'"

"It's probably a girl." I shrugged and pointed to his coffee mug. "You make extra?"

He got up from the table and grabbed a glass from one of the cupboards. "No, I didn't. You can't have caffeine."

"What?" I frowned at him.

"It's maybe bad for the baby. I just looked it up."

I grabbed his phone and saw that he had in fact been looking up things I couldn't eat and drink. "It says one cup is probably okay."

"You willing to bet her health on a 'probably?'"

"Are you willing to risk your health on a 'probably?'" I shot back, ready to find a knife and stab him if I needed to. I was tired, like bone-dead tired, and I'd slept well.

Which meant the baby was growing.

And I was in for the long haul.

He sighed. "One cup, then."

He poured the coffee and gave me a glass of water too. I grabbed the water despite my hedging. I guessed I'd be doing more research before sipping caffeine for the next nine months.

I stared at his phone. "This list is long, probably too long for me to remember." I clicked on deli meat and read that I could harm the baby if there was listeria in it. "Oh, my God! I...Oh, my god."

"It'll be fine."

I glared at him. "You don't know that." I clicked on wine—it could cause death or fetal alcohol syndrome. I shot up and combed my hands through my hair. "When's the last time I had a drink?"

"Calm down."

"Calm down?" I racked my brain for the last time I'd even taken a sip but couldn't remember. It'd been a long time; I'd shied away from alcohol when I took over the bratva. I thought my aversion was just because of all the responsibility, but maybe it was my body too. "Oh, God. What are we even doing?"

"We're doing this." He stepped in my path and pointed to my belly, then motioned between us. "And this…together." His tone was authoritative, firm. "Don't worry. I'll remember the list."

"Rome, we're in the fucking mob. We don't have the time to remember all this! And even if you happen to remember it, you're not always going to be with me. You can't be by my side all the time." I swerved around him and stalked up to the counter, looking for my phone. "We should call the doctor."

"For what? We were just there." He leaned his hip on the counter and waited for me to say the words.

I knew some people thought abortion was a dirty word. Sometimes, I wondered how my mother's life would have turned out had she aborted me. So many lives were dismal, tragic. Was a life like that worth it? Could they have been spared?

We stared at one another. Rome's gaze was harder than normal, more determined. I figured mine looked scared or unsure.

Either way, I couldn't get the words out. They clogged my throat, then ran away so that I couldn't say them.

I sighed. If I couldn't say them, I wouldn't do them. My body was closing in on the fact that I was about to embark on protecting my dream and my baby at the same time. I wrapped my arms around my stomach. "I guess we can call him to set up the regular visits, then."

The first smile of the morning that whipped across Rome's face had my heart pounding loudly.

"Rome," I said in warning. "We have to set boundaries."

He nodded, the smile somehow spreading even wider as he walked toward me. "Sure, babe. Set your boundaries."

I held out my hand, and he walked right into it and farther still until he was up against my chest.

"I'm serious too. Set all the boundaries you want." He nestled into my neck like he could care less about the gravity of the situation. "I'm going to rip them all down anyway. The monster doesn't like any boundary between him and you."

"The monster needs to get on board, asshole. We can't be stupid with a baby on the way."

"We'll be smart by staying together."

"The bratva doesn't want that," I said, but my hand was rubbing his chest. "They want me standing on my own. They want you all bowing to us."

"I'll bow to you any day. I just need you bent over too while I do it." He grabbed my ass and rubbed his cock into me.

My body had been more than sensitive to his advances lately. "You need to stop with that too. I read women can be more aroused early on in pregnancy. Everything is sensitive."

"All the more reason for me to be tempting you, woman."

"No. We need to focus on other things."

"How about I fuck you and then we focus on other things?" His hand was already inching up my thigh.

"Rome, contact the damn doctor," I said, but I sounded breathless. He laughed against my collarbone and then shoved himself away from the counter and from me.

My body revolted, but I gripped the edge of the granite to make sure I didn't jump his bones.

"Fine. We'll get some appointments out of the way, Kate-Bait."

I nodded and wiped a hand over my face, trying to rid myself of the nerves. "I would like you to ask him how to keep my stomach from growing to twice its size and stretching me all the way to Zimbabwe."

"Woman, I don't think we can avoid that." He grabbed his black phone from the table and sent out a text message.

"Well, then, I have to go shopping. For all things baby."

He hesitated for a few seconds on that one. I knew he hated shopping. The man could barely handle me at a boutique, let alone running around looking for maternity wear. "Probably need to discuss this with all parties."

"Why?" I shrugged and then smiled, because I knew it would press his buttons. "I got you. You'll protect me, right?"

He shook his head at my goading and then looked me up and down. "You really want me to go? Why don't you call Brey and Vick?" The question came out high like I was crazy and like he was a little scared.

"If I call Brey and Vick, Jett and Jax will be coming. I'm the head of the bratva now. They aren't letting us out of their sight. Should I go with other men to shop for your baby?"

That side-eye from him came quick. "And the queen reigns. Let's get you fed and out of those ratty socks. We call the doc and get some updates. Then we go."

"What is with all men and trying to get rid of these socks?"

"What other men?"

"I used to wear them at Bastian's."

He scooped some scrambled eggs he must have made before I woke up onto a dish for me. He smacked it onto the table harder than necessary. "Fucking Bastian," he grumbled and pointed to a chair for me to sit.

I plopped down in front of the eggs. "That was months ago, Rome."

"It could be years ago for all I care."

"You've been with other women. You don't see me getting all hot and bothered."

"You don't have to see them every day like I do Bastian."

"I wasn't with him. We kissed. That's it."

"That's it, like your mouth isn't fucking gold." He stood over me, one hand on my chair, one had on the table. He didn't wait long before he crushed his lips to mine. I took in the kiss, smiling. This morning was a blip of sunshine on our dark radar.

I pushed him away after a minute, knowing we wouldn't get anywhere that day if we kept doing what we were doing.

225

"I'll remind you again, I only ever kissed him. He never fucked me, okay?"

He jerked back and quirked his head. His voice came out low. "Nor will any other man ever again."

His hand went between my legs to rub my pussy. I rolled my hips, practically ready to screw him there at the kitchen counter.

"Jesus Christ. No wonder you're pregnant with my child."

My body wanted nothing to do with shopping. I curved my back, pushing my tits out for him to see.

He groaned. "I swear, either I'm dreaming or your tits are growing already."

My hands slid up my top to cover them and squeeze. "They're more sensitive too."

"Fuck the store. You can order whatever you want." His hands flew off me and then went under my armpits to lift me onto the table. He grabbed the chair from the table and sat in front of me, a predatory smile on his face. "I'm hungry."

"You already ate. We should go." I crossed my arms over the baggy t-shirt of his I wore.

"That's not the meal I'm starved for, Kate-Bait." He scrunched the material up at my thighs and then snaked his hands under the shirt and over my belly to my tits. He didn't rub them nicely. He pinched each nipple and rolled it between his fingers. I gasped, and I knew we wouldn't be going anywhere if I spread my legs further.

I did anyway.

CHAPTER 18

KATIE

THE EXTENSIVE SPEWING of Russian from Ivan's mouth made it clear he wasn't exactly happy about the conception of his great grandchild.

"It could be a boy." Doubtful, but I knew how to work a situation. "Would that be better?"

The swearing in Russian continued. Rome and I stood there patiently.

We'd decided to tackle Ivan before another doctor's appointment. There wouldn't be a way to keep the news under wraps much longer with the underground gangs leaking it anyway. Every one of our partners needed to get on board. Especially Ivan.

Especially my only living relative.

"It's the wrong blood, Katalina."

"There's no right or wrong." I planted a hand on my hip and decided to wait him out. The more he simmered now, the less he'd spout off in the future.

"There were so many plans. Too many ruined layers." He laser-focused on my stomach. "That seed has ruined everything."

The motion was fast, faster than I expected, especially because I hadn't expected it at all.

Ivan's gun was at my belly as quick as Rome's gun was at Ivan's head.

"Don't fuck with me, old man," Rome growled, his other hand holding Ivan's jaw so that the barrel of his gun dug hard into Ivan's head.

"This baby should be dead." His cold azure eyes shot daggers into mine.

Showing weakness would have fed him.

I didn't gasp; I didn't step away either. I stepped forward, pushing into his line of fire.

Tempting him to pull the trigger would rile him. He'd only pulled the gun to prove he had one, never intending to shoot. He just wanted my fear.

It whipped through me fast enough, though. Fear roared through my veins like a lit match to a dry forest. It grew fast, like gasoline-and-kerosene-poured-on-it fast. The impact almost crippled me.

This was real fear, not the kind I used to have. Before, I was in the mob, I was in men's beds, I was in a dark alley all alone without any thought of losing anything. I had nothing to lose. That's what made so many in the mob dangerous. They were willing to do anything because their life didn't matter to anyone else, barely mattered to themselves. They lived, breathed, and died for the only thing that was relevant: their mob family.

This was different. It wasn't fear for my mob family or even my own life, but for an innocent bystander, one that I suddenly loved more than myself. Was it evolution or the animal in me? Maybe. The maternal instinct was visceral and vicious.

I almost fell to my knees, begging for the life of my baby, a tiny little human I didn't know yet but wanted to know more than anything in the world.

I *almost* did.

Strength was finding what had been bred into you and digging it up at those life and death moments. My father bred love into me. He died for me so that I could protect and love the way he had.

Rome and I deserved to breed that love into someone else too. If Ivan took away our opportunity, how would we get to see the monster and my mayhem mixed up all together in one tiny little innocent body?

The more I stared at that man protecting the hell out of me, willing to go to bat for me, willing to believe in me, in our baby, in the future of what we could create, the more I wanted to see the offspring I created with him.

I deserved that. My father deserved that. Rome deserved that.

And Rome should have gotten a medal for his restraint in those moments. He was ready to kill my grandfather, but waiting for my move.

The little girl in me that had been silent since her innocence was stolen wanted another little innocent human to have a chance. It was her time to shine.

The longer that gun was held to my belly, the less scared I became. How dare he think he could do this to me after all I'd done for the bratva already?

"You feel small, Katalina? Helpless?" Ivan asked in a voice that snaked around my bones and tried to constrict me with fear.

"I've always been small, grandfather." Dante had taught me well enough to know that I had to act fast. I maneuvered like we'd practiced, one hand quick to knock the gun from his grip with a hit to his wrist while I snapped my body out of range. My other hand snatched the gun from his loosened grasp. "But never helpless."

The disarm wouldn't have worked on someone younger or more alert, but Ivan had gotten comfortable in his role and his old age. He didn't think I'd do it, and it left him vulnerable.

Rome's jaw ticked at my move, but he didn't comment. I'd hear about my actions later, surely. Right now, the battle I waged was between Ivan and myself. He'd been the teacher, the enforcer, and the bratva boss for as long as he could remember.

Now, he needed to step aside. He needed to accept the choices I was making for the bratva and for my own life as queen.

"You're quick, but you won't be quick enough for the bratva you rule, Katalina." He sighed and lifted his hands in the air, knowing there was no way out with us aiming both guns at his organs.

"I only have to be quick enough for you right now, Ivan."

"I've taught you enough, huh? Spare my life for that at least. I won't bless that child though. You know I can't do that. You are full of hormones and carrying a baby. No one will respect that." He shook his head in disgust at what he believed would ruin me. "I didn't see your weakness until now. Your father loved you too much, Katalina. You have some notion that you can make him proud by changing how we do things and that you can love a baby like he did." The man scoffed, phlegm catching in his throat. "You can't fill my shoes, Katalina. I'm not sure that you ever would have been able to."

"Fill your shoes?" A laugh escaped from deep in my gut. The Russians barely trusted him. He had no good ties to the families in other cities, and the men under us were circling like sharks, ready to attack as soon as they saw blood. "What have you accomplished? Have you solidified contracts with the Stonewoods, made peace with the Armanellis?"

"You had a leg up on all that. It was because of your—"

"Careful what you say, Ivan." Rome finally spoke, backing me when he couldn't take the blatant disrespect any longer. "Choose your next words very carefully. You're speaking to the woman who's carrying my child."

Ivan glanced at him. "You going to stand beside her when the bratva bring her down?"

"It would take the whole international bratva, Ivan, and even then, you couldn't fight the tsunami coming your way. The tide is changing. Get on board or drown."

Ivan threw up his hands and stormed past us.

Rome and I stared at each other, the guns in our hands hanging at our sides for a moment.

A laugh bubbled out of me. I slapped my arm over my mouth. "I'm sorry..." He looked at me like I was insane. "I might be a little hormonal. Or this shit is just funny. I'm pregnant and having to point a gun at my grandfather?"

He shook his head as I started laughing harder. "You've got a problem, Katalina."

"Come on, Rome." I walked up to him so I could wrap my arms around his waist and look up into those mean eyes of his. "It's sort of funny."

"It's sort of fucking scary, woman." He sighed into my hair. "I'm going to lose my mind before this is all over."

"I think we lost our minds a long time ago." I rubbed my face into his shirt, taking in his smell, taking in the place I felt safe.

"Ain't that right. Let's call Bastian and the boys and make sure everyone's on board with merging. We need the bratva and the Armanellis of Chicago on the same page all the time now. We watch each other's backs, everyone on the damn boat. And let's make sure it doesn't sink like the Titanic."

His gun at my back and the gun in my hand at his, I got up on my tiptoes and kissed the hell out of him. "Buckle up, monster. We've got a rollercoaster from hell to ride through."

CHAPTER 19

KATIE

THE MEETING DIDN'T go smoothly. That rollercoaster ride was bumpy, rough, and took more coaxing than we'd originally expected.

It took a week of ironing out details. I updated Brey and Vick, letting them know I was pregnant. Vick called and left a voicemail saying I needed to immediately call her back. She knew I wouldn't. Brey's call I answered. We didn't talk long, and she probably heard the stress in my voice because she didn't pry.

The big players were informed, but Ivan didn't help at all. Thankfully, Maksim and Luka had pull. Others had signed the contracts and were already seeing the financial benefits of working with the Stonewoods and the Armanellis.

I knew we'd have those that rebelled. Bastian had already dealt with a unit within his family. He'd made an example out of them. And I'd been informed of two of my men plotting against my reign. Rome wanted to sneak into their homes in the middle of the night and torture them. His overprotective nature overpowered his sanity sometimes.

"We're not doing that," I told him. "I've got Maksim and Cade working together on it. Everything will be fine."

"Damn, it's weird to think of those two working together. For any of us to be working with the bratva is something. Remember, though, sometimes logical ways don't work, woman," Rome said, his hand sliding around my thigh as I put my hair up in front of the long mirror near my bed in the penthouse. He still sat there, rumpled from a night of fucking me into satiation.

That was a feat at this point. My drive to have him had increased daily, probably from being pregnant. Or having him near me all the time.

He did little things. Rubbing my feet while we talked on the couch. Bringing me water while I talked on the phone for hours on end about the details of this damn merging.

When he saw my fatigue, he took the phone away from me. I fought him for it, but he was a tattooed bear of a man.

He cared for me like only he could.

Which was why I was getting ready to go out. "I'm not going to worry about it. I've got shopping to do, right?"

He groaned, but he'd been the one to bring up the fact that we still hadn't gone. "I guess I've got to get you something to wear to cover these, huh? We haven't gone shopping yet." He stood up and slid his hands under my shirt to grab my boobs.

"They're getting out of control," I mumbled, looking at him in the mirror, wrapped around me.

"My dick is out of control looking at them. You need baggier clothes. Or less cut-up tops."

"Or maybe we just embrace that I'm going to be huge everywhere."

"I'm okay embracing that. I want to see it." I felt his length growing against my ass. "I'm counting the days 'til it happens. I just don't want anyone else seeing it. So let's move your ass."

He smacked it and walked away. I almost whimpered because I wanted to get lucky before we went anywhere. Or maybe we didn't have to go at all. The idea of draping a big bag over my body because it was going to be ginormous left a bad taste in my mouth.

"Get your mind out of the gutter, Kate Bait." He glared back at me. "We're getting you some damn maternity clothes."

Fuck me. "Are you just going to wear what you wore last night?" I eyed his naked chest and abs. His clothes were balled up in the corner of my room, definitely wrinkled.

"I'll go grab a shirt downstairs," he mumbled, almost to himself, but I heard him, way too loud and clear.

"Downstairs? Like to your own place or…"

He immediately glanced everywhere but my face.

"Rome, are you fucking living under me?"

Instead of showing any remorse, he crossed his massive arms over his chest and stood there like a damn Adonis in his briefs. "Your security was shit."

"How long?"

"How long what?" His jaw ticked because he knew exactly what I was asking.

"How long have you been a freaking stalker?"

"I've been stalking you since the day I met you, Katalina. It's never going to stop. I have a sick fetish that I'm somewhat proud of at this point. And I'm never going to allow my queen and my baby to be at risk."

"You're fucking crazy."

"As are you," he shot back and I couldn't even hide the smile. He stalked toward me and pulled me into him to devour my mouth.

God, would the zap I felt every time he connected with me ever dull?

He told me to meet him at the front of the building. I got ready quickly, and then we drove to a boutique that Rome claimed was perfect for security purposes. On the way there, I told him he had to get rid of his apartment.

"Does that mean I can move in with you?" He fluttered his long eyelashes at me in jest.

I rolled my eyes at his out-of-character playfulness. "It's probably a little fast for—"

"I've known you since you were barely a teenager."

"True, but—"

"You have our baby in your belly."

"Okay, I know that but—"

"I'm going to fuck you every night for the rest of your life. No one else."

"Rome, now that is—"

"The truth." He gripped my thigh, pressed the button that raised the partition so his driver wouldn't witness his hand sliding up to cup my pussy. I practically cried out when his fingers rubbed back and forth. "This here is mine. Forever and ever. 'Til death do us part. Want a ring so I can move in?"

I'm sure my eyes bulged. "Are you seriously insane?"

"I'm efficient." He leaned in and licked my neck, literally licked it like I was his favorite piece of candy. "I intend to get to that point anyway. We could skip to it."

"No. I don't even know if I like you being around, let alone living with me."

"You will." He chuckled into my collarbone, and then he grabbed me by the hips and pulled me into his lap.

"We have to go get this baby freaking clothes, Rome."

"I have to make this baby's momma happy before we do so that I can move in with her." His hand slid up to my jeans button and I let him unsnap them. I wasn't fooling anyone. I wanted his fingers on me. He slid my panties to the side and took my ball of nerves in between his thumb and middle finger. He pinched and rolled in an intoxicating rhythm as he sucked on my neck. "How wet do you have to be to say yes to moving in together?"

"This is fucking blackmail," I moaned and rolled my hips into his hand.

"It's just a reminder, baby. A reminder of who calls the shots between you and me."

"Pretty sure that's me," I panted.

His stare grew dark, possessive, and controlling. Rome liked me pushing his boundaries, I knew from the way he smiled like I'd just handed him a prize. He stopped what he was doing and grabbed my hips to flip me onto my stomach. I was over his lap like a child. He shoved my panties and jeans down just enough that my ass cheeks were at his mercy.

He slapped them.

Hard. So hard that I wondered if the driver heard it and my yelp after.

"What the fuck, Rome?" I asked, but it came out as a purr.

"Who owns this?" His fingers went to my slit, so wet now, he would have been able to slide his fingers in without a problem.

I whimpered, my head in the seat.

It wasn't the direct answer he wanted. He smacked my ass again, and I couldn't hold back the moan. "You think you own it, or is this pussy mine?"

"Rome…" I breathed out, wiggling in his lap, trying to get his fingers to slide into me rather than back and forth over me.

I felt him shift, his hard length pressing into my stomach. Then suddenly, his teeth bit down on my ass cheek, most definitely leaving marks. His hand gripped my skin there, plumping it up so that he could take all the bites he wanted. "This ass, this pussy, this little virgin hole"—his thumb pushed where I knew I'd never let a man enter—"they're all mine."

I tried to push myself up to respond, but his arm bore down on me. "Rome—"

"Tell me they're mine. And tell me we're moving in together so I can reward you instead of punish you."

His thumb was working my ass, and his fingers were sliding back and forth over me, just hovering at the entrance. I couldn't hold out if I tried. "I'm yours, you wicked fucker. You can move in. Now, give me my reward."

His fingers shifted, his thumb went deeper, and he held me down as I arched and rolled. I clawed at the car seat and hit a high faster than I was proud of.

I climbed on top of him and took what I wanted, or maybe he took what he wanted as he met me thrust for thrust.

After we rearranged our clothing and straightened our appearances, he mumbled to me, "Stonewoods might be coming."

"As in Brey and Vick?" I glared at him. That meant acknowledging the 'mommy club' side of having a baby. I'd avoided it. I hadn't seen them since the news of the baby, and even speaking to Brey on the phone had been a strain. Fortunately, like a good friend, she was quick to back off. Vick wouldn't be able to do that, though.

I sighed and texted them to confirm they would be coming.

When we walked in, I was a little taken aback by the lux décor and the pastel colors of the clothing.

"You're pregnant!" Vick squealed so loud that everyone in the boutique winced and the saleslady jumped. She barreled in through the glass doors ahead of Brey, Jax, and Jett.

Everyone exchanged hugs and handshakes as I mumbled for Vick to keep it down, but the woman was vibrating with so much excitement, I swear she looked like a high-maintenance chihuahua shaking over having its first treat.

No one was calming her down. Jett stood back with Jax and Rome, all of them in suits, not really wanting a part of our conversation for the next hour.

I wanted no part of it either, quite frankly.

"Neither of you had to come," I mumbled as I picked at one of the pieces in the store. The clothing was made of silk, all pastels and bright shades, and the price tags were gold colored, no doubt representing how much each piece would cost.

"Of course we did," Brey responded and nudged my shoulder. "The guys thought it would be good to start here. For security purposes, right?"

She caught me scrunching my nose and I didn't even care. "Not for me, that's for sure. You both wear these kinds of outfits, but I don't."

Brey side-eyed me and looked down at her attire. It was a flowy white top with black pants. She wore green earrings that made her eyes pop, but that was it. "I'm going to go with no comment."

We both glanced at Vick who was energetically throwing clothes over her arm. "We can try on all these outfits! We'll have to add some extra color, but the material is perfect. You're going to—"

"I'll fit in them for two weeks. I'm shopping for maternity clothes." I pointed at the pyramid of clothing draped over her shoulder. "Those will fit me for two days."

"You're tiny. I don't think you'll pop in the first trimester." She turned to Brey, her eyes razor sharp with determination. "When did you start showing?"

"Probably five months."

"How far along are you, Katie?" Vick was like an investigator for a top crime show.

"They think eleven weeks now," I answered. "But I'm not here to shop for—"

"You're the queen of the bratva now. Let us spend the money."

"You're married to Jett Stonewood, Vick. You've been spending money like it grows on trees for a while now."

"Not true." She turned to Jett. "We keep a tight budget, don't we, babe?"

"Pix, you have every piece of clothing from every boutique in this city. I don't know what budget you're talking about."

"Excuse me, you told me the sky's the limit for some, but not us. That's what you said." She smirked at him.

He rolled his eyes. "That's our *company's* motto."

"Well"—she shrugged and stared at us like an innocent, wide-eyed doe in her Tiffany blue designer dress—"shouldn't we try to live by your company's standards?"

The stars in his ocean blue eyes and the smirk that people rarely saw from the CEO had one of the salesladies sighing.

I rolled my eyes instead. "I'm not wearing anything over your shoulder."

Rome ambled over to me, and his eyes trailed up and down my body. I felt the heat in his stare as he took in my attire.

All black, cut at the sleeves, ripped dark jeans, and lettering across my chest that said "I'm not interested."

"New store, Kate-Bait?"

"I don't know why we're here in the first place."

"We needed to establish security. They're in place up and down the streets now. And"—he turned to the saleslady—"she needs new stilettos with some support and comfort."

"Not possible," Brey, Vick, and I mumbled at the same time.

The saleslady wasn't paying attention to anything he really said, though. Her gaze had focused on his mouth, his full lips, his straight teeth, and that dark stare that held most women hostage. "I'll call the owner. We can get a custom shoe made. I'm happy to assist in any way I can."

"She's happy to assist, all right," Vick mumbled, but she couldn't have whispered even if she was in that movie where they had to be quiet the whole time in order to survive.

The saleslady returned only a few seconds later, and her walk was catlike, trying to lure every one of our men in the store to look at her. If it hadn't been for me, she'd have sunk her claws into Rome the second he walked in. She placed her hand on his forearm when she got close enough to him, like I wasn't there.

Or like I was trash.

She thought that because I wore clothes that were beneath her boutique and didn't perk up at the silk on her hangers, I could be ignored. She thought that because I checked the price tags, I didn't have the money to spare on them.

She leaned in close to Rome, and I saw his jaw tick as he crossed his arms. "Could I have your number, please? The owner will call you with the designer on the line to see exactly what's—"

I held up my hand to stop him from responding. He wanted her attention about as much as I wanted her giving it. But I got to handle this confrontation; I wanted it. "I need the shoes. Would you like my number?"

"Your number?" she squeaked, like she'd forgotten all about me. "Oh, I think it's better if the owner talks to the one who's buying."

I narrowed my eyes. "You think I'm not buying my own shit?"

Rome draped his arm around my shoulder. "Don't disrespect my woman. Call the owner and give me the phone."

She glanced around, her hand now a little shaky, but she dialed the number. "Yes, hi. A customer would like to speak with you." She nodded and then handed over the phone.

Rome turned with me toward the door and exchanged smirks with the Stonewoods. We still had anonymity. They didn't. They knew what was about to happen, though.

"It's Rome." His voice rumbled into the phone. "I didn't think it was necessary to let you know I was coming in."

He paused. "Next time I will. My girl needs shoes and she only wears stilettos and combat boots."

"I wear flats sometimes." I never really did. Not anymore. It was either combat boots or stilettos now. Probably boots for the rest of my pregnancy.

"What size?" Rome asked me.

"Size 7."

"She likes red bottoms. I have a few more requests, so tell your designer to call me."

He waited again, and I figured the owner was telling him to go to hell. No one was getting that designer on the phone. We all knew who he was.

"Of course I know who he is. Tell him who I am and have him call me. She needs boots too, ones that go up her leg to hide the ratty socks she wears underneath."

I smiled at his ridiculous request. When he hung up, he handed the phone to the woman whose eyes were now wide with fear. "Thank you for your customer service today."

Vick glared at her. "We will never be back."

Brey sighed and hooked her arm into Jax's as we left the store.

Walking down the busy avenue suddenly felt different. People moved out of my way like they knew I carried a dangerous weapon. They leaned in to each other and whispered when they saw us. But it wasn't the Stonewood men attracting the attention this time. It wasn't the Stonewoods a girl turned and snapped a photo of.

It was me.

"Does everyone know something I don't?"

"The shop assistant probably alerted social media that the Stonewoods were out. And that we were too."

"No one knows who I am..."

"They're starting to, Katalina. Chicago's starting to realize you're their queen. You're about to feel their fear, their love, and their respect for you all at the same time. This city is intelligent, and it's alive with the determination to amount to something more. They'll kneel for you as long as you feed that determination."

I rubbed my hand over my belly, a habit I was quickly adopting. "I have to do that for them and for who I'm growing inside me."

"And you'll do it like a ruler should. Remember, you're Cleopatra, huh?" His finger brushed at the side chain of my necklace.

I took a deep breath in. "You believe in me more than I believe in myself. More than the bratva and more than the Armanelli Family. You might want to take that as a sign that you're not thinking straight."

"I take it as a sign that I'm still the best at my job. I know what people are about to do before they even do it. It's what keeps us safe."

I stopped on the sidewalk and let the Stonewoods keep walking on ahead of us. I turned Rome to face me, and people fanned out around us as they passed. Looking into his dark eyes, I saw a love deep enough to kill sound and movement around me. The world melted away, faded into the darkness, was muted out by the man in front of me. He didn't expect me to be in fancy clothes or hold me in the light where he thought I belonged. He just accepted that I would rule the darkness and do it well. He didn't question whether I could handle being a mother and a leader; he assumed I would because his trust in me was more than I had in myself.

Would he know what I was about to do in this moment?

Would he be able to keep himself safe before I acted?

I stepped forward and wrapped my arms around his neck. He frowned, but before he could stop me, my lips were on his. I was wrapping my legs around his torso and he was gripping my ass to get me even closer.

I kissed him in broad daylight for the bratva and the Stonewoods and the Armanellis to see.

I kissed him like I had the confidence to, the right to, the power to.

Because I did.

CHAPTER 20

KATIE

"IVAN, I'M NOT going to apologize." I lay on the couch, phone to my ear, legs up, contemplating how many holes in socks were too many. The holes were only on the calves, none really in the bottom, and I still liked that the tops read "Fuck" on one and on the other "You."

The lecture from my grandfather continued. He'd heard about me kissing Rome in front of all of Chicago. Everyone had, really. My security, the Armanelli's security, and the Stonewood's security had eyes on us.

I'm sure a few cameras went off. The people we were with were infamous enough and now maybe I was too.

I didn't care. The statement had been made; the news was out. "Ivan, you retired to your bedroom during the last meeting. Do you recall?"

My question was met with silence. I heard a rustling on the phone, as if he was getting up to leave whomever he was with for a more private setting.

"Little girl, you still have a lot to learn. Don't wash your hands of me so quickly."

"The last time I saw you, you left after holding a gun to your great grandbaby's head. I can't figure out why that is. You've known all along that we were going to be bound to the Armanellis in some way. So what if Rome and I have this child?"

"Ack." He dismissed my idea with just a sound. "You don't trust the one who gave you power."

"Power isn't given, Ivan," I replied and stuck a finger in one of my sock holes. It was probably time for a new pair. "You actually taught me that. Quite frankly, it only took a bullet to the thigh for Konstantin to give me the power. And I'm taking the rest in my own way."

"You're treading on thin ice. You're not merging leadership by having Rome's baby." There was a beat of silence. "It should be Bastian's."

Ah, there was the wrinkle in the suit, the chink in his armor. Therein lay the frustration. My grandfather wanted pure blood. The highest leader in the Armanelli Family tied to his own.

It pissed me off so much that I disclosed what Rome and I had found out through a call on one of my blood tests. "I forgot to tell you, you can officially call the baby a girl now. She's healthy in case you're wondering."

He grumbled over the phone line but I smiled at the news. Finding out the baby was a girl brought some sort of weird recognition and reality down upon me. I wanted to meet her so badly, see the innocence and perfection I created.

"She's worthless. Not the right Armanelli." My grandfather carried on.

"And, have you forgotten that I'm a mutt?"

He sighed like he knew his argument was null and void. The traditions of families and their bloodlines didn't make sense. They never had. No one's blood was as valuable as their actions or loyalties. His own son had been disloyal in the end. He was a testament to that. Just as Rome's father had been a testament and Mario too.

Family was only as good as their loyalty to you, not their blood relation.

Power shouldn't revolve around a birthright.

His voice was low and ominous when he said, "I don't forget anything, Katalina. Not in the way people think I do. I remember enough to know when to test the bratva and when not to. You're making your own bed."

"Are you saying you won't help me tuck in the sheets?"

"I don't deal with messes, darling. If you choose this path, have that baby, be with that man; I will wish you the best. But my hands will be tied when it comes to the repercussions."

I shrugged and let the apathy roll through me. It stopped in my gut and bloomed into worry and fear. Something grew there that I couldn't shrug off. My neutral ground had been lost, lost to a little soul growing innocently in my belly. The doctor had let us know I was officially 13 weeks along now. My morning sickness had subsided and I had been feeling a wave of normality. But now I was being threatened by the old head of the bratva.

"Ivan, there will be repercussions either way. What's done is done. You can consider yourself officially retired."

I didn't hesitate to hang up the phone. Cutting ties with the man was easy. I hadn't known him long enough to mourn his loss. I texted Maksim and a few others that Ivan should not be included in meetings in the future, that he needed to focus on his health. Ivan replied in the group chats that he appreciated my blessing.

It was all for show.

He was seething mad and probably plotting something against me. It didn't matter.

I got the call that afternoon. The last part of the government and the police force had signed off on the contracts with our lawyers. Our state would be held to a new standard regarding sex trafficking, along with about a billion other things, but that was the one are that mattered to me. The lawyers had been hired for this very reason. The partnerships were ironclad, the contracts written by the best in the world, and the government, along with the big players in the city, were all in the know.

If someone acted out, every partner brought them down, legally and with the government behind them.

Rome turned the key in the front door minutes later. I didn't sit up when he came in, just

looked at him from my spot on his couch. We'd finally agreed to pass the time between my penthouse and his. And by his place, I meant the one with the panic room. I made him get rid of the damn apartment under my penthouse.

Crazy man.

Crazy man that I loved.

This place with the cream tones and the muted colors appealed to me, not because of the design, but because of that damn panic room. It was a little home of mine, a place where I'd felt safe in a weird sort of a way. I'd found comfort there with him and Edgar Allen Poe, with him curled up next to me doing nothing for a time.

"I heard the news, Cleo." He was smiling, a big bag at his side.

"Did you now?" I swung my legs back and forth in the air, the "fuck" and the "you" written on them flying at him over and over.

"Want to celebrate by opening your gift?"

I turned on the couch and sat upright, a bit intrigued with what was in the bag. "You were out buying gifts?"

"I was at the club, setting up. The opening is in the next few days. There's something in here you can wear to it."

I hummed. With all that was going on, I'd forgotten that the man I now lived with was opening a sex club. "I'm not sure how to feel about my future baby's daddy participating in this exclusive endeavor."

"You feel fine about it because you are who you are," he said as he came to sit down next to me.

"And who is that?"

"The woman who's got my soul pinned to her own."

"If you say so." I glanced down, not really sure I wanted to explore the subject any further. I had to let it settle. I'd bottled my feelings for so long, I wasn't used to owning and expressing them now. "Anyway, I'll bite. What's in the bag?"

He waggled his dark eyebrows at me. I pursed my lips, trying my best not to smile. The man was bringing me gifts and doting on me like we were actually together. It wasn't really established. I was having his baby, and we were sleeping and living together. Yet we hadn't said the words that would seal the deal.

"A couple things."

I rolled my eyes and grabbed for it.

He pulled it back. "Now, now. Don't get impatient. Maybe we should feed the baby in you first. What do you want for dinner?"

"Oh, get fucked, Rome. Give me the bag."

"Don't I get a please?"

"You get a give-it-to-me-or-leave." I crossed my arms over my chest.

"This is my place, woman."

"Until you knocked me up. Now, what's mine is yours." I smiled but it was a bunch of saccharine bullshit we both knew was going to be followed up by something foul. "And when that's the case, I make the call."

"Hmmm...we'll see." But the man handed it over with a dopey look on his face.

Maybe it was the moment that got me or the fact that I was pregnant, I wasn't exactly sure. Suddenly, though, the words bubbled to the surface and I couldn't hold back saying, "I appreciate you. I appreciate this space with you. I appreciate the gift and the standing by me."

"You shouldn't appreciate it," he said softly. "You should expect it. Every woman deserves that, right? And a woman like you probably deserves a lot more."

"A lot more?" I raised my eyebrows, already backtracking with a sly comment. "What's in here anyway?"

I pulled open the bag and saw no clothing. "Looks like I'm going naked to the sex club."

"I'm not buying your ass clothes when I know you'll throw them away or rip them all up to make them your own. You handle that."

I hummed because he was probably right. Plus, my eyes had locked onto the beautiful brown box I knew and loved with the crisp white cursive writing and the big L showcasing the name of the best designer in shoes. I'd have red bottoms now for sure. I'd had plenty of them over the years. Men liked to hand them over as a gift.

These felt different, though. These had been bought with my baby in mind.

I pulled one box out, along with the one under it and another, smaller one. I narrowed my eyes at Rome, looking at the smallest box first.

Was this what I thought it was?

My heart thumped so loud, I felt the beats in my temples, in my ears, throughout my body. My hand shook as I grabbed the edges of the lid. The sturdy cardboard slid off and in that box was a deep red dust bag. I glanced at Rome who was sitting there next to me, arms crossed, waiting patiently.

"You didn't," I whispered.

But he had. We both knew it.

I lifted the bag and saw two tiny little combat boots. They were black with red bottoms and they looked just like the ones I wore every now and then. Tiny dual zippers popped in the color silver, next to little itty bitty shoelaces. I flipped them over to showcase the red bottoms.

I slapped a hand over my mouth but couldn't really hold back the choked-up sob that escaped my lips.

"What the fuck is wrong?" Rome moved quickly, ripping the box from my hands and kneeling before me.

"I just...I didn't...She didn't feel real until just now."

In some ways, I'd pictured her. I thought about what it would be like and I imagined how much I would love her and how protective of her I was already. I rubbed my stomach like I was trying to reach her, trying to feel what it would be like.

Those shoes, though—they were real and they were so tiny.

"She's very real. She's as real as you. And she's going to be just as beautiful too."

"Oh my God," I practically sobbed and dropped my head to his shoulder. "Don't say shit like that. You're supposed to be a monster and an asshole."

"I am," he grumbled. "Sort of. Not exactly when it comes to her, though." He brushed his fingers over my belly.

"Oh really?" I rolled my eyes, lifted my head from his chest, and smeared away the makeup that was probably running down my face. "Well, if it makes you feel better, I'm not my normal callous self about her either. I've been secretly reading all these damn studies to make sure I'm doing everything right."

He nodded like that was completely normal. "Me too."

"What?" I glared at him. "You didn't tell me…"

"I've only brought you specific food-based recommendations. You're on a multi-vitamin, but we need to make sure of other things too."

"Like what?" I was curious to hear if he'd been reading the same stuff I had.

"Supposedly you can't go in sandboxes or some shit." He shrugged.

"Right? Oh my God. I was reading why. What the fuck is that about?"

"A damn parasite that comes from animals in there."

"We're going to turn into germaphobes after all this."

He chuckled. "Finish opening your damn present, woman."

255

"They're both for me?" One side of my mouth went up. "I wonder what they could be."

"Those two"—he eyed them carefully—"are weapons."

I pulled back to look at him, my hands on his shoulders. "Huh?"

He grabbed one and set it on my lap as he sat down in front of me. He pulled out the combat boot first, a larger version of my future mini-me's. He hit the bottom stud in the middle of where my Achilles tendon would be. Fast as lighting, two large blades on the side shot out.

"Shit," I gasped out.

He did the same with the stilettos. Then he tapped my nose. "Weapons, Katalina, for the queen of the bratva."

"I shouldn't need those. I have security."

"You have yourself first. Remember that. Don't trust a single person except yourself if I'm not with you. Ivan's made his intentions clear."

"People build trust by exchanging it with one another, Rome. I have to trust these—"

"Never trust the bratva. Never trust a man that's envious of your power. Every man beneath you is. The Armanellis, the Stonewoods, we're on your level. They are not. I promise you that."

CHAPTER 21

ROME

FIREWORKS LIT UP the sky like it was the middle of the city of Chicago.

The shimmering of each firework reminded me how beautiful this place was, the potential in it, the life that was breathed into it by each driven person. The buildings had been made by hard workers, by CEOs busting their asses, and by our families ruling where we needed to.

This club's opening was going off with a bang—quite literally—because the Stonewoods had backed our family time and time again. The elite members knew exactly why fireworks were going off, but the city thought it was the Stonewoods providing them a show, entertaining the city of Chicago. Those elite members, some of whom had paid millions already for access, smiled on their way in. A couple stopped to tell me that the fireworks were a nice touch.

I was aware. As men and women filtered in with clothing bags and those who wanted to change immediately were escorted to the fitting rooms that lined the back, I took in what I'd made. I was just as much of a mastermind as the Stonewoods. Our underground club shimmered with the sparkling diamonds in the ceiling underneath the brightest lights. Pole dancers, Cirque De Soleil performers, the best strippers, and even some back-up dancers for celebrities were in cages, on hula hoops in the air, and dancing within the crowd. Yet the lighting was dim in the private nooks and corners for the clientele that wanted them.

I'd already seen a politician come from his fitting room in all black leather and walk off with a dancer. A couple grabbed hands with another couple dressed in luxurious lingerie and underwear. The night was young, but we had already handed out keys for sex toys within Cartier-style boxes, brought out kama sutra furniture, and lowered bondage tables for our guests. More would be dispensed throughout the night, dependent on requests. Spreader benches, fem dom chairs, saw horses, and spanking benches were all options. Nothing was off limits if people were willing to push their boundaries.

I shook hands with a big wig who wore a collar and not much else. "I'm pleasantly surprised by the turnout," he said.

"You underestimated me?" I asked from my seat at the bar. I didn't see the need to mingle, wasn't even sure I wanted to be here.

Clubs and bars weren't my scene. I owned them because they were effective at bringing in clean money and because I enjoyed controlling a place where people could let their guard down.

Now, though, the woman I loved was meeting me here. Instead of coming with me, she wanted more time to get ready. Frankly, she just wanted time, because Katie had fluttered about the whole day in holey socks doing God only knows what.

I should have had some sort of idea. I'd watched her ass in her black shorts the whole day doing it. Still, when it was time to go, I realized she hadn't even attempted to get ready.

Now I had to wait.

My freaking baby's mother would be walking through a damn sex club and I knew for a fact she would be the hottest thing in here.

I smiled when one of my favorite bartenders ambled up to me. "It going smoothly, Bonnie?" I asked.

"Sure thing, boss. Can't complain yet." She was working around the center of the bar, where a waterfall cascaded from the chandelier above. We'd had the chandelier custom-made so that the water could move around the crystals and there was a platform inside that allowed a dancer to move within it. It was grand, over the top, and just what we wanted. Tonight, we were paying the woman in there very well to wear only a diamond bra and thong that shimmered under the dim lights.

"How are you doing down there, Rome?" the dancer called from above. "Sure you don't want to come up here for a dance with me?"

"I'm good, Whitney." I lifted my glass to her and took a small sip.

Bonnie let out a loud laugh. "I cannot imagine you up there. I kind of want to, though. I'm happy to get you a ladder."

"I'll pass. We meeting goals?"

"It's looking good. We're making money hand over fist and everyone seems very happy. You never gave me an update on who was who here, so I'm treating everyone the same."

I nodded, looking out at the crowd. "That's what I want you to do." A rockstar walked by, eyeing up my bartender.

"There's a lot of big money here. It makes me wonder what I should be saying yes and no to."

"Only exactly what you want, Bonnie." I met her gaze and held it, making sure she understood what I was saying. This club would never be a place where anyone would do something they didn't want to do. This club was a place where instead you could go and do exactly what you wanted and find a person that would do it with you. It was also going to be a place where politicians, bigwigs, and CEOs would come to discuss business because we would all know each other's secrets.

I let the night roll by. I nodded to some and said a hello to others. It progressed as it should. Some were getting spanked by a woman half their size. Others were getting whipped, while still others were getting tied to a table.

Fantasies were coming alive and morphing into reality for so many. My only concern now was that Katie wanted to visit. I didn't want another man looking at her or even considering fucking her.

I felt her before I saw her. The hairs on the back of my neck stood up. I turned slowly on the barstool and watched as she stalked toward me, her tiny body swaying to the bumping of the bass. Every man's eyes turned toward her, even if they didn't want them to.

At this point, Most had some inkling of who she was, who she'd become.

A woman who tied three large, powerful entities together wasn't to be preyed upon. Instead, she was the predator and she walked like it too. Finally, Katalina was commanding the type of respect she deserved.

She radiated it, emanated it, and wore an invisible crown made of all the hardships and thorns she'd had to experience to get there. It was a jagged, sharp-edged crown that could make someone bleed, die, give up...but she'd survived.

She'd taken it all and learned to reign.

She wore a cut-off shirt that didn't belong in this type of establishment. Everyone had on their best attire or hardly anything at all, but Katie had decided to stroll in with a grungy shirt that made her look like a little tomb raider. The graphics across her chest were skulls with flowers, and the white lines popped against the strobe lights. The picture matched the tattoo on her side, skulls and flowers woven together. Somehow, she made it all work with her dark eye makeup. Her rejection of luxury wear drew even more attention, because it proved she couldn't care less about all the people below her. She didn't have to dress up; she didn't have to do anything.

When she reached the bar, she didn't say anything at first. I saw the way her movements were fluid, her back relaxed. Yet in her eyes, there was irritation.

"What's going on?" I demanded the answer immediately.

"Great turn out for the first night," she said, ignoring me. She took in the atmosphere. We'd made the center bar a deep mahogany, but some of the back bars had pure glass so that patrons could see their hands and legs beneath.

Mirrors lined some of the walls. People liked a show, especially their own. Katie didn't say whether she liked what she was seeing or not.

It was then I realized two bratva men had walked in behind her. "Who are they?" I jutted my chin toward them.

"Extra security."

"We don't need extra. I'm here with you."

"The bratva considered that." She sighed and ran a hand through her black strands. "They don't exactly trust you yet, though."

"Interesting. You're holding my blood in you and they don't trust me with it? It doesn't matter, though, because it's not their decision, Katalina." I narrowed my eyes at them. I wasn't sure if they were here because she agreed to it or because they were going against her command in order to watch her every move.

It felt like the latter, considering the way she narrowed her eyes at them.

"It's a joint one, monster." She rubbed her face and tried to get rid of the anger. Then she smirked at me, probably because she saw my jaw clenching. "It's just the beginning of a transition. They'll get used to it, huh?" She shrugged and relaxed a bit in the shoulders, and it cooled the temper running through me for a moment.

"Well, you saw the opening. I'm not inclined to stay with you while the whole place stares us down. So let's go. And your guards can go the opposite way." I waved them off.

She rolled her eyes. "Rome, they're providing security for me. Extra safety."

I glared at both of the guards. "You think they're any good at that?"

The men glanced at one another, not sure what to do. They were young, highly untrained, and not ready to do anything other than collect intel.

I had the answer to my question. "You want them to continue to follow us?"

"I'm not sure there needs to be any following."

"Because?"

"Because I'd like to stay for a drink."

"You can't drink." My gaze flicked down to her belly where she rubbed immediately. There wasn't a bump there. Not yet.

"Of soda."

I kept my eyes on her. "Should you even be drinking that?"

"Are you fussing over a damn ginger ale, Rome? I'll drink what I want. One sip of carbonation and sugar isn't going to hurt the baby."

"So, you did read up on it?" I tried not to smile.

We were already crazy parents, already out of control.

"Oh, shut the hell up." She stomped her foot. "I realize I'm getting a little obsessive about what I can and can't do so as not to harm the baby."

I sighed. I was too. We were helicopter parenting before the child had even gotten to the viable pregnancy stage.

"If we go, I can stop that habit of yours for a little while."

"Really?" She tilted her head. "How so?"

"You don't need to ask the question when your pussy knows the answer, Katalina."

She glanced behind her. "Want to say it louder for the people in the back to hear? Jesus, Rome."

A laugh rumbled out of me. She thought I cared? I didn't give a damn at all. This was my place. "Katalina, the whole world knows you're having my baby. What's there to hide?"

The two bratva men near us scoffed a little more loudly than Katalina liked. They weren't her normal security.

"Where's the guy that normally drives you?" I revisited the irritating topic of conversation from earlier that night.

"Maksim? He flew to LA for some business. I think we could have allies out there in time."

I nodded, but that wasn't what I was worried about. Not all her men had been put in their place. They had a look of hunger, of unease, to them that I didn't like.

"You two can leave." I shot daggers at her security.

"Oh, Jesus," Katie muttered and then waved between all of us. "Vladimir and Trent, meet Rome."

None of us exchanged any niceties.

"We're driving her home," Vladimir responded. His eyes held hatred, the kind my monster fed off. I knew the look because I'd had it on my own face before.

"She's staying with me. I'll be taking her. You got a problem with that, talk to Maksim. Or is it Ivan you report to?"

He spat on the floor of my club. I stood up, ready to rearrange the look on his face and make him aware that his disrespect wouldn't be tolerated.

"Vlad, go home," Katalina said, her tone reprimanding.

"I'm supposed to stay with you to protect—"

"I can protect myself. I'm also the one who requests whether or not I have security. I don't want it now."

The man started to protest again.

She cut him off. "I'm not asking you. Don't disagree with me again."

His anger was palpable as he and his friend retreated.

There was a shift in the air, something foul was there now. It reeked of betrayal and dishonor.

CHAPTER 22

KATIE

W E SPENT ANOTHER week together with no hiccups. The doc came and told me I would be showing soon. He also said the heart sounded strong and gave us pictures of the fetus.

I handed them to Rome and told him to do something with them. We both stared at them like foreign objects, not sure how to handle precious baby memories when we barely had precious memories of our own.

We decided one could go on the fridge and the others we'd put in an Edgar Allen Poe book on one of our shelves for now.

"Is it morbid that we're putting life into a book about death?" I asked.

"It's shining light where there's darkness. It's poetic if nothing else." He stared at the books. "Remember when I read to you."

"Maybe you should read to me again." I waved him on and we went to the panic room. We lay in that bed like two lovebirds, as if we weren't mobsters. He rubbed his hand over my stomach at one point and asked, "Do you feel her in there yet?"

"No kicking or anything. But—it sounds weird, I know it sounds so fucking weird—I feel her heart. She's brighter than us, Rome. She's so freaking bright and full of joy. I'm going to deliver joy into this world and she's going to wrap all our hearts up in it."

He didn't say anything. He stared at my stomach with love, though. His fingers rubbed back and forth and then he pressed down on her before he lowered his head and kissed my skin. "Made from darkness but pure light. I'm going to be obsessed," he murmured.

My heart warmed and my mind buried this memory somewhere safe with all the memories I had of my father, of his love, of his own heart. It was where that memory belonged.

I didn't have a lot of good in me left, but I felt the good spread here, with Rome, talking about our baby together.

I wanted to freeze us in that moment because I knew our lives wouldn't stay this perfect.

I walked on eggshells for days after. I didn't want to disrupt our happiness. I tried to stay in, tried not to rock the boat.

But I was the bratva queen.

He was the underboss of the Italian Mob.

Something was bound to happen.

Rome had a big event a few nights later at New Reign. He wanted me to come. I'd grumbled that I'd think about it and that Maksim would be available if I wanted to get ready and go.

I didn't.

Rome had winked at me and said that it would be good, that other Pahkans and families would be there, that I should make an appearance. I fake-gagged and he laughed as he swung the door closed behind him.

I got the call only an hour later.

One of my guys had been trafficking, not just one or two women but truckloads of them.

My stomach rolled with the news. It'd been someone close, one of the men who'd done security for me the night of the opening of New Reign.

He'd made small talk with me. He'd smiled to my face.

And betrayed and lied behind my back.

I gave Maksim the news and he delivered the message that I wanted everyone to meet immediately at the bratva's facility. It was near the lake, in an allotment of empty warehouses that weren't really empty at all.

I didn't say a word to Maksim as he maneuvered the SUV there. The rage pulsing in my veins screamed loud enough.

The bratva had disobeyed me again, and Vladimir had headed the operation. He'd questioned my authority and gone against the contracts. Change was always hard. It was like packing your bags and leaving the comfort of your home to walk into a pitch-black abyss, knowing you would never get that comfort back. Why leave that warm bed, that cozy blanket that smelled just the way you wanted it, for something completely unknown. Everyone could say it would be better but no one could promise it.

The bratva knew the grass hadn't been greener before. They were human. They knew the darkness that lurked in the shadows of the unknown and they wanted to cling to the tradition and home they'd had before.

So Vladimir rebelled. I knew he hadn't acted alone, but he'd have spearheaded it. He'd smuggled in women under the guise of a legal shipment for one of the Stonewoods' many businesses within the aerospace field.

It put us all in jeopardy. And it signed his death sentence.

We pulled in to the facility's parking and my heartbeat quickened. I was new to it all, wanted to call Ivan and ask him to come with me.

I knew I couldn't though. Ivan had made his intentions clear.

When we walked through the doors, Maksim stood close to me, ready to do damage if anyone acted out. The bratva were all sitting, heads hung low, and two of them had Vladimir in their grip.

"The bucket over there contains a liquid that will eat away at his skin," one of my guys said, proud of himself for getting it.

I cringed at the notion and at the look in his eyes. Was I getting soft? How could leadership have made me so? I rubbed my belly and then fisted my hand, sure that I had to maintain a cool head about this, had to enforce a rein that was fearful where only the strongest survived.

"Vladimir, you made your choice."

"I didn't!" he screamed, wiggling in the men's arms as they dragged him back toward the steel bucket. "You saw my wife. I held her just last night. She wants kids, a family."

"You ripped a daughter from a father and mother. You think those women you sell aren't daughters, wives, mothers, those longing for a family too?"

"They're addicts. They don't have anywhere else to go. Most are grateful." His eyes narrowed and he went limp in my men's arms, causing them to loosen their grip. "One told me 'thank you,' Katalina. She would have got on her knees for me."

"What?" I whispered, and my gut turned as a sick smile spread across his yellowed teeth.

"Screw it. I'm going to burn in there anyway. Let me say it like I mean, huh? She was a whore like you. All of them are. You're vessels for us to use to make money. You belong in the damn truck with them." He glanced at my belly. "Blood of the bratva or not, you need to be fucked into submission and that bastard of a baby needs to learn the way of the world too."

He ripped his arms from the men and sprinted toward me. My security wasn't what I thought they were. They ran with him and Maksim shot one and collided with the other, wrestling him to the ground. My body was on high alert, ready to defend what I loved but hadn't met yet. My baby would see the light of day.

I was sure of it in those moments.

Vladimir went for my neck and I let him come, bracing for my chair tipping over before we sailed backward with his momentum. He expected me to flail and try to remove his hands, but I yanked him close by his shirt and wrapped my legs around his back. Up my skirt was a knife, and it would be so easy to grab, so easy to have it at his throat.

I wanted him to suffer, though, wanted him to feel the damage, the pain he'd inflicted on the dream I'd grown to love. The women in the busses were my daughters, my mother, me. They were who I was and who I would always be. The little girl in me screamed for torture and punishment.

My red-bottomed shoes had been custom made for blood. It took just the right angle, but the sharp blades sprang from the sides when I pounded the back of my shoe into his spine. I stretched my legs out and brought them down again hard.

The chortle from him and then the guttural scream satisfied the mother in me.

His hands flew from my neck to scrabble at his back, but by then, I'd latched on. My arm had wrapped around his neck too, and I clung tight as he stood up and tried to shake me off while I kept bringing my stilettos down on him.

"No, stop! Stop!"

"You'll be dead when I do," I whispered in his ear, and his face paled. "The last thing you'll think of is my name, Vladimir, and how *this whore* fucked you. Fucked *you* into submission."

My legs were wet with his blood now, the spattering and gushing making it clear to me why he'd fallen to his knees. I pulled us backward and he fell on top of me, mumbling curses in Russian. As his eyes glazed over, I knew what the end result would be and didn't need to witness it.

I shoved him off. Silence stretched over the room. I didn't spare him a second glance as I got up and righted my skirt. "Who's cleaning?"

"I will, Katalina." Another member of the bratva on my left said quietly. There were a few here that had let the show play out. I didn't blame them for that. This was the queen making her mark to them. They had to know I could lead and defend myself.

Maksim had two dead bodies near him and was straightening his clothing too.

"Don't save his body. Burn it and throw the rest in the river. Tell his family the manner of his death left no remains, and set up the wife with an account." I walked to the door, and the only sound that could be heard was the shoes clicking across the floor. When I looked back, the blood stains were prominent on the cement, imprints of a mother fighting for her daughters.

"I'm so sick of this bratva thinking I'm a whore. Is this what you all want? Me to fuck you all into submission? Pick you off one by one and bleed the fear from you? Do you all want fear rather than mutual respect, friendship, love?"

"No, ma'am. I just think they're all scared of change." Maksim answered.

"They should be scared of death, of sacrificing their place in the family because of what they're used to."

Maksim nodded. "Many are under the impression God will save them once they do die."

"God couldn't save the innocent daughter in my stomach, let alone any of you. We're all sinners. Born to the blood of our ancestors and we chose this place. My baby will not. She'll be born with the blood of this bratva and the Armanelli blood flowing through her. She won't be able to wash her hands of it, no matter how hard she tries. So you change what you can without relying on what you cannot."

"Are you saying we can't make God save us?" Maksim lifted a dark eyebrow.

"No, you can't. And you can't rely on an afterlife either. But you can change the life you have here. If you don't work for change, you'll never see it."

"Katalina, we're all trying to push change." The man at my left murmured.

"How? You didn't say a goddamn thing."

"It wasn't the right time. You can see that, can't you?" He answered, like that was a good enough reason.

"Wasn't it Martin Luther King who said that your silence becomes your betrayal?"

He stared long and hard at me. I let my words sink in. The moments ticked by. He could either stand with me loudly or fall back silently. "You're right."

"That I am," I said and proceeded to walk through the door, ready to slam it shut behind me. "Tell your brothers that. And make sure they understand that Vladimir just secured his seat in hell. If anyone else wants to go with, I'm happy to send them."

CHAPTER 23

ROME

HER EYES, AS silver and beautiful as the moon, were hollow. I immediately scanned her for injuries, for something that was wrong. I looked at her straightened hair swishing with each step, the strong jaw against the hoodie that shrouded her neck, down to where she'd sliced off the bottom of it to showcase her small waist. Her black jeans hung low on her hips and were frayed right above those designer heels, the ones I'd gifted her.

They were stained.

I knew those stains better than anyone else.

Blood.

I left my drink at the bar and met her halfway. "What happened?"

She took in the club, not meeting my eyes, but instead scanning everything that was going on in the room. "I wonder if you didn't tell me about your club because you didn't trust me."

"Trust you with what?" I said, trying to at least grab her attention.

She shook her head as if in disgust but didn't say anymore.

"I'm calling Bastian," I announced.

"No need. I did already. Everyone will be here soon."

Katie before the bratva felt nothing. She moved through the world letting everything roll off her back, even when it was the craziest shitstorm barreling through.

Katalina, now, after the bratva, felt every single thing. She felt her pain. She felt her reign. She felt everything. She felt the weight of this damn city and it was a heavy one.

Yet, the numbness in her gaze and the way her hands didn't shake meant something had driven her back to the hole she couldn't be in anymore. She needed to feel, she needed to know her power.

She couldn't shut down again.

"Okay. Let's talk about what happened then."

She shook her head and walked past me, past the throngs of people mingling and getting lost in one another, to the bar. She asked the bartender for a water and when one was handed to her, she took two gulps before turning to me and asking, "Do you think the monster is in you or in me? Have you ever thought about that? Have you ever wondered about whether or not I'm too far gone to come back? Because I do.

I wonder if I've been wronged so much that I've forgotten my dad's love."

"What are you talking about Katalina?" I knew exactly what she was talking about. I just knew it wasn't true. She had to be stronger than all of us. We needed her to be better than we could ever be. "Tell me what the fuck happened. I'm going to find out anyway."

She fisted her hand, but I took it and pried her fingers open to thread them through mine.

"I just don't know how I can do that, lead the bratva and be a mother. I don't know how I can kill and still love. I'm furious and I feel it down to my bones. Am I supposed to turn around and love a daughter after something like that?"

I shook my head at her. "Did you kill for love? That's what families do, that's what any family would do for someone they love. "

"Is that what keeps you going? Knowing that we're doing all this for the family, for people that we love? Seems like everybody does it for pride or for money and greed. "

"Is that what you think of Bastian, Cade, and me? You think I took Mario... No, let's go way back. You think Marvin was for that?"

She tilted her head, her hair falling like a smooth waterfall down her shoulders as she thought about it. I wanted to drag her out of there, tend to her needs, tear her from the line of fire. If she'd done what I thought she had, word would spread and the exclusive members of this club would be judging her by the end of the night. It was the last thing we needed.

"Did you love me then?" she whispered.

"I loved some part of you since the moment I met you, Cleo," I admitted. "I was chained to you since day one."

"How do we chain everyone together then?"

"We have to gain their trust, Katalina. Or you reign in fear and power alone. That doesn't last."

She hummed low and murmured, "Maybe it'll last long enough for me."

The music pulsed through our veins and swayed the crowds and their extracurricular activities. Katalina spun on her bloody red-bottomed shoes and stalked away.

"Goddamnit," I grumbled into my drink and shoved away from the bar. I made my way to where she had disappeared. It looked like she was about to enter the fitting room areas but had been stopped by Bastian, Cade, and Dante walking in. She pushed past them.

"Did you check your phone?" Cade asked me, his stare piercing me instead of his phone in that moment.

I didn't answer him, but pulled my phone from my suit pant pocket. His text read "Vladimir is dead. Trafficking. She did it herself and made a show of it."

There's something deep inside you that grows and morphs into something ugly when the people you love are in danger. "Was she protected? What happened?"

"Her men lost control of the situation." Bastian pulled at the collar of his shirt. "Or they let him loose on her."

The beast, the monster, the demons in me roared. "Who

had eyes on her while I was at the club today? That was supposed to be you, Cade."

"She handled it," Cade said without even a damn hitch in his voice. "We have to trust her to handle it."

Bastian clamped a hand on my shoulder but I shrugged it off as he said, "She's one of us now. It's our job to handle it, Rome, but we have to let her handle it too or she won't ever really lead them."

"She has my baby in her belly," I rasped like any one of them would understand, but the oxygen had been stolen from me. It was replaced by suffocating animosity toward everyone. "Don't any of you get that? One innocent life between all of us. We got one."

They all looked every which way except into my eyes.

"I don't have to explain the gravity of this. I won't because you all know. If we don't protect my baby, I will drag this city to hell. I don't give a fuck if she's a queen or a damn god. We protect that innocent life in her by intervening every single time there's a risk."

"We can't do—"

I grabbed Cade by his shirt collar. "Don't tell me what we can and can't do."

He didn't even flinch. We all saw Cade as the quiet, good-natured tech geek but I saw the screw that was loose there sometimes. At that very moment, he laughed hard in my face as I pulled him close. The tattoos on his hands were stark black against the strobe lights and I read that chaos on them as he pried my fingers from his shirt. He laughed crazily the whole time.

When he'd freed himself, his laugh died abruptly. "Remember I watch every single movement everyone makes. I study you all. She was safe. I care just as much about her as I do any of you. So fuck off."

I shoved past all of them while Dante and Bastian tried to tell me to calm down.

My body, my soul, my monster was on a new mission. My tyrant had been in danger and I needed to know that she hadn't been harmed.

As I walked past the tall podium where hosts were dressed in skimpy costumes ushering people in and out of the fitting rooms, I told them to lock it down.

They immediately jumped to get the area closed off, and I breezed past to find Katalina.

She stood in front of a mirror, wearing that dress from so long ago, the one with feathers curving around her breasts. She'd cut the waist and the skirt too. The fabric stretched tight across her tits and I eyed her flat stomach, wondering when it would grow like the other parts of her had started to.

"You're not wearing that out there," I said.

"I'm not in the mood to be bossed around, Rome."

"I'm not in the mood to kill anyone tonight, either."

"Neither was I, but here we are."

"I heard." When she didn't say anything in response, I snaked my hand around her waist and ran my fingers over her stomach. "She's an innocent bystander in all this."

"Exactly. So I have to find a different way to keep her safe. What we're doing isn't working."

"Building trust is going to take time."

"We're running out of time," she shot back. I saw her mind working, saw her searching for a target. I knew I wasn't going to like the bullseye she found.

"Dressing like this and flaunting yourself in front of these people isn't going to help. I'll end up tearing someone's eyes out."

"I don't think anyone understands my commitment to you all. I think the bratva think they can sway me. They tried to scare me tonight. They wanted Bastian's partnership eliminated, they wanted that contract gone. And some of them conspired to try to make it happen."

"They'll come to understand."

"Or we make them. We can show them how bound we all are."

"Katalina..." I said her name low in warning.

She spun to stare at me with fury in her eyes. "What?"

"When you fuck around in a sex club, you're not in control. People let their demons out to play and get lost in fantasies. They keep their secrets close until they're here and can act them out. This is a place where you see the most raw side of a human."

"You may have more experience in a club, Rome. But I've been attuned to what sex does for a human for a very long time. I know how the sway of my hips can draw a man's attention; I know the way I lick a finger can bring a man to his knees. Sexual desire is a pleasure and a weakness. What better way to connect with them?"

I couldn't control grabbing her hair and pulling her face close to mine. She needed to understand how serious this was, "If you open the box, I won't be accountable for my actions after."

A slow smile crept across her face. "That's perfect, Rome. I'm not taking accountability either." She leaned in and nipped my bottom lip. Then she kissed me hard and I met bite for bite. We shared something between us right then. We'd always been equal but I tasted her anger and wanted whatever she did. I was going to support her tonight in any way I knew now.

I loved her. Every crazy, furious part of her.

Once we calmed a bit, she turned to grab a pair of black lace gloves off the small stool in the fitting room. She slid them on slowly and then pointed to her back. "Now tighten my bodice so we can get this show on the road."

No further prompts were needed from either of us. I yanked the ribbon harder than necessary. I tied her in so tight, I hoped no one would be able to get her out. It was only a matter of time though.

Tonight, I knew as well as everyone else, the devil and all our demons were coming out. I wanted to show the bratva just who they thought they could have her forget, and she just wanted a show, period.

We'd succumbed to the darkness and were about to let it envelope us. That was the allure of a place like this. As we walked back out, I saw that they'd dropped the rings from the ceilings so that guests could start using them. People draped themselves across them, folded around them, and fucked around them too. We snaked through the crowd, Katie glancing at sex scene after sex scene. A woman let two men have her on a couch.

I nodded at her when she waved. "She's opening her 10th spa downtown this month."

Katie nodded and stayed close to me to talk. "She's definitely celebrating the right way."

"With both those men?"

"To each their own. You can't really go wrong with more than one, right?" Katie shrugged.

I saw the way her eyes lingered, how she licked her lips. Katalina was contemplating it, and that was the allure of a place like this. It opened your eyes to possibilities you thought were impossible. A woman could have more than one man, you could dress the way you fantasized, you could tempt and punish however you wanted. There was a labyrinth of possibilities, and as the lights flashed and strobed over everyone, you caught glimpses of all that could be.

"You think more men would hit you harder than just me, Kate Bait?"

She dragged her metal-colored eyes up and down my body. "The more, the merrier." She swung her gaze to a velvet booth sequestered off in the corner where a celebrity was eating out her friend. She smirked at me and kept moving like what she'd said hadn't fried every nerve in my body, hadn't made me want to slap a leash on her and drag her home.

Katie needed to learn that she was the queen of the city and that I, along with everyone in this town, would bow to her, except when it came to us. Between her and me, I ruled. I could bring that woman to her knees with pleasure in seconds. She might fight me on it, she might act like other men would do just as well, but in the dark recesses of her mind, she needed to be sure.

Tonight, I had a feeling, we were going to see that happen. Everyone here, everyone that mattered, would understand that Katie was tied to the Armanelli Family in a way no one else could be. She held the hearts of all of us men in a way not even I wanted her to.

Tonight, we would worship our queen to make everyone understand that they bowed to her or we would destroy them.

Even if I wasn't going to like it.

CHAPTER 24

KATIE

ROME AND I meandered around. He followed me as
I turned corner after corner to see the dark sections
of the club and witness all the aspects of it. There
were orgies and roleplay and sex toys and pure uninhibited
freedom. The bass vibrated through you with slow, melodic
music or fast up-tempo beats.

Every beat had me thinking of something else.

Had Vladimir acted alone? Who was on his side and who
was on mine?

Did I call Ivan and tell him that I'd taken a man's life in
front of the bratva? The leadership of it all was foreign to
me. I knew it was my place now. I knew I'd taken the role,
but when someone goes for so long without ownership of
even themselves and then without true equality, it's normal

to falter. It's normal to feel like you may not be able to handle it, that you're not fully equipped.

Yet I'd been through it all for a reason.

I'd learned to dissociate, I'd learned to survive, and I'd learned to control my mind in even the most horrific situations.

Now, I stood in one of the most surreal ones, next to a man who was willing to do whatever it took, with a baby in my belly who would bring innocence to families without a trace of it, in a club that allowed us to explore our most sinful thoughts.

"This is like a dream, Rome. I don't know how it can all be real, how any of you can get away with having all this happening under one of the biggest buildings in the city," I said to him at one point.

He nodded like he understood how one would think that. "We've got the best lawyers as you know. And obviously some of the most influential people in the state are here. Everyone signed NDAs and contracts with us. We hold all the cards and none of the responsibility. We wouldn't have it any other way."

The funny thing was, I knew this was how it worked. Deals were made by leaders of the world in back alleys and in the basements of the biggest buildings in town.

"Guess it's a good thing I'm here to start making all the necessary connections," I said, rolling my eyes. My mind was numb to it all, my body tired from the fight to become a leader. I needed a drink but couldn't have one. I needed a bed but couldn't rest in one. I needed a break, but leaders didn't get one.

The strobe lights morphed to a red light pulsing to the beat of a hypnotic song. I didn't see the sexual aspect of it. Just the red.

Red that spilled everywhere when I'd taken Vladimir's life. So much blood since I walked away from the Armanellis. So much death. And still, they didn't understand. This partnership was supposed to help everyone. We'd brought in more companies that wanted legal business partnerships than ever before. They would have more money in their pockets soon.

I'd keep striving. I'd keep pushing until everyone saw the benefit. "Who do I need to chum up to while I'm here?"

"Chum up to?" Rome's brow crinkled in confusion.

"Yes. I doubt Ivan will show up. I know some of the bratva will attend later. Most of them probably will if Maksim has anything to do with it."

"Why do you say that?"

"I told him to get on board or be ready to sink. I expect him to share the message with others. I'll confirm their alliances at some point, but who else is a necessity here? I see the chief of police walked in and there's a few business owners. Anyone else?"

Rome stared at me for a minute, his gaze penetrating my soul and pulling me to him like a gravitational force. He didn't say a word, but his hand came up and rubbed my cheekbone. "No one, Katalina. You don't have to do anything for anyone."

I turned around the club, took in everything. My eyes landed on the waterfall, at the stage the was at the very top. "I want to go up there."

His jaw ticked before he turned away from me. We were building to something I knew he wouldn't like. It was the only way though.

Would he desert me here? Would he let me go through with it?

When I didn't immediately follow him, he looked back at me and waved me forward. "Let's go, woman. Time to give them all the show you want."

"You know?" I asked as I walked toward him.

"I think I know that we're going to crown you tonight. No one will question where you belong after that." He said the words softly, like he'd resigned himself to them.

I narrowed my eyes at him. "The monster going to be okay with this?"

"We'll have you any way we can, Cleo." He tilted his head toward the stairs.

As we headed up the polished staircase, I gripped the railing a little harder than necessary. I felt the smooth material at my fingertips, the way the gloss filled in all the rough edges.

I swung my gaze to the top and saw that Maksim had arrived. Others within the bratva were behind him. They'd all met Cade, Bastian, and Dante. Rome left me behind, my ascent too slow for him, or maybe he wanted to give me a view of the bratva and the mafia standing there together.

All their eyes were on me.

I held their attention, grasped it in the palm of my hand, felt the power I possessed. Didn't they all feel it too? How we'd woven ourselves together and made an omnipotent entity, assigning ourselves the responsibility to do good with it? For the city, for the people, and for us.

Rome motioned to someone and suddenly the whole club dimmed and the waterfall glowed red from the spotlight focused on it.

The men at the top of the staircase had the center stage, and I knew I would too as I walked toward them. Chairs lined the balcony, but there in the center, close to the waterfall, stood a throne. Completely made of crystal, it sparkled, the centerpiece of the scene. I realized as I took my last step that the railing post was topped with a small crown that was the exact replica of the one on the back of the throne's frame. It glittered, beautiful and terrifying all at the same time.

Bastian stood behind it, just out of the water's reach, and stared at me. "May I sit?" I asked him as I walked up.

He didn't answer at first. Instead, his eyes dragged up and down my body. I held myself more languidly, sashayed toward him to give him that sign.

It'd been a long time since I'd seen that look of hunger in Bastian's eyes. He'd leashed it and packed it away for other women. He'd moved on from me, I knew that. I wasn't ever really sure he'd totally and completely lusted over me the way Rome thought he had. Yet the look was back, like he knew he'd have me if offered.

I smiled at him. This was my time now. I did what I wanted without anyone having control over me.

I'd come to make an impression, come to feed my rage. What that meant, I wasn't sure, but these men would be a part of it.

I glanced at Rome, at Maksim, then at Cade and Dante.

I heard Rome's low voice as his eyes bore into mine. "You said there was no better way to celebrate. She had two, and you can have all the men you want. Is it what you want?"

We had a silent argument then. He was goading me, I knew that. I was making a show of my power, he knew that. We just weren't quite sure which was more important. He sucked on his teeth and then a small smile crept across his face. "I'll prove you wrong in the end, Katalina. I'm all you want."

I smiled back and quirked a brow at him, taunting the beast. "Maybe we need to show everyone then."

Rome stalked toward me, like he was ready to dominate me and make me his. "I should punish you for acting like I'm not enough," He murmured the words so only I could hear.

"Punish me here? I'm taking my pleasure, not punishment."

He hummed low, "I'll punish you at some point for all this and it'll be the most pleasure you'll receive in a long time."

I felt my nipples tighten at his words. "I'm not even sure this will help them see how we'll be bound forever, Rome."

"It'll help you in one way or another." He looked me up and down. "Or is this a line you won't cross?"

I narrowed my eyes at him. He wanted a fight. Or he wanted to dare me, to push me out of my comfort zone. I didn't know his end game but I knew mine. I was showing this city that no one overstepped my rules. I made them and I was bound to the one I loved. Rome had my heart and I had his.

It pushed me over the edge. "Cross the line," I commanded.

No other command was needed, but everyone heard me say it, knew I was the one in control here. His hand shot out and grabbed my arm to yank me the rest of the way to him. He devoured my mouth, branded me with a searing kiss that had people gasping. The audience was growing. I heard murmurs from the floor below us and the bratva behind us talking amongst themselves.

The music pumped through my veins as I surrendered to his mouth. Rome always took control here and I let him because I knew he wasn't like any other man I'd been with.

I pulled away from him and glanced around at the men before me. They weren't like others either. Somehow, they'd all stepped up. Maksim had risked his spot in the bratva for me, Dante still trained me, even though I was the enemy, Cade protected my location, and Bastian had signed on to a partnership with me.

I'd made them all a family. I'd put them in front of bullets, put them in harm's way, and they'd risked their lives and families for me.

"No turning back when the bomb goes off, Rome," I murmured in his ear.

"I'm about to detonate it, honey. I'll be in the explosion along with you. No turning back."

I took a step away from him, my heart suddenly in my throat as I walked around him toward the throne. This wasn't something I'd ever done.

I twisted to take everything in and saw that almost every single person in the club had turned our way. Some had drinks in their hands, some were set up to watch the show and pleasure themselves, and most were already mesmerized, small smiles on their faces.

Bastian's heavy hand went to my shoulder to shove me down. He leaned forward and I felt his hot breath at my ear. "Do I get a taste of you after all?"

I glanced up at him and fluttered my eyelashes. "Bastian," I tsked. "You're only here to do what I ask, nothing more and nothing less."

The crowd whispered at my controlling these men. It was a testament, a show of who really ruled this city.

Cade swung a chair around and I pointed to him, "Cade, get video."

He squinted at me before he nodded. I heard the sound of the record button and knew that would be his way of participating. He'd have the footage, he'd maybe enjoy it, and he'd put it out there for whomever needed to see it.

Rome's face didn't hold a smile or any real emotion when he leaned in to whisper something to Cade. His black suit and tattoos peeking out at his neck and wrists reminded me of what a hot devil would look like, someone you'd sell your soul to even though you knew you'd be banned from heaven forever.

He walked forward slowly, eyeing Dante, Maksim, and Bastian. "Who thinks they deserve to see how demanding Katalina can be?"

I turned to see them all smiling, wolves in the night sharpening their teeth.

"Katalina." Rome reached my knees. They were closed as if no one deserved access. He pushed his pant leg in between, spreading them and causing my skirt to inch up. "I wonder if you're ready for me yet."

He knelt down in front of me, and his hand slid up my thigh. My breath caught in my throat as he held my gaze. "I'm not going to enjoy this, Kate Bait. It's going to kill me to have anyone watch you, to share this."

"I know," I murmured to him. "The monster in you doesn't do that well."

His jaw popped up and down like he was holding back saying a million things.

Rome knew just as I did, this was the place where real deals were taking place. This was the stage that would solidify how connected we all were in front of everyone. Contracts and paperwork be damned.

"I love you and you're mine," he said. "This is one time."

I nodded and smoothed my hand over his cheek. "Never again after this."

He yanked me forward on the chair and my skirt rose high enough to bare me to most of them. He lowered that dark head of hair and sucked hard on my bundle of nerves. I immediately grabbed hold of his skull, my legs opening further for him.

My body didn't care who watched; my mind turned off at the touch of his mouth. My monster ravaged me like only he knew how. His tongue lapped at my entrance where he could taste how wet I already was.

I held on tight, trying my best not to orgasm too fast. And when I didn't, he raised his head and made eye contact with Bastian behind me. "Guess she's going to be stubborn. If we can't show everyone how much pleasure we give you, Katalina, they'll most likely think we don't deserve you, right?"

I nodded without responding, trying to follow what the hell he was talking about, but he'd slid one of his fingers up my pussy and was pumping it so slow to just the right beat that I could barely see straight.

"What next, Katalina?"

I scrambled, trying to gather my thoughts. I stared into the eyes that I trusted more than anything in this world. I gave him trust, that's what he deserved and I would show everyone that trust tonight. "Dante, have someone bring a table and lubricant." I said loudly, not breaking eye contact with Rome. Then, I bit down on my lip when he moved his fingers in me back and forth. I continued commanding the room. "Bastian, untie my top."

I felt Bastian's hands at my back and Rome's mouth was on my clit again, sucking while he slid yet another finger into my pussy.

I gasped when Bastian's breath hit my ear suddenly. "You're beautiful, love. This city belongs to us now," he whispered. Then I heard his feet retreat.

My eyes fell shut as I rubbed my own hands over my breasts. I heard a few moans in the crowd, knew people were starting to really enjoying watching. Rome heard it too. I felt it in the shift of his tongue, how the pace had quickened and become rougher, how his hands on my thighs dug in like he wanted to make sure I knew his monster wasn't happy with other eyes on me.

I got lost in the beat of the music, in my own euphoria One of the most powerful men that I'd ever known, one that could snuff out a life in a heartbeat, was publicly deifying me.

Cade's voice broke through my fog as he said, "Come for the camera, love. Show the world how you own us."

My eyes shot open.

Dante was moving a black leather table near to me. Maksim's jaw had dropped along with those of other bratva members.

This was what no one would ever forget.

I wouldn't either. I'd been delivered to another world where the men put me higher than themselves, got on their knees for me, worried about my comfort rather than theirs. I owned what they would do and maybe I had for a long time. I just hadn't seen it.

Men and women surrounded us, some pleasuring themselves while they watched us, others pleasuring each other.

The spotlight remained on me. On us. On my pleasure. On the fact that we'd all made this decision together. My boys stood there ready and willing to show the world just what we were made of.

This was a team now, a unit that most would never be able to penetrate. These boys were mine and I was theirs in a way that everyone was about to truly see.

"Katalina, don't make us wait for you," Cade commanded yet again.

This time, with Rome's masterful hands twisting in me with the rhythm he knew I liked most had me flying over the edge into a straight free fall.

I didn't see stars. I saw darkness down below and I dove straight in.

I belonged here, I ruled here, and I knew that I would be worshipped here always. In darkness lay my light. It would be where I had equal footing and where my baby and I would thrive.

A few members clapped at my release, like they really thought we were putting on a show for them. Yet they'd faded away, they weren't important anymore. Rome and I had gotten lost. I was doing this for my own power now, my own pleasure, and in celebration of finally finding a place where I'd always be an equal.

They were moving as a hungry wolf pack. These men were somehow my givers. They'd found their place with me, a place to seek out my comfort, my security, my strengths and weaknesses, and indulge all of them.

"Give me your eyes, Kate Bait?" Rome murmured into my thigh. I stared into his onyx eyes, so full of need that I almost told him to take me away from everyone else.

"This isn't what I planned—"

"It's what was bound to happen. We've all wanted your pleasure and everyone needs to see." Rome looked at the others. "You want to get on that table? Maybe we shouldn't cross that line here."

"Rome." My lazy gaze fell on him. "I determine my own lines, no?"

He leaned over me, his hands on each arm of the throne, and glared at me. "The baby in you is ours. That makes this body of yours just as much mine. You'll always be mine. I don't dip my dick anywhere else."

I raised an eyebrow. Rome's dirty talk was authoritative, and my pussy clenched as I pushed him further, seeing that possessive animal in him come to life. "I didn't tell you that you couldn't. I make my own lines."

I started to stand up, but Rome shoved me down. Then he dove down to suck on my neck. Hard. He bit and scraped his teeth on me. He left marks, painful ones, before he dragged his tongue across them all.

He gripped my chin and jerked my head toward him. "Mine. Say it."

"I think you'll have to prove that," I whispered to him.

Dante spoke up from the side. "Prove it here, right?"

He patted the table and walked over, nodding. "Right here."

Rome shook his head. "You haven't had enough in front of everyone? Just say you're mine and I'll take you out of here."

He smiled at me like he enjoyed daring me. He knew I wouldn't concede and people watched as we stared one another down.

"I belong to me," I said. "I say when I'm done, Rome. And you listen."

Just a foot away, the table of dark wood waited, unforgiving. The first board was slanted diagonally so that I would be upright but at a good angle to have someone hit me doggy style with a lot of force. Dante directed me to put a leg on either side of the two boards attached to the bottom of the slanted board. The dark leather padding on them pushed against the back of my knees and lower thigh, keeping my legs from closing.

My ass and pussy were bare underneath my skirt. If someone lifted it or put their hand a little ways up the skirt, they'd know, I was open to be fucked. Ravaged and taken advantage of.

Dante asked, "Are you comfortable?"

I winked at him. "Why wouldn't I be?"

He hummed low. "Some days I wonder how much your body can take."

"Guess we're about to test that out."

Rome motioned to a hostess and she delivered tools on a silver tray. I turned to see Rome picking up a paddle.

He chuckled when my eyes widened. "I'll use it on you one day, huh?"

I was panting just thinking about it. Still, I taunted him. "Or maybe not. I don't think you deserve to punish me that way."

He took his time lifting my skirt high enough for my ass to show to everyone. He smacked me hard with his open palm.

"Jesus," I yelped.

Rome then dipped his finger inside me and rolled it. My ass moved immediately with the motion. Rome chuckled, "Damn, you're always so wet and ready for me aren't you?"

"Shut up," I ground out, wanting his finger to just keep going, to keep hitting me in all the right spots.

He didn't continue though. Suddenly he pulled out and leaned forward to whisper into my ear. "Should we show everyone who you belong to now? Forever?"

I eyed the tray. I looked at him. I wondered if I'd ever want anything more than him in this moment. He was doing what I wanted, putting on the show in front of everyone, showing them all how we were bound together. "You better make this so good for me and for our city to see."

He chuckled like he enjoyed the challenge. That same finger was at my ass, probing my one virgin hole with a firm motion.

His finger was wet from my slickness and I gasped when he shoved it in.

My face was toward the damn balcony; I could see everyone watching me. They looked on as I took that finger. I bit down on my lip and tried not to cry out immediately. Rome's other hand expertly rubbed my clit and I tried not to orgasm right away.

My body was tight though, not ready for this new place to be touched.

"Trust, Katalina," he murmured in my ear as he grabbed the lubricant from the tray. "You either have it or you don't."

301

I turned to glare at him and I felt his finger leave me only to be replaced by a cold sensation. "Oh, my God," I moaned as Rome pinched my clit and probed me over and over again as if he really did want all my trust.

I felt my body opening, but when he stuck two fingers in, I clenched.

He smacked my ass. "Katalina, relax."

I breathed out and let the pleasure and pain zing through me. I closed my eyes and focused on it, focused on this city watching us, at me showing everyone who we were, at Rome being by my side for it all.

Another ass smack.

I cried out. All the stimulation, just the right amount of pain, my body unexpectedly took over and I climaxed, even though I'd thought there wasn't much left in me.

I rode Rome's hand and pushed my ass harder into his fingers.

"She's ready for me," he murmured. I didn't know if it was to himself or to the crowd or to me.

I felt such a sense of loss when he pulled his fingers from me that I practically whimpered. Then his dick was up against my asshole and I felt the cool lubricant on it, nudging into me.

His hand worked my pussy and just as Rome started penetration, his fingers thrust in and out of me. The rhythm had me rocking back and forth on Rome's dick while he nudged further and further in. My sensitive breasts rocked with the rhythm too and my hands went to them, squeezing them for more pleasure.

I felt more of the cool lubricant being added to my entrance. He was taking his time, making sure he didn't fuck me raw.

He slid two extra fingers in my pussy and curled them. I moaned and rolled my whole body. It gave Rome a moment where I was open enough for him.

He thrust in further and I sucked in a breath. "Oh, fuck."

"That's right. Bigger than you expected when I screw you here, huh? Remember I own you. You own me, baby."

I was gripping the edge of the table, so close to screaming in pain but also in ecstasy. He'd hit a place I couldn't describe to anyone in the world. I'd never felt it before. I was empowered and completely helpless all at the same time.

"Say you're mine," he commanded.

I didn't hesitate. I wanted him all and I wanted him now. "I'm yours. And you're mine."

"That's"—he shoved the last inch of himself into me—"right."

The initial shock of him filling me pushed me over the edge, and he pumped into me over and over as I thrashed and took the high I needed from him in front of everyone.

I felt his cum shoot into me with one last thrust and knew this solidified the bond we all had on another level.

The crowd was clapping around me, like somehow we'd won them over from this show.

I knew we had. Deals were made in the basements of sex clubs by the rich and the famous. This was how.

I relaxed onto the table as Rome pulled out of me and barely lifted my head when he murmured an order for me to be taken to the back on the table to clean up and recoup.

Rome said he'd be back in minutes, that no other man better touch me in that time.

The monster was now back full force, ready to rip apart anyone who wanted a piece of me.

He'd done the show. He was over it now.

He bent down and looked at me before they took me to the back of the club. "I'm in love with your crazy and I'm in love with your ass. I'll see you back there in a minute, huh?"

I smiled at him. It was one of those smiles I felt deep in my bones, like we'd done what we set out to do. That things would be right now. That we'd move forward instead of back.

Rome didn't meet me in the next minute. Or the next hour. No one saw where he'd gone after he'd said a few words to Bastian.

My monster had vanished.

CHAPTER 25

KATIE

W E'D SEARCHED UNDERGROUND gang's communications for hours; we'd sifted through security cameras in the club and watched footage in every which way we could.

Rome couldn't have just disappeared. Something was fucking wrong.

Cade finally found footage through a phone he'd tapped in the club. It was illegal and not something I'd ever repeat, but I wanted to just about die when he told me he'd gotten something.

I almost did die when I saw the recording. We couldn't identify the person that had drugged Rome or the men who'd dragged him away.

Yet I saw, just like everyone else who watched, that there was a gunshot to his side, I was sure of it. The camera angle only caught him flinching in the slightest, but the way the man held the gun to Rome's side, it was obvious to me that he'd been wounded.

Drugged and shot.

If he wasn't dead, he was near to it.

I called everyone. I sent Maksim out looking. I even drove to Ivan's to find him gone. When I called him, he acted oblivious. His tone gave him away, though. I hung up and told everyone to focus directly on him. Most of the bratva was still inside the club. Most of them hadn't acted with Ivan. Some had, though.

Some I would have to punish.

Just hours later, my phone rang again, and when I saw Ivan's name, chills ran down my spine.

"Meet me where we always do, granddaughter. Let's get this show on the road."

I hung up on him and moved fast. I held back the Armanellis because it wasn't their fight. When I got to the meeting place, most of the bratva had arrived. Everyone had been alerted in some way or another.

I may have earned the bratva's respect or at least convinced them that I was as tied to the Armanellis as I ever would be, but Ivan had to accept that too.

He didn't want to.

He stood in the center of the facility with all our eyes on him, gun in hand and a beaten and drugged Rome on the floor next to him.

He motioned me forward. I went fast and willingly. My life didn't matter, but my baby's and her father's life did.

He smiled at me like we were a family, like he loved me, like we could make all this work. "Here is your choice. Choose me. Not him."

He handed me the gun in my silence.

"You don't pull the trigger, Katalina. You'll lose the power. You'll lose everything. This bratva won't back a weak woman who's susceptible to her emotions and her sexual drive." He gripped the gun in my hand and pointed it directly at Rome. Rome swayed as he sat on the floor, his face marred with bruises, with dried blood, with pieces of flesh missing. They'd destroyed him in the past couple of hours.

They'd left him alive for this moment.

For me to end him. To bleed out the man who'd put me on the pedestal and given me the confidence to rule in the first place.

For me to prove to them all where my loyalties lay.

How do you choose between everything you love, everything you want, and everything you've dreamed of?

I'd wanted to think a queen wouldn't have to. I'd wanted to think we had it all lined up. But deep down, I knew it wasn't like that. During those moments that felt too good to be true, I'd wondered when it would all go to shit. I'd walked on eggshells, looking over my shoulder for the moment that would destroy it all.

It was this moment.

Surrounded by the men I'd tried so hard to lead, I saw it all for what it really was. "You never truly wanted to give up the bratva."

"I wanted a union of the bratva and the Armanellis."

"We had one."

"We had a partnership, not a blood union. And it was a hollow one, filled with idiocies and unnecessary rules. We don't follow rules. I'm a lion. Not a sheep. And you made me a fool with your spectacle. You showed them you were the whore we always thought you to be."

No one was there to save us. No one was there to save me.

Was the bratva a family of love or wrath? I had to find a way to make them tap into it.

"You want me to tell you that you are the lion, Ivan? That you're the king? Why did you bring me in then?" I looked at him one last time, searching for a weakness and praying I'd found it. "Do you remember the year my mother died? Do you remember how?"

He glanced at me with a look of disdain, but I saw the sliver of fear, the slight chance that he'd underestimated me and I pounced on it.

"Tell us how it happened."

He glanced around with eyes wild and frantic. "It doesn't matter! They're gone."

"You took your own blood, didn't you?"

"No!" he screeched. "You did! I didn't kill Dimitri."

"Are you sure?" I asked again. Because I knew. I'd been in the meetings with him and his doctor. He'd willingly let me listen in. His long-term memory was fading, and even thought they'd increased his medication, no one knew how long it would continue to help. I knew that right then, I'd found a weakness.

"Of course I'm sure."

I turned the gun in my hand, staring down at it as if contemplating his statement. "I wonder, is anyone else here concerned that we're taking lessons from a man who's trying to rid himself of his own family and who doesn't even have his memory?"

A few of the guys looked at one another. I had their attention.

Ivan shook his head. He even chuckled to himself before he said, "You can't sway the bratva against me, Katalina."

"Against you? I've been ruling. You've been retired. Remember? You asked for that. And hasn't everyone got a bigger cut? Haven't your families been protected?" I turned to one of the bratva's members that I knew had been at the club the whole night. "Akim, when was the last kill? Didn't the Armanellis just save your son's life, give him extra money?"

He glanced between Ivan and me. He sighed and shrugged. "Yes." Quick Russian flew from his lips when one man asked for clarification. Suddenly, that man's gaze on me changed. The look of disdain grew to one of love.

"And Nico, we just bought your mama a house, no?"

He nodded. "She's happy."

"And she's safe. Safe because of contracts I put in place that are legally binding between some of the biggest players in this country."

"Shut the fuck up!" Ivan lunged at me but I swung my weapon his way so fast, a few of the bratva gasped.

"Don't come for me unless I ask for you, old man. I'm not in the mood."

"You threaten me?" He seethed, his lips curling up over his teeth like he wanted to bare them in warning. "You think a gun will protect you from us?"

"From us? You mean from them? The bratva?" I looked at each of the men sitting in their seats. I glanced at Rome and wondered how much time I really had to play this game. He'd fallen onto the cement, blood seeping slowly from his clothes. I didn't know where from. I didn't know how long the wounds had been open, and I didn't know if there was irreparable damage.

"This gun won't save me." I suddenly felt numb to it all.

Rome's breathing was labored. If the hospital couldn't get to him in time, if they couldn't heal him, bring back the monster I loved, if I couldn't share my life with him, then what was it all for anyway?

"Nothing will save me if he's gone. I'll burn this whole city down. Do you understand? The father of my child is bleeding out. I won't stand for that. I'm this empire. I built it through blood, sweat, and tears. Off my own back and on my back, I worked my ass off. I'm the queen of the bratva now. Me. This is power and I'll reinforce it now in the way you all want to see it done. With fury if I have to. We save my family, my partner, my baby's father because family is family. The bratva is the bratva. You don't agree, then you let me crumble and bleed out with him."

Ivan's eyes flared like he wasn't sure of my words.

It didn't matter. I was sure.

I turned to them all and held up my gun. "If Ivan and you all want me gone, you want to fend for yourself in the dismal place you've been all these years, then do it." I set the gun down on the cement floor. The metal clicked loudly as I let the handle fall. "I won't fight you. I won't even beg you. Take my life, shoot me down."

Ivan eyed me curiously and then his smile came slowly. It crept across his face, centimeter by centimeter, like a bull finally seeing his target and knowing he'd won. "You tried, little girl. You tried. A woman can never rule, though. Had you birthed a boy from real Armanelli blood, maybe your family would have stood a chance."

"Maybe." The first shot rang out. I didn't flinch. "Maybe, but I would have had to sell my pussy for a seat when all I needed to do was rule with it instead. Love conquers evil, you fool."

Another shot rang out.

His eyes bulged when it registered.

I wasn't the one bleeding.

He was.

"No..." he whispered, grabbing at his first bullet wound.

I caught him as he was about to fall to his knees and whispered in his ear. "Respect the ones you love and they'll fight for you, bleed for you, kill for you. You never lived by the Armanellis' oath but you should have because now even though you bleed, I won't bleed with you."

I dropped him to the floor and jumped over him to run to Rome. I yelled out for help to get him in a car.

Maksim felt for a pulse. "Katalina, I don't feel—"

"Get him to the hospital. Now." I wouldn't listen. I wouldn't give in.

Not now.

Not when we'd been so close.

That little feeling that something was going to go wrong was roaring now. I wouldn't let it take over though. Rome had put enough confidence in me to keep me from falling down now. He'd held me up when no one else had. He'd believed when there was no belief left.

I'd do the same for him.

CHAPTER 26
ROME

THE FIRST VOICE I heard was Bastian's. "If she wants to order them for the room, we don't care."

"Well, I do. There's no point to a hundred bouquets of flowers. Men don't care about flowers." Jett's voice sounded perturbed.

"He will. Those flowers sort of smell like Katie. So he'll love them," Vick said in a lighter tone than everyone else I'd heard so far.

Silence stretched long enough for me to grow concerned. I didn't know what the hell I'd woken up to, but the fact that Katie wasn't answering had me opening my eyes.

"Where's Kate-Bait?" The second the words left my mouth, the second I opened my eyes, everything came back to me.

She jumped up from my bedside to hover over my face, squeezing my hand. "You're awake," she whispered.

I didn't answer her. I took in her curls, the way they fell around her face, how they almost bounced with the slight tilt of her head when I didn't respond.

"Can you hear me?" she asked, a frown forming fast.

"Of course I can hear you," I grumbled and winced when I tried to shift in the bed.

"What the fuck, Rome? Then answer me!" She shoved me in the shoulder and I winced.

"Jesus, woman." I didn't ask or even wait for a sorry. I'd be waiting forever.

"I'm scared as hell." Her voice shook as she said it. A steadying breath seemed to calm her a little. "Can you feel your legs?"

"Right. We need to know, do you think you're paralyzed? Do you have amnesia?" Vick called out loudly from the foot of my bed.

"He's not deaf, Vick." Brey had inched her way up and grabbed my other hand. "Glad you're talking, Rome."

"Well, I'm convinced at this point, Katie wouldn't have been had it any other way." Vick kept rambling. "She'd have found the serial murderer inside her. She's stacking up more bodies than you at this point and had you died or been permanently injured, yeah, that would have sent her over the edge."

Jett rolled his eyes and grabbed her elbow. "Let's go."

"What? Phantom, you know I'm right." Vick looked affronted.

"We're going, Vick." Jett motioned to the room and everyone started walking out, but Katie grabbed Brey's hand and those two stared at one another. Bastian patted my leg before he left.

Vick and Jett followed the rest out as Vick yelled, "I'm still ordering the flowers. You'll want them before they discharge you!"

Brey shook her head. "She's out of control."

Katie nodded but didn't say anything for a long time. She sat there holding Brey's hand over my chest, and I let the silence stretch, knowing she was working through something.

"I'm used to plowing ahead, guys. I'm used to not feeling anything and then having to move on." Her moon eyes glistened with tears that hadn't spilled yet. "I'm feeling way more than I usually do," Katie whispered to her friend over me. It was a plea from her, a question I couldn't understand between two friends who'd known one another long enough to share an unspoken bond.

"It's fucking awful." Brey's fingers squeezed Katie's. "I think you told me once, though, that it doesn't get better but it doesn't really get worse either, right? This will be kind of like that. Pregnancy and the kid and worrying about this guy here—it won't get better in the sense that you'll always worry. But it won't get worse either. You'll get to *feel* that freaking love, Katie. You wouldn't trade that for anything, right?"

"I don't think Rome would let me even if I tried," she choked out.

"Not gonna happen. You can handle it," I grumbled.

315

She squeezed my hand and Brey got up to leave, waving at both of us but not saying a word.

"Hm..." I stared at her hair. "Maybe your hair's out of control."

"Yeah, no time for straightening with you in the hospital."

"That's all it took to get them back?"

She rolled her moon grey eyes at me. "The curls? They don't scream lethal, do they? They're too wild."

"They're fucking beautiful. *You're* fucking beautiful to wake up to."

"Not in a hospital." She sniffed and looked up toward the ceiling. "Jesus, we're in a hospital and you were dead. Dead for too fucking long."

The way her voice shook, how she tried to hold back her fear, I wanted to comfort her. "I'm fine," I ground out, sure as hell I was about to die from the pain in my side.

She sucked in a breath and jerked her hands away from me. "Sorry. Sorry."

I shook my head and waved her off. My pain didn't matter. I tried to lift my head but felt the pain in my side too much.

I tried to sit up again. The pain ripped through me; the wound screamed for me to lie down. The sweat started to pour from my body. I didn't care. I tried again, and this time Katie gasped as I shoved up from my elbows and we saw the wound had bled through from my back onto the sheets.

She moved toward the door, "We need a fucking doctor right now."

I grabbed her hand before she walked away and yanked her back toward me. I gripped her upper arms and straightened her stance so that she faced me directly. I took in every inch of her. She had a bruise on her face that I ran my thumb over, and she had a cut on her lip that I dragged a finger down. "My baby still in you?"

I'd blacked out when they'd shown up with her. I knew they'd brought her there to kill me off. Ivan wanted her removed after he discovered she wouldn't deliver him the great grandchild he'd always wanted. I knew she'd be tested, but I knew she'd find a way too. That woman was badass where I couldn't be, even without any of us by her side.

She jerked out a nod and her chin trembled before she sucked in a quick breath and straightened, blinking back her tears. "She's in there safe and sound."

"You have to offer yourself and her on a platter for me to be here?"

"In some way, I guess. I didn't fight him. I told him to let the bratva pick. I wasn't going to fight it out with him. This is a chess game, not a fist fight. I did what I had to do."

"Don't ever do it again, got it?"

"I'll always save you, monster." Her stare was hard, unmoving.

"Save my baby and yourself first, Cleo."

"My blood is your blood, monster. I bleed, you bleed. You bleed, I do too. We need you."

"Well, you got me, I guess. The queen reigns, huh?"

"The bratva took down Ivan for me. They drove you here."

"No shit?" I said, surprised. I knew she could do it. I just didn't know when or if it'd be before I died. Ivan wanted my head. I thought for sure he'd get it after that injection and being shot.

"Yeah, no shit. Next time you decide to bleed out, I need you to make sure you do it slower."

I laughed at her order and then wheezed when the pain hit me like a freight train.

"Jesus Christ. You need pain meds."

I grabbed her and pulled her mouth down on mine. "I need you."

"You got me. Forever and ever."

"You did it, Cleo," I whispered as I stared into her silver eyes. "You won their trust."

She shook her head, her mess of curls weaving back and forth. "No, Rome. We earned it."

KATIE

"**I**'M NOT WATCHING her for another hour," Bastian screamed into the phone.

"Another hour?" I heard Dante sound off from afar. I winced. "Might be two hours."

"What the fuck, Katalina?" Bastian roared into the phone. I heard my little girl giggling in the background. He murmured something to her and then roared again. She squealed in delight.

"You'll be fine," I said with a smile.

"Put Rome on the phone. He'll listen."

"You're right. He will. Which is why he's not getting on the phone." I eyed the man sitting next to me at Heathen's Bar, his very first bar down the street from where I'd gotten a tattoo not too long ago. He was all broody male and sitting with his brow completely furrowed. Those dark eyes held worry and fear and dread all wrapped into one big daddy package.

"Do we need to leave?" he asked, already standing.

"Sit down." I grabbed his tattooed forearm and pulled him back to his seat. "She's fine."

"No! She's not. Well, she is, but I'm not. She doesn't listen to anything, Katie. Ivy, don't you dare spill—" Bastian swore fluently away from the phone. "She's smiling, woman. She's worse than you and Rome combined."

"I'll see you in two hours." I hung up before he could argue.

"What's wrong?" Rome asked immediately, his jean-covered knee jumping up and down.

"Nothing. He just hates babysitting because Ivy doesn't listen to him." I shrugged.

"She's not hurt?" His shoulders hadn't relaxed and his hand was now fisted on the bar. "We should leave. We're too far from home if something happens."

We'd taken this trip to see how Heathen's was getting along. It was hopping and doing well. Cole and a pretty brunette were making drinks while college kids buzzed in and out from the patio. The lights twinkled outside, mixing with laughter and a cool breeze.

"You needed to come see this place off," I murmured. He was giving it to Cole; it belonged to that guy anyway. He was here night after night. From every call Rome made to this bar over the years, I knew that Cole had his heart and soul invested here. Rome's was invested in other areas.

"Look, we've got guards up Bastian's ass for Ivy's protection, Rome. Not that she needs it. Dante's there and Cade probably is already on his way over. She's fine."

"She's a goddamn angel and we need to protect her," he grumbled and I gave him that look you give people when they've fallen off the deep end. He sighed heavily. "I'm being overprotective."

"You're being obsessive and crazy."

Rome wasn't just that though. He barely let me hold our daughter when we were home together. We'd moved into his place. Sometimes the panic room had perks and I wasn't about to pass them up by staying where I was. We'd turned the guest bedroom into a nursery. Little Ivy didn't love her room much or maybe she loved her father's arms more. That girl screamed for long minutes from the moment she learned she could. Rome would be across the hall in a matter of seconds. He'd rock her back to sleep or mix her a bottle of formula.

Now, he was giving away bars, trying to teach our guards what it was to be an enforcer. He wanted to give Ivy her daddy. The standard he held himself to was exhausting.

And amazing.

And hot.

I downed my drink and hopped up from my bar stool. "Time to go."

"Go where?"

"I want a tattoo."

"Oh, for fuck's sake, Kate-Bait. We don't have time for that."

"I think we do. And I'm getting what I want or I'll tell Bastian to keep the little minion from you."

"We both know that's not ever happening. I'd hunt him down."

I gave him a big smile. "I have a feeling you'd find him too."

"You bet your ass." He finally smiled a little when I wiggled it in front of him, and then he rolled his eyes and waved to Cole. "Keep it in line or call me when you can't."

Cole smiled and nodded, no other communication because that was how their relationship had always been.

We ambled down the street, and I took in the cool air whispering through my hair. "Remember when you walked me here last time?"

"Unfortunately."

"I didn't think we'd end up here back then. I was set on killing the chemistry between us."

"That would have been impossible. I'd stared at your ass far too long to forget it."

"See, but you were much more committed to having me forget you, forget the family, back then."

He rubbed the scruff on his face and smiled. "Woman, the monster in me was willing to do that. We've always warred over you."

I walked on in silence, waiting for him to continue his explanation.

"My head has always known you were made for more than all of us. You had those crinkled up papers with all your notes on how to make your father comfortable. You had a heart, one that had been loved and nourished from a young age. None of us did."

"Just because you weren't loved like my daddy loved me doesn't mean you couldn't do it yourself."

He chuckled and pulled me to his side by my waist. "I know that now. I know that now because of you. You gave me Ivy. You tamed the monster."

Those words had my heart veering off course. I was so damn in love with him that I held onto my crazy idea until Zane was in front of us giving me a tattoo of Ivy's name on my wrist. I sat there while Rome held my hand like he had before.

He finished and cleaned his gun.

"Zane, can I try?" I pointed to his tattoo gun.

His gaze ping-ponged between Rome and me, then he narrowed his eyes at me. He either knew something I didn't or he just trusted Rome. "Fine. Button's here. You dip in ink. I'll have to clean up what you mess up. Be gentle on him or it'll end up jacked."

I'd been watching him do my wrist and took the gun to mimic the same steps. I drew a straight line across my wrist under Ivy. It was messy but it was there.

"That'll do just fine."

Zane spun on a heel and left us alone in the parlor again.

This time, I wasn't going to hold back. I was the queen and I did what I wanted. I tilted Rome's head, ready to tattoo my name on him. "You said you were ready to take my name on your neck. Tonight's the night."

The man shook his head before he chuckled. "Give me the tat, Cleo. I'm yours forever, anyway."

I did just that.

THE END

Bastian's story is coming!
Pre-order ***Soul of a Sinner*** today.

Subscribe to Shain Rose's newsletter
to be the first to know when:

shainrose.com/newsletter

Keep in touch by joining
Shain Rose's Lovers of Love Facebook Group:

facebook.com/groups/shainroseslovers

Meet the Billionaire Stonewood Brothers

INEVITABLE

A second chance romance that spans childhood to adulthood. When Jax saves Aubrey from a fire her father started, will they be able to overcome the trauma and focus on their love for one another?

REVERIE

An angsty, enemies-to-lovers standalone romance where opposites definitely attract. When Jett acquires Vick's company, everyone is wondering if they have what it takes to survive the tension in the office.

THRIVE

A captivating friends-to-lovers small town romance where Mikka and Jay will have to face their dark pasts while indulging in small town delights.

ABOUT
SHAIN ROSE

Shain Rose writes romance with an edge. Her books are filled with angst, steam, and emotional rollercoasters that lead to happily ever afters.

She lives where the weather is always changing with a family that she hopes will never change. When she isn't writing, she's reading and loving life.

FACEBOOK PAGE:
facebook.com/author.shainrose/

BOOKBUB PAGE
bookbub.com/authors/shain-rose

TIKTOK:
tiktok.com/ZMJcuQP8Q

GOODREADS PAGE:
goodreads.com/shainrose

INSTAGRAM:
instagram.com/author.shainrose/

WEBSITE:
shainrose.com

AMAZON AUTHOR PAGE:
amzn.to/37Nfejt

ACKNOWLEDGEMENTS

To my readers, thanks for getting me. Thanks
for spending your time on my words. None
of this would be here without you.

THANK YOU!

Made in United States
North Haven, CT
05 July 2024

54422221R00187